Notturno

Notturno

GABRIELE D'ANNUNZIO

TRANSLATED AND ANNOTATED BY

STEPHEN SARTARELLI

PREFACE BY

VIRGINIA JEWISS

YALE UNIVERSITY PRESS ■ NEW HAVEN & LONDON

A MARGELLOS
WORLD REPUBLIC OF LETTERS BOOK

The Margellos World Republic of Letters is dedicated to making literary works from around the globe available in English through translation. It brings to the English-speaking world the work of leading poets, novelists, essayists, philosophers, and playwrights from Europe, Latin America, Africa, Asia, and the Middle East to stimulate international discourse and creative exchange.

Yale University Press books may be purchased in quantity for educational, business, or promotional use. For information, please e-mail sales.press@yale.edu (U.S. office) or sales@yaleup.co.uk (U.K. office).

Set in Electra type by Keystone Typesetting, Inc., Orwigsburg, Pennsylvania.
Printed in the United States of America.

Library of Congress Cataloging-in-Publication Data
D'Annunzio, Gabriele, 1863–1938.
Notturno / Gabriele D'Annunzio ; translated and annotated by Stephen Sartarelli ; preface by Virginia Jewiss.
    p. cm. – (Margellos world republic of letters)
    Includes bibliographical references.
    ISBN 978-0-300-15542-6 (cloth : alk. paper)
    I. Sartarelli, Stephen, 1954– II. Title.
    PQ4803.N6513   2012
    853'.8–dc23   2011042667

A catalogue record for this book is available from the British Library. This paper meets the requirements of ANSI/NISO Z39.48–1992 (Permanence of Paper).

10 9 8 7 6 5 4 3 2 1

CONTENTS

by Virginia Jewiss

Gabriele D'Annunzio's *Notturno* offers one of the most extraordinary stories of literary creation ever conceived. On January 16, 1916, D'Annunzio's plane, a flying-boat on a wartime propaganda mission over Trieste, was forced to make an emergency landing, and D'Annunzio suffered a detached retina in his right eye. In an effort to protect his remaining good eye, his doctors ordered him to remain immobile, both eyes bandaged, in a dark room in his house in Venice. Confined to bed and blackness during the damp Venetian winter, Italy's most celebrated living author nevertheless insisted on writing. To keep his sentences from overlapping and running together, he invented a "new art," or rather, revived an ancient one: "Then I remembered the way the Sibyls used to write their brief auguries on leaves scattered by the winds of fate." D'Annunzio recorded his own brief thoughts not on leaves but on thin strips of paper, each wide enough for just one or two lines of writing, which his daughter Renata, whom he affectionately called Sirenetta, prepared for him. Following his three-month convalescence, the thousands of scraps of paper he'd filled were gathered and revised, again with the help of Renata, and published in book form in November 1921. D'Annunzio chose the evocative title *Notturno*, a musical and artistic term that conveys both the dreamlike, pensive quality of the work and the disturbing darkness in the author's soul.

Unlike the ancient Sibyls or blind prophets who peer into the future, D'Annunzio used his blindness as a prism through which to view his past hopes and present despair. Burdened with grief for his comrades and guilt for his infirmity, he "sees" in the recesses of his deadened eye man's ravaged flesh and enduring soul, and he describes death—in all its grotesque glory—with unflinching coldness and heartfelt longing. Fragments of his past surface and reshape themselves in his imagination: the loss of comrades, his mother's embrace, summers by the sea, travels in Egypt, walks in mist-enshrouded Venice, fiery Rome, and his home town of Pescara. *Notturno* is a diary of darkness and light, a labyrinthine journey through time as memory, fantasy, and hallucination blur in the searing pain of his eye. In a tone that oscillates between lethargy and zeal, he promotes his self-styled myth of the poet as hero, casting himself as a Nietzschean *Übermensch*, yet simultaneously revealing his doubts and fears. D'Annunzio agonizes over his own living death of inaction—he compares his narrow bed to a coffin—in contrast to what he considers to be the glorious fates of his fallen comrades, all while fanning hopes of redemption for himself and his country.

The work is divided into three "offerings," and the patriotic and spiritual notions of sacrifice suggested by that term gather force as D'Annunzio's sight is gradually restored with the coming of spring and Easter. Yet much of the originality of this work lies not in a unifying theme or redemptive finale but in its tendency to offer up disparate memories and conflicting sensations. Reminiscing about a dead friend, D'Annunzio notes that "there is a place in the soul where the river of darkness and the river of light flow together." A hymn of loss and recovery, *Notturno* unfolds in a fluid space where hope and despair constantly converge: the book closes with an image of flames against a night sky, and of dying embers ready to be rekindled.

The physical limit imposed by the size of the paper strips on which he writes lends an extraordinary lyrical quality to D'Annunzio's reflections, which together create what can only be defined as a prose poem, the first of its kind in Italian. The staccato phrases, with their narrative sparseness, are surprisingly versatile for expressing grief, mutilated flesh, the chop of the water in the Venice lagoon. And they stand in stark contrast to the distinctive, highly wrought style of D'Annunzio's earlier works. Heralded as a masterpiece when it first appeared, this hauntingly beautiful and highly experimental composition helped inspire a new mode of writing, and it remains the most unsettling and timeless of all his prose works. The first complete English version of *Notturno* ever to be published, this volume offers a fresh and startling perspective on one of the most significant but later somewhat eclipsed figures of late nineteenth- and early twentieth-century European literature.

D'Annunzio's fame during his lifetime can hardly be exaggerated. He published his first poetry at age sixteen, marking the beginning of a long and prolific literary career that also included novels, plays, and short stories. Sensual, psychological, and rich in lavish descriptions, his works earned him the informal title of

Italy's national bard. Yet his writings have often been overshadowed by his flamboyant life. D'Annunzio was a charismatic, theatrical, and eccentric individual, for whom art and politics were inextricably intertwined. He was born in 1863, shortly after the tumult of the Italian Risorgimento, which brought about national unification, and died in 1938 in a fascist Italy intent on expanding beyond its borders to found a new Roman empire. His patriotic passion, love of adventure, and thirst for renown complemented and at times complicated his role as author. A daredevil pilot, a fervent ultra-nationalist, and a indefatigable seducer, he flew with Wilbur Wright in 1908, campaigned for Italy's entry into war, carried on scandalous, public affairs with the likes of Eleanora Duse, and was an early sympathizer of Mussolini.

Though already fifty-two when World War I broke out, D'Annunzio volunteered for combat and was granted special permission to carry out missions in the infantry, cavalry, navy, and air force. It was on one such mission that the accident that caused his blindness occurred. In 1918 he organized the famous "Flight over Vienna," making an epic seven-hundred-mile round trip in order to drop tricolored propaganda leaflets, the text of which he had written himself, onto the enemy city. After the war he was adamant that the port city of Fiume—a former Venetian possession and now Rijeka in Croatia—be assigned to Italy. In September 1919, D'Annunzio led a bold mission to seize the city, which he held against international opposition until forced to renounce his claim over a year later. His expulsion from Fiume marked his withdrawal from active politics, leaving the field open to Benito Mussolini, who adopted much of D'Annunzio's bravado and bellicose theatricality.

D'Annunzio's controversial public persona and political agenda later compromised his literary reputation. Despite his criticism of the Axis alliance and his eventual divergence from Mussolini, his image was inescapably tainted by his early association with fascism. After World War II many of his works were dismissed as proto-fascist, and his literary style had fallen out of favor. Though he remains an ineluctable figure in the Italian literary canon, his works have never regained the prominence they held during his lifetime.

Nevertheless, D'Annunzio's importance to readers today is far more than one of literary influence or historical significance. His voice in *Notturno* is relevant precisely because of its disturbing combination of ardent nationalism, patriotic zeal, and sheer beauty. Though the techniques of warfare have changed dramatically since D'Annunzio's day, as have the cultural and political conditions that prompted his daring feats, his troubling and inspired meditations continue to speak to the conflicting emotions, expectations, and realities of war: the deep bonds that form between comrades in arms, the imperatives of patriotism and peace, the yearning for glory and self-preservation, the view of death as redemptive release and pointless tragedy. *Notturno* rises above the specificities of any particular conflict or political perspective to get at the heart of man's unceasing search for beauty amid the ruin of war.

by Stephen Sartarelli

Gabriele D'Annunzio saw himself at once as the culmination of the ancient Italian literary tradition founded by the medieval vernacular poets and as the herald of a new Italy fusing adventurism, militarism, and a sort of "vulgar Nietzscheanism" with the nation's storied excellence in the arts. His language is dense with allusions, archaisms, and high rhetoric and may appear dated to the contemporary reader, despite his many efforts to absorb modernist trends into an already highly syncretic approach to composition.

I have tried as much as possible, within the limits of contemporary tastes, to preserve the often antiquated style of his poetic prose, and in this translation the reader will therefore find spellings, diction, and syntax somewhat unusual even for a text written nearly a hundred years ago. Moreover, combined as it is with a free use of literary devices inherited from French Symbolist poetry—parataxis, synaesthesia, extreme allusivity—and the imagery of an already industrialized modern world, the archaism will, no doubt, seem all the more pronounced. Such, however, was the nature of D'Annunzio's contribution to Italian letters. His is a poetics of accumulation and contradiction sustained primarily—one is tempted to say only—by the stylistic mastery holding it together.

My purpose here has been to allow this tension, and its rich, difficult harmonies, to find a voice in the poetic registers still accessible to our American English in the twenty-first century.

The translation is based on the 1995 Garzanti edition of *Notturno*, edited and annotated by Elena Ledda. That edition was based on the *editio princeps* published by Treves (Milan) in 1921, except for a few corrections of typographical errors and omissions.

Notturno

FIRST OFFERING

Et in tenebris
Aegri somnia[1]

I am blindfolded.

I lie supine in bed, my torso immobile, head thrown back, a little lower than my feet.

I raise my knees slightly, to tilt the board propped up on them.

I am writing on a narrow strip of paper with space for one line. In my hand is a soft-leaded pencil. The thumb and middle finger of my right hand rest on the edges of the paper and let it slide away as each word is written.

I can feel the edge under the tip of the little finger on my right hand, and use this as a guide to keep the page straight.

Elbows motionless at my sides, I try to keep the movement of my hands extremely light, so that their play extends no further than the wrist joints, and thus none of their shaking is transmitted to my bandaged head.

My pose feels in every way as stiff as that of an Egyptian scribe carved in basalt.

The room is devoid of light. I write in the dark. I trace my signs in the night, which lies solid against both thighs, like a board nailed in place.

I am learning a new art.

When the doctor's harsh sentence cast me into darkness, assigning me in darkness the narrow space my body will occupy in the grave, when the wind of action grew cold upon my face, almost obliterating it, and the ghosts of battle were suddenly barred from the black threshold, when silence fell within me and around me, when I quit my flesh and rediscovered my spirit, from my initial, confused distress the need to express, to signify, was reborn. And almost immediately I began to look for a way to avoid the rigors of my treatment and deceive my stern physician without disobeying his orders.

Speech was forbidden me, especially crafted speech; and I failed to overcome my age-old aversion to dictation and the secret reticence of an art that wants no intermediaries or witnesses between the material and the person shaping it. Experience dissuaded me from trying to write with eyes closed. The difficulty is not in the first line, but in the second, and in those that follow.

Then I remembered the way the Sibyls used to write their brief auguries on leaves scattered by the winds of fate.

I smiled a smile unseen in the shadows when I heard the sound of Sirenetta cutting paper into strips for me, as she lay on the rug in the adjacent room, by the light of a dim lamp.

Her chin must be illuminated as it was by the hot sand's reflection when we lay beside one another on a Pisan beach in happier times.

The paper makes a regular swishing sound, calling to mind the surf at the feet of tamerisks and junipers parched by the libeccio.

Under the blindfold, the back of my injured eye burns like the summer noontide at Bocca d'Arno.

I see the wind-rippled, wave-wrinkled sand.

I can count the grains, plunge my hand in it, fill my palm with it, let it flow through my fingers.

The flame grows, the dog days rage. The sand glistens in my vision like mica or quartz. It dazzles me, makes me dizzy and terrified, like the Libyan desert on the morning I rode alone to the tombs of Saqqara.

My eyelids are unprotected, completely exposed. The tremendous heat burns under my brow, inescapable.

Yellow turns to red, the plain is transfigured. Everything becomes bristly and jagged. Then, like a creative hand shaping figures from malleable clay, a mysterious breath raises reliefs of human and animal forms from the blinding expanse.

Solid fire is now worked like chiseled stone.

Before me is a rigid wall of red-hot rock, carved into men and monsters. From time to time something like an enormous sail seems to flap, and the apparitions flutter. Then everything scatters, swept away by the red whirlwind, like a cluster of tents in the desert.

The edge of the torn retina curls, burns like Dante's paper, as the brown slowly effaces the words written on it.[2]

I read: "Why have you twice let me down?"

Salty sweat drips into my mouth, mixed with the tears of my smothered lashes.

I am thirsty. I ask for a sip of water.

The nurse refuses, as I am forbidden to drink.

"You shall quench your thirst with your sweat and tears."

The sheet sticks to my body like the shroud that swathes the salt-speckled drowned man hauled to shore and left on the sand until someone comes to identify him, to close his frothy lids and bewail his silence.

When Sirenetta approaches my bedside with a cautious step and brings me the first sheaf of paper strips of equal size, I slowly withdraw my hands, which have been resting for some time on my hips. I can feel they've grown more sensitive; there is something unusual in the fingertips, as if a glowing light had collected there.

Everything is dark. I am at the bottom of a hypogeum.

I am in a coffin of painted wood, narrow and fitted to my body like a sheath.

The other dead are brought fruit and focaccia by their families. I, the scribe, am given the tools of my office by my compassionate daughter.

Were I to rise, my head would strike the lid, the outside of which bears a painted likeness of me as I once was, eyes limpid and open to life's beauty and horror.

My head remains motionless, wrapped in its bandages. A desire for inertia holds me still, from my hips to the nape of my neck, as if an embalmer had indeed practiced his art on me.

At once my hands find the right gestures, with the same infallible instinct shown by bats when they graze the jagged walls of their dark caverns.

I take a strip, feel it and measure it. I recognize the quality of the paper by the faint sound it makes.

It is not the customary paper the craftsmen of Fabriano used to make for me, one page at a time, with a watermark of my motto, *Per non dormire*, which now seems as dreadful as an unending torture.[3] This paper is smooth, a bit stiff, sharp at the edges and corners. It is rather like a scroll, one of those sacred scrolls the painters used to put in their panels.

My hands feel almost religious as they hold it. A virgin sentiment renews in me the mystery of writing and the written sign.

I hear the scroll crackle between my trembling fingers.

My anxiety seems to blow on the glowing ember behind my eye. Sparks and flashes fly in the whirlwind of the soul.

I feel the compassionate girl's hand on my knees. I raise them slightly to receive the board. To me, in darkness, it is like a votive tablet. The strip of paper is laid out on it. I take the pencil between my thumb, index, and middle fingers, the middle still furrowed from persistent work. *Nulla dies sine linea.*

I tremble before the first line I am about to trace in the shadows.

O art, pursued with such passion, glimpsed with such desire!

Desperate love of the word inscribed for the ages!

Mystical thrill that sometimes fashioned the word from my very flesh and blood!

Fire of inspiration suddenly fusing the ancient and the new in an unknown alloy!

The hand weighed the material. The material had color, shape, timbre.

The quill was like a paintbrush, a chisel, a musician's bow. Sharpening it was a glorious pleasure.

My humble, proud spirit trembled at the sight of the thick, untouched ream to be transformed into a living book.

The quality of the lamp oil was chosen as if for an offering to a stern god.

And during the hours of felicitous creation the hard chair became a creaking prie-dieu under knees bearing the violence of a stooped body.

Now my body is in a coffin, cramped, laid flat.

Yesterday my spirit thrashed like a great eagle caught in a trap. Today it is composed, attentive, astute.

Yet my heart beats wildly.

I feel the paper. My hand twitches as it holds the pencil, almost painfully.

All at once, in my burning field of vision the figure of Vincenzo Gemito appears, such as I saw him in the early days of his madness, climbing up a rocky, blinding slope, where demonic herds of goats nibbled on parched grass, to his prison.[4]

I see him in a room as narrow as a cell, pacing continuously between the door and window like a caged wild animal.

A great head with a mane of hair and beard like a prophet gone mad in the wind of the desert, barely supported by a slender, bent body and two legs broken by fatigue, held upright by an unyielding stamina, as Michelangelo's legs must have been upon the Sistine scaffolds.

Right hand in his pocket, he gesticulates with the other and never removes the first, as if it were paralyzed.

I am moved by the same pity and anguish that assailed me

when I learned that for years, ever since the start of his dementia, he had kept a piece of red modeling wax hidden in his hand and endlessly repeated, with his thumb and forefinger, the motion a sculptor makes to soften and taper it.

Stricken in the head and stripped of the power to create, all he retained was that instinctive gesture, that moulding motion, that habit of the Cellinian craftsman, master of lost-wax casting.

And here he is now, in the inferno of my bandaged eye, living a terrible life.

He looks at me from the depths of a desperate sadness.

He has grown old. His hair and beard are white, unkempt, ravaged by storms and destiny, like the kingly locks of Cordelia's father.

His hand is no longer hidden: he is holding the scrap of red wax between his thumb and forefinger. Fleshless, all nerves and bone like some sickly root of the soul, the hand repeats the motion without cease.

Now his head vanishes, then his body, devoured by the fire under my eyelid, which burns as in a foundry.

The hand remains, only the hand, as if it belonged to some victim of the blaze.

And the wax does not melt: there it is, red as a clot of blood, between the ceaselessly moving thumb and index finger.

The vision becomes so intense, so harsh, that I struggle not to cry out in fear and pain.

Madness flashes through my brain.

I have the urge to tear my eye from its socket, that I may see no more.

I am inside the night, my night of flames and torment.

Sirenetta has left my side. In the adjacent room I hear the paper rasp gently as she cuts it.

Overcoming the tremor, I place the tip of the pencil at the edge of the strip.

For a brief moment I have the confused impression of gripping not a wooden pencil but a piece of lukewarm red wax. It is a moment of indeterminate horror.

At last I write on the invisible scroll.

I write these words:

"O sister, why have you twice let me down?"

Anxious, I call my watchful guardian, who comes running.

I say to her: "Here, see if you can read what I've written."

She takes away the strip, which sounds like a palm frond.

Silence.

The seconds seem eternal, marked by the beats of an anxious heart.

I listen.

In the other room, a melodious voice reads without pause the words I have written, which must surely seem sibylline to her.

"O sister, why have you twice let me down?"

The first time, she overshot glory by a hair's breadth, killing my comrade, who had vowed with me to go on a journey of no return.[5]

The second time, in a fateful game of hours, she granted another the magnificent destiny to which this same man had assigned me, admitting my divine right to the honor.

An angel or demon of night blows on the blaze inside my lost eye.

Countless sparks spatter in the wind.

My head is bent backwards, abandoned, dangling in the void.

I no longer feel the pillow, I no longer feel the bed.

I hear a confused rumble, I hear the roar of the aeroplane, I hear the crackle of combat.

A brusque, compassionate hand has pushed me aside. My head has been punctured: it hangs down in the void, over the vibrating edge of the cockpit.

Over me falls the shadow of the right wing; the propellor's airy star is my crown.

Now not fire but blood spatters everywhere. Not sparks but drops. The heroic pilot is bringing the sacrificed poet back to the fatherland.

O boundless glory!

What divine or human hand ever cast a more august seed into the furrows of the earth?

In the speed of war the endless blood scatters like grain in the wind.

Each spurt divides by the thousands, like the mist of a crashing waterfall forming a rainbow. It does not flow but flies, does not fall but rises.

What is Orpheus's head, floating upon his lyre, compared to this sublime aspergillum?

The new myth is more beautiful still.

I see my face transfigured in the centuries of greatness to come.

The soul does not flee but still hews to the wound like radiance to the flame that bursts and fades in the gunfire, stopping and resuming, subsiding and then flashing again, held by nothing but an invisible bond that the will to burn makes stronger than the storm.

Long sorrow now become sudden joy, long misery transformed to purity's pinnacle, the soul gazes upon the wondrous face that now is truly its own, the face it so wished to possess but could not.

It knew death was a victory, yet never one so great.

Immortal, it is yet radiant in death, and the wind of the mournful flight cannot extinguish it.

Flesh was its weight, and is now its rapture.

Blood was its turbulence, and is now its freedom.

It is borne by the body in an élan of creative beauty.

No believer's or martyr's head on the block was ever so beautiful as this head on the fragile edge of the morning's abyss.

No wounded eagle ever bloodied the light so fiercely with its flapping feathers.

The blood eternally glistens the way the milk of the goddess gleams eternally white in the night.[6]

Behold the earth, behold our destination.

The last drop scatters in the rumble of flight.

On wings unscathed the heroic pilot bears the bloodless body of the sacrificed poet back to the Fatherland.

The news is swift as a thunderbolt and remote as the memory of a great deed.

Every shore of Italy shudders like the cloth of her flags.

Glory kneels and kisses the dust.

Why are the blind portrayed as seers facing the future? As those who reveal what is to come?

Just as Tiresias dipped his divining lips into the blood of a black ram slaughtered over a ditch, so have I drunk my sacrifice for several nights; and I see not the future, nor live in the present.

Only the past exists, only the past is as real as the bandage in which I am wrapped; it is as palpable as my crucified body.

I feel the breath and heat of my visions.

In my wounded eye, all the substance of my life, the sum total of my consciousness, is forged anew. It is inhabited by an evocative fire in continual labor.

He who approaches my bed is less alive than the dead man who stares at me with embers for eyes, as if rising from a burning sepulchre in Hell.[7]

I write not on sand, I write on water.

Every word I trace vanishes, as if abducted by a dark current.

It is as if I can see the form of every syllable I record through the tips of my index and middle fingers.

But only for an instant, accompanied by a glow, a sort of phosphorescence.

Then the syllable dies out, disappears, lost in the fluid night.

Thought runs as though across a bridge that collapses behind it. The arch resting on the bank is destroyed, then at once the middle arch falls. As dread reaches the opposite bank, escaping in fear, the third arch gives way and disappears.

I write like one casting anchor: the hawser pays out faster and faster, the sea appears bottomless, and the fluke never manages to catch, nor the hawser to tauten.

Like a rapturous melody arising unexpectedly from some deep orchestra; like the revelation of a line of verse awakening the soul's secret sound; like the message of the wind that is the speed of infinity in motion; with a spirit without mooring, a body without form, a bliss resembling terror, I feel the world's ideality.

My comrade lies on the island of the dead, down there, behind the briny brick wall, behind the mournful curtain of cypresses.[8] He is in the quadrilateral of earth where sailors are buried, laid neatly inside the leaden coffin that I saw sealed by a hissing flame.

He lies under a funeral pillar of Istrian stone planted at the head of a pile of turf.

His pillar is like a sundial, where Icarus's arm extends like a bronze stylus indicating, over the carved name, the only hour: the hour of ultimate bravery.

My comrade is dead, buried, released.

I am alive, but precisely situated in my darkness, like him in his. As I breathe I feel my breath pass through purplish lips, like his in his first hours, opening a mouth made almost senseless, hardened by the metallic taste of the iodine circulating in my body.

I am like him in my injury as well: I see again the sheet of cotton covering his right eye socket, shattered in the crash.

Thus are his death and my life one same thing.

From his stillness down there, what I loved in him reaches me here; and from my stillness here, what in me was worthy of his love goes out to him.

Though I suffer, and though he suffers no more, the flesh dissolves for both of us, as our spirits rejoin.

Between his last word, which I heard on the receding shore, and his livid, gelid hand, which I grazed with my lips an instant before the coffin lid concealed it from me—between that voice and that coldness, was I alive with him? Or did I die with him?

There is a place in the soul where the river of darkness and the river of light flow together.

It is the place where our friendship lives on. Where our images are reflected and merge.

He is no longer an apparition; he is a constant presence who pushes away all who draw near.

But his first apparition comes back to me in an aura of terror.

It is the eve of his burial.

My grief remains caught in his ravaged flesh.

It is the evening of St. Stephen's. His fire is lit. I am seated where he used to sit. From time to time he annihilates me. I lose myself in him.

I no longer hear what the living beside me say.

Cinerina is there, with her strange, brilliant face, which makes me think of the young Beethoven, and her unusually big eyes, whose gaze is enriched by melancholy and irony blended together as in some mysterious collyrium.[9] Manfredi Gravina is there, too, to console me and help me believe that I still have friends in the world, still have comrades sworn to war.

"What's the weather outside?"

Cinerina says that when she came at seven, the sky was clear and full of stars. Manfredi says that there is dense fog now.

It is ten o'clock. Time to go. Renata is sleepy.

I put on my big gray cloak, over my heavy aviator's tricot. Every act, in the anteroom, is repeated as when he was there. But his small black cape is not hanging from the golden peg, nor do we hear his pleasant, ironic voice.

We go out. We chew the fog.

The city is full of ghosts.

Men walk soundlessly, wrapped in mist.

Vapor rises from the canals.

On the footbridges, one sees only the white stone border of each stair.

Some drunken singing, some shouting, some sort of row.

Blue streetlamps in the mist.

The cry of aerial sentries muffled by the fog.

A dream city, otherworldly, a city washed by the Lethe or Avernus.

Ghosts approach, brush past, vanish.

Renata walks ahead of me the way she did *then*, and Manfredi walks beside her. They are talking the way Renata and my comrade used to talk. Now and then the fog comes between us.

We cross the bridges. Small lamps glow like will-o'-the-wisps in a cemetery.

The Piazza is filled with fog, the way a tub is filled with opaline water.

The Procuratie Vecchie are almost invisible. The top of the campanile dissolves in the vapor.

The Basilica is like a rock in a hazy sea.

The two columns of the Piazzetta look like two columns of smoke rising from twin piles of ash.

On the Riva degli Schiavoni, the lamps of the moored boats.

Light music at the Caffè Orientale, behind the opaque doors: a dance melody.

Drunk people singing.

Wandering ghosts.

The dead are out tonight, as on All Hallows' Eve.

We say goodbye in the lobby of the Albergo Danieli. I am hoping Renata will sleep tonight.

I head back to the Casa Rossa, alone. My friend is with me, in spirit. Deep sorrow seeps from my heart.

I look at the quay where his skiff used to dock, where every night we would shake hands and say: See you tomorrow.

A man in the Piazzetta turns around at the sound of my footsteps.

He turns around again, then walks away, becomes a smoky shadow, disappears.

I enter the arcade under the Procuratie, illuminated by the blue lamps. I am astonished to hear a large family speaking of everyday things, with the sluggish stupidity of people who have been drinking. Are they alive? Are they dead? I pass them. They become shades.

From there to the bridge of San Moisé, as I shudder to think that I shall have to pass in front of the Vicolo della Corte Michiel, I notice that someone is walking beside me noiselessly, as if barefoot.

The person is the same height as my friend, has the same build, the same gait.

He is wearing neutral, nondescript clothes, grayish in color, and a beret, also grayish.

He is silent, unusually so, as if there were no living voice or breath inside him.

No sound of heels, or shoes, or sandals.

I have an instinctive feeling of terror. I slow my step. I see him before me.

The gait is that of my comrade. Soon he is at my side again, there, in front of the passage that leads into the Corte Michiel. The street is deserted.

I light my pocket torch at the turn and slow down. I manage to keep a distance of two or three meters. He never turns around.

His step is so silent, so strange, that the few passersby stop for a moment to look at him.

We are at Santa Maria del Giglio. The fog enters the mouth, fills the lungs. It floats towards the Canalazzo and accumulates.

The stranger becomes grayer, more weightless. He becomes a shadow.

Now I quicken my step so as not to lose him.

In front of the house where one always hears a piano in the evening, in front of the antiquarian's house, he suddenly vanishes.

He did not fall into the canal, did not cross the bridge, did not enter a doorway. All the doors and shops are closed. I explore them with my torch. I retrace my steps, to make sure.

Then I run up over the bridge and rush down the calle, to make certain I am not mistaken and that he is not still in front of me.

The calle is deserted. So is Campo San Maurizio.

Perhaps I'll find him in the narrow little street that leads to the

Casa Rossa? My heart flutters. A sheet of fog grazes my cheek. A band of drunkards yells in the distance, at the end of the wharf.

I have sunk my lips into the fullness of death. My grief has sated itself in the coffin as in a feeding trough. I could not stand any other form of nourishment.

I relive those mournful days, hour by hour, instant by instant. With eyes blindfolded, I try to see. With forehead aching, I try to understand.

What has happened seems unjust.

Even the harshest necessity can seem beautiful.

But there is nothing beautiful about this unforeseen event, other than what my passion bestows on it.

We knew the danger to which we had freely devoted ourselves, a freedom visible only to us, in a few fleeting smiles. We knew that ours was a desperate endeavor, and we had no desire to flee a glorious fate.

In the final days our figures loomed large on the gloomy seas' horizon. The melancholy energy of our departure exalted the preciousness of every passing hour.

Constancy in living action, in the inertia of Venice, in the mist of a vanishing city that seemed emptied of even the last scraps of life.

Action's double edge, honed each day, seemed to cut through the opaque, lazy mass of sadness all around.

A manly duo, battle's duo, reborn in the creation of the human wing, pilot and fighter, altitude's weapon, heavenly weapon, wielded by a single will, like the young Greek's double lance.

Each comrade *is* the other.

There is no nobler bond in the world today than this tacit pact that turns two lives and two wings into a single speed, a single prowess, a single death.

Love's most secret, unexpressed shudder is nothing compared to certain glances which, *in lighter moments,* reconfirm to each the two men's fidelity to the idea and gravity of the matter at hand: tomorrow's silent sacrifice.

Now the death that should have taken two has taken one, only one, in violation of the pact, the offering, in violation of justice and glory.

The pinnacle of glory, for the winged duo, is the holocaust: the sacrifice in which the victim is consumed by flames.

Their true fate is fire.

Their rumbling wing becomes a flaming pyre.

As in the eighth circle of hell, they are two men "inside a fire," but the fire is not divided. High in the air they did not speak. And they needed no brief exhortation to make them eager.[10] Nor did they speak in the flame's collapse.

As the flight was only cerulean silence cadenced by the rhythmical song of combustion, so the holocaust ends in black silence.

Heroism demands that the winged duo, if overwhelmed, should be utterly consumed.

Whosoever surrenders, and gives up his wings, can be said to sin against the nation, the soul, and the heavens. Luckless or shameless, he loses all right to glory.

Borne up by fire, the aerial combatant is an incendiary in life and in death.

Blessed are the two heroic comrades whose bones blend indistinguishably on the stretcher like smoking embers!

The anguished days, the sleepless nights return.
The past is present, with all its details, all its vicissitudes.
I suffer my sorrow again, cry my tears again.
My friend is unburied and reburied.
A gesture, a word, a smell, a light, the hum of a propellor, the gleam of a bayonet, the fold of a flag, the dripping of a candle, a hand turning livid around fingernails almost white, a blurry stain on the floor, the roar of flames shooting out from the seam in the lead, the boom of the first shovelful of earth upon the coffin, echoing into eternity: the grim horror of it all, in all its details, is mirrored in my implacable lucidity.

And sometimes I see myself as he might have seen me from his coffin.

Sometimes I am both the corpse and the one contemplating it.

Bright flashes of light burst in rapid, spasmodic succession, as on that August night when, clutching each other like blind men, we walked along a quay inundated by the heavy downpour, smarting from the incessant lightning that struck whenever we opened our eyes.

I must request a respite, that I may study his face, such as I saw it that last time. I want to find in me the distant part of me that knew, perhaps, that it was to be the last time, when I myself did not know.

How did I wake that morning? What dream accompanied my soul to the threshold of daylight?

Like trees in oblique sunlight, our acts cast long shadows behind them which no one can measure.

And so I rise and get dressed; I don my cape and my courage, as every morning. Nothing can keep me at home. This house is less than a temporary tent. I am free, and I have a plan. My plan is everything to me.

Life has no worth but that of a spear in the hand about to be hurled. At once the bones feel lighter. Of all the flesh, only the heart is alive.

I go out. This little house has an iron door that shuts quickly behind me.

Bora. Rain. The canal is howling.

The Sant'Andrea motorboat idles noisily along the quay. I have brought my suitcases and sack of messages with me.[11]

Rough waters on the lagoon.

Splashes.

I chat with the Sicilian motorman.

He tells me about his shipwrecks in the Pacific and off the coast of Trieste.

When I arrive at Sant'Andrea, Beppino is waiting for me.[12] He's wearing his new suit, a blue, gold-buttoned jacket, and breeches tucked into his bootlegs. A strange feeling. My myopic eyes don't recognize him immediately. Something indefinable hovers between us for a moment.

I disembark, walk down the pontoons onto land. With that almost deferential politeness he has always maintained despite our familiarity, he accompanies me along the muddy quay, where the bora is blowing fiercely.

We enter the wooden house.

Very hot in the hallway.

The stove burning red.

He takes me into his small study, shows me the mistletoe he was given and wants to bring with him on the aeroplane for good luck. He asks for the suitcases and sack to set aside.

It is time for lunch.

Three French officers come over to our table.

Flowers, special dishes, elegance, all in my honor!

I sit down beside my comrade.

General conversation. We talk about mystery, the occult, and then about luck, talismans, fetishes, hexes. Beppino listens; from time to time he interjects a fresh comment, original and profound.

We rise to get coffee. He shows me some cheerful prints that will adorn the corridor. We talk about books to put on the shelves in the mess hall; we talk about Sant'Andrea, the new constructions, the coming spring . . .

With us are Manfredi Gravina, Gigi Bresciani, Alberto Blanc.

We talk about the device invented by Gigi Bresciani.

The "usefulness" of failure.

The young Veronese's physical type: blond, skinny, pale, with sideburns, thin lips, and blue eyes, rather like an English petty officer from the time of Horatio Nelson.[13]

Beppino amuses himself flustering Alberto Blanc, maker of incendiary bombs and telemeters.

Somebody mentions Miraglia's fury when the Japanese Commission was announced. We talk about the Japanese "psyche," then the Chinese one.

Manfredi speaks insightfully about the great Chinese lord, about how impossible it is to become intimate with him, and his impenetrable politeness.

It is two o'clock. Time to leave. The motorboat is ready.

A black cat hides under the sofa. During the meal, he ate out of a bowl with such gusto that his tail was moving the way it does when cats are in heat.

The table near a window and a stove.

The window is ajar because the heat is too intense. It blows open with each gust.

The cold gray light in the refectory, on the flowers.

The bora was so strong that the motorboat's engineer thought it would last at least a week!

The motorman is from Siracusa. We talk about the sun, the heat, the oranges, the almond trees in bloom, Taormina. I see the Latomie again, the theater, the Venus, the Ram . . .

We get up to leave. Beppino accompanies me. He is on guard duty this evening. We talk about solitude, its restfulness.

He will go to bed early and sleep long. We, too, Renata and I, will be alone, having declined Alberto's invitation to go out to a trattoria, since our friend cannot come.

Crossing the pontoons, still in his company, I descend into the motorboat with Manfredi, Albert, and Gigi Bresciani, who seems pensive.

Beppino is happy to come to dinner with me tomorrow, the last supper before the flight of no return . . .

"Now let us dine and drink, my friend, for tomorrow we'll be food for the fish."

His eyes laugh with a childlike cheer.

We say goodbye. He's on the edge of the pontoon platform, looking at me.

I turn round two or three times to wave to him. He disappears.

It is cold, drizzling, and windy. I am wrapped in my great gray cape.

The lagoon is yellowish and choppy. A black barge with a reddish sail passes.

I remain silent while my friends talk. They're talking about him. Manfredi suggests a practical joke: he proposes, for Carnival (will it be a carnival of butchery? a Mardi Gras of massacred fatness?), that we have some sailors dress up as Serbian officers, tattered, filthy, and seedy, and send them, in the guise of a "Serbian mission," to visit Sant'Andrea, so we can enjoy watching the commander fly into a rage . . .

A burst of hilarity almost tender, so much do we love him, so much do we relish his whimsical grace.

The ashen damp deadens the laughter and pleasantry.

High walls. Enormous machines.

We enter the Arsenale. Luigi Bresciani goes to work around his combat aircraft. Manfredi Gravina returns to the Admiralty. The will shines through the melancholy of a moment that is no more.

Taking leave of Alberto, who is insistent about dinner, I tell him to come to my place at seven, and that, depending on my mood, I shall tell him then whether I think it better for me to go out or stay home.

A dull sadness. Life snaps suddenly, like a taut rope. Which is difficult to reknot.

Renata, too, is sad. I decide we should go to dinner with Alberto, to distract her. She, too, regrets our friend's absence. It is as if we can no longer enjoy ourselves without him.

I write to Cinerina to tell her to come.

Renata goes to get dressed.

We go out around eight, into the darkness, holding hands.

Shyness and distaste before the glass door of the trattoria, through which we can see people eating and smoking. I feel like turning back.

Someone comes up to me to encourage me, and leads me into the other, quieter room, where Alberto and Manfredi are waiting for me.

Terrible food, listless conversation. Renata is sad. Alberto is in a dark mood and says little. He makes an effort: he feels discouraged, he feels old! He is supposed to leave on furlough tomorrow morning or evening.

We are brought some insipid fruit. Life has suddenly lost all its flavor. The room is cold and white, as in a hospital. A stranger is sitting at the table beside us: he watches and listens with an expression of curious stupidity.

We forgo coffee, which we will take instead at the shop of the Barretteri. We head out into the darkness, gloomily. Manfredi tells us how every time Miraglia comes out of the trattoria onto the quay, he bangs his nose against the wall.

Moments later, we begin to see the moonlight. Exiting the arcade, we come out into the Piazza and under the spell.

The moon is almost full. The air is cold.

The Merceria darkens, narrow and cluttered. Even before we reach the Ponte dei Barretteri, we can smell the spirited fragrance of the coffee, the way one can when passing certain little Arab cafés.

We climb the steps and go inside. The red-haired girl looks over at us, as if searching for Beppino, our usual companion, who is not with us.

We take our coffee standing. Alberto drinks some cedar water, which seems to perk him up.

As we go out, Manfredi and Renata walk ahead. From the few words that reach me, I can hear that he is telling her about the years he spent at the Academy in Livorno with our friend.

When we reach the Ponte della Paglia, Renata says she doesn't feel like going home so early.

The Riva degli Schiavoni is bright with moonlight. Through the closed doors of the Caffè Orientale comes the sound of a stringed instrument.

We accompany Manfredi Gravina back to the Arsenale. We go to look at the Lions sent as a gift to the Republic by Francesco Morosini, conqueror of the Morea. We linger, trying to decide which is more beautiful.[14]

We separate and come back over the bridge.

I walk Renata back to the hotel. We feel sad, as if we had wasted the evening. (The previous evening we had accompanied Beppino to the quay, where the skiff was waiting for him, but he had come back to escort Renata all the way to her door.)

I go home alone.

I stop, as usual, in front of Santa Maria del Giglio and touch the bas-relief of Zara.[15]

I think of my friend, alone on guard duty at Sant'Andrea.

A restless night. I wake up at three, unable to fall back asleep. I read until five. Then I drift off again, into a superficial sleep.

Through open windows, the sun strikes my pillow. A clear, windless day. Ideal for undertaking the great flight.

An obscure anguish grips my heart. I chafe at the thought of losing this unexpected opportunity. My thoughts keep turning back to Sant'Andrea. I would like to go have breakfast there, to question my comrade; but Manfredi said yesterday that he was going to stay in the city.

I begin to write him a letter asking him please to telephone Sant'Andrea. I stop when Renata arrives.

I am so anxious and taciturn that she asks, "What's wrong?" I have no answer.

It is almost midday. The sky is blue. I look at the plants in the garden: there is only the faintest of winds. I hear the rumble of an aeroplane passing over the Canalazzo.

Why so much darkness gathering in my heart? Am I ill?

We go down for breakfast. I do not speak. I am obsessed. I eat mechanically.

Renata has arranged some flowers in vases: red roses, jonquils, violets, carnations. Beppino, as promised, is coming to dinner this evening. Renata smiles. It will be just the three of us, in keeping with our cherished custom.

I have no desire to go pose for my portrait in Cinerina's studio at the Zattere.

But Cinerina is waiting for me. It might be the last image of me. Renata wants to come along. We leave.

Spring warmth along the bright quay.

Gray torpedo boats at anchor.

Three numbers written in chalk on the red door of the building that houses the studio: 41, 5, 9.

Renata leaves me there and turns back. I go upstairs.

I am unable to dissemble my dark mood. Cinerina is there, all eyes, all chin, no longer a woman but a will to art, in her white canvas smock and with her sober paintbrushes in hand. I assume my pose, lost in thought. She speaks for the pleasure of chatting. I don't listen. An indeterminate amount of time passes; brief, no doubt.

We hear someone come up the wooden staircase and knock at the door, calling for me.

The voice is Renata's. I open the door.

Renata is pale and upset.

"Come. There's been an accident."

"An accident? Miraglia?"

I immediately think of him.

"Come downstairs. Genua's here. He'll tell you."

I descend the stairs, heart racing. I find Memmo Genua in the doorway, distraught. He tells me he has learned, from the telephones in the sentries' posts, that the aircraft flown by Giuseppe Miraglia plunged into the sea and that the pilot is in grave condition. The mechanic, Giorgio Fracassini, our Fracassini, can't be found! He may have sunk to the bottom.

I race back up the stairs, take leave of Cinerina, who is upset. I go back down.

Genua, Renata, and I start running along the Zattere in search of a gondola or any boat at all.

Miraglia has been taken to the Navy hospital. I continue to question Genua to find out the truth.

My knees buckle. My tongue is tied. I leave Renata in Campo San Maurizio and continue down Via XXII Marzo. I pass before Beppino's house, at the entrance to Corte Michiel. People look at me. I am unable to control my terrible anxiety.

We encounter a sailor walking hurriedly. Genua stops him. I do not hear what he tells him. I approach. The sailor was on his way to my house. I learn that the body has been transported to Sant'Anna hospital.

The body! He is dead.

Genua holds me up.

I start running, to find a way, any way, to my destination and flee the curiosity of the passersby. The sailor rejoins us and offers us a motorboat, which is waiting at Santa Maria del Giglio. We go.

St. Mark's basin. Blue.

Sky everywhere.

Shock, despair.

The motionless veil of tears.

Silence.

The throbbing of the motor.

Here are the Gardens.

We turn onto the canal.

On the right, the shore, with its bare trees, and something funereal, remote.

Before us, in the low sky, the stupid, obscene form of a captive hot-air balloon, silver in color.

It is about three o'clock in the afternoon.

We arrive. I jump onto the pier, then go inside.

I ask the officer on guard about Giuseppe Miraglia. I am shown a door. I go in.

On a small bed on wheels lies the corpse.

Head bandaged.

Mouth clenched.

Right eye injured, livid.

Left jawbone shattered; signs of swelling.

Olive-colored face: an unusually serene expression.

Upper lip protruding slightly, a bit swollen.

Wads of cotton in the nostrils.

The look of an Indian prince in a white turban.

Hands folded on the chest, yellowish.

Both feet wrapped in white gauze.

The right foot is broken. The thumb on one hand is broken. One leg is broken. A number of ribs are broken.

He is wearing his blue jacket with gold buttons, the one from yesterday.

People try to drag me away. I refuse. I remain kneeling. I ask to be left alone.

When I am alone, I lean over the deceased and call him several times. My tears rain down on his face. He does not respond, does not move.

I fall to my knees again.

The noise of the day.

Motorboats throbbing on the canal.

Muffled sounds of footfalls on the floorboards.

A sailor enters with a bundle of candles: he puts one at each corner of the bed.

Luigi Bologna enters, then Carlo della Rocca. I cannot move, cannot stand up.

Somebody places a bouquet of flowers at the feet of the corpse. I think I recognize Silvio Montanarella, the youngest aviator.

Two sailors enter with fixed bayonets, take up position at the head of the small bed, and do not move.

Another sailor pins a large, warship's flag to the back wall, opposite the window.

A flag is unfurled over the headboard as well.

After I know not how long, a sailor comes in with another bundle of candles and opens a door in the wall in front of me.

The door had been closed.

I hear some shuffling. Two sailors are carrying a stretcher with the body of Giorgio Fracassini on it, found after a two-hour search through the shredded canvas and tangled wires as the aeroplane was being transported back to Sant'Andrea.

They cross the threshold and lay him down in the small room next door.

I rise to go see him. I lean over the body.

Memories of the day in Trieste, his recommendations concerning the gasoline pump, his cleverness in hiding the twenty-first tricolor pouch . . .

He looks asleep. His face is composed, severe. He is wearing his dark-leather suit.

He looks like a monk who has found bliss in passing. That masculine face, almost always shiny and dripping with sweat, with its fearless blue eyes, smooth brow, and aquiline nose, has found peace, ennoblement. It is truly at rest.

I go back into the adjacent room and find my friend's body covered with a black pall with a gold cross on it.

His face is covered with gauze.

A sailor is about to remove the flag from the headboard and replace it with a small Red Cross flag. I prevent him. He was taking it to hang on the wall of the next room.

I arrange the red and the green to the right and the left, over the black pall.

The magnetism of the warship's tricolor flag.

The white boltrope, the slipknot . . .

The men go off to look for another flag for Giorgio.

Umberto Cagni comes in, accompanied by other officers. I glimpse him through burning eyes. He approaches, uncovers the deceased's face, murmurs something I don't understand. He goes to see the mechanic as well. Then he draws near to me as I force myself, back to the wall, to overcome my horror. He takes my hand, shakes it, and in a rough, soldierly, almost violent voice, says: "Good day!" And he leaves.

The bursts of the motorboat's engine. The craft driving away.

Here comes Manfredi Gravina, and then Alberto Blanc. I don't move. A sailor puts a black cushion, from the prie-dieu, under my knees.

Night has fallen. I hear the first cry of the sentries: "On the lookout overhead!" I think of Renata. I think of the flowers she put in the vases for our friend.

I stand up. I go outside, onto the wharf.

A golden moon shines low in the sky, in front of me.

I step down into the skiff and go back up the canal.

The wall of Gardens, the bare trees on the bank, the balloon's black nave.

Genua accompanies me, to pick up the parcels I have prepared and hand them over to Alberto Blanc, who is supposed to take them to Rome.

Death is with me, the smell of death. Renata is waiting for me: she knows everything. We embrace, weeping. She wants to come and see him.

I go into the dining room to get the flowers. Three places have been set! I gather all the flowers from all the vases, and carry them with me in a single bunch.

I return to the death chamber.

The candles burn. Their little flames flicker, mirrored in the blades of the bayonets. The two sailors stand guard, immobile.

I arrange the flowers on either side of the corpse. I feel the shape of his hips, his legs.

I lay the white jonquils on the red and green parts of the flag.

I uncover his poor face. The right cheek is swollen and blackening.

The mouth looks closed.

Reality, at moments, eludes me. I reflect. Close my eyes. I imagine him alive, as he was yesterday; then I look at him and see him there, inert, lifeless. Can it be?

The wake begins.

In front of me is the door to the other death chamber, where Giorgio Fracassini lies. It is illuminated, the shadows quivering.

The two sailors, immobile; the stiff gleam of the naked bayonets.

The swashing of the canal below, under the window.

The cry of the sentries.

A strange atmosphere, like a mass of impenetrable crystal, envelops the corpse.

Around ten o'clock the commanding officer arrives. He enters with a brisk step. He masters his emotions. Kneels, prays. He stands back up and goes into the room where Giorgio Fracassini lies. He shakes my hand in silence, leaves.

I hear the throbbing motor of his launch. Then all falls silent again.

Around midnight, Commander Giulio Valli arrives. He sits down beside me, talks about the deceased.

Sorrow, affectionate regrets.

He confesses that Giuseppe Miraglia had been asked to give everything in his power, and more.

In the early days of the war, with only a miserable little aircraft and an old Mauser pistol, he took to the skies alone against the enemy, he defended Venice, he explored Pola![16]

Valli talks to me about the confidence the aviator had in me, and about that which he inspired in me himself. Two days earlier, Giuseppe Miraglia had told him: "If I suggested to Gabriele D'Annunzio that we fly over Vienna, he would simply reply: 'Let's go'; he would settle into his seat and never look back."

The commander expresses his regret for the destruction of this duo, which had such grand designs and was capable of carrying them out. Then he speaks of the man's goodness.

My sorrow welcomes his measured words, circles round them like a whirlpool and seizes them.

Giulio Valli is a man of refinement; philosophical, steeled by irony, indulgent, strong, and flexible, able to understand and appreciate a character such as Giuseppe Miraglia's.

At about two in the morning, he leaves. I tell Luigi Bologna and Carlo della Rocca to go rest. Silvio Montanarella is supposed to come at four.

A new notion of time. The struggle between the living image, continually created by memory, and the motionless body.

When the anguish becomes unbearable and the black pall seems empty to me and in my love I imagine my companion placidly asleep in his bed in Sant'Andrea, I stand up and lift the gauze. The bloated face appears. The mouth is more closed than ever, more tightly sealed. The bronzelike color darkens.

I am exhausted. Carlo comes downstairs in his black smock and pleads with me to get some rest. I resist.

The guard of sailors is changed every two hours. They are almost all handsome, big, and stern, and have the noblest expression of sorrow. They wear leather cartridge belts, dark blue uniforms with light blue collars, and cloth berets.

Bells chime five o'clock. The next sentry cries out, the distant ones reply.

The swashing continues.

My feet are frozen on the naked floor. The cold is in all my bones.

I rise to go throw myself on a bed in a room on the second floor.

A sailor accompanies me through the shadow-filled corridors. A helmsman sleeps outside the door to the room, sitting, his arm on the back of a chair, his face in the crook of his elbow.

I go inside. The room is white. The bed is white.

An electric light over the bed is on. I dare not turn it off, however blinding.

I use my great gray cape as a blanket. I cover my head to block the light. I am dead tired but unable to sleep.

When I close my eyes and begin to doze off, I see my friend, alive, coming towards me. I start.

I dream that he is entering the Casa Rossa. I say to him: "Is it you? Have you come back?"

He uncovers himself, unwraps the black cape. It's not him: it's a mask, one of those white plaster masks the Venetians used to wear with the domino.

Time passes, I don't know how much.

I hear footsteps in the corridor. I hear trumpets sounding reveille in the barracks nearby.

My head hurts. The back of my neck and occiput throb painfully.

I hear the shuffling of the sailors cleaning the hospital corridors.

Is this the day? Once again reality eludes me.

Is it true? I bound out of bed and wet my eyes with a handkerchief dipped in a pitcher of water. I go downstairs.

I get lost in the hallways and stairways. At last I find the death chamber. I enter.

A haze of flowers and wax.

The black pall, unchanged. The corpse's shape, unchanged.

The two sailors standing guard.

The sounds of the day, outside. The horns, the bells, the city reawakening, life inevitably beginning again.

Good Silvio is there, red-eyed.

The pain in my head becomes so fierce that I can no longer stand it. I call for the launch and go out on the pier. I look out upon the cold ashen morning.

I return home, exhausted. I undress. My uniform smells of death to me. My underclothing has the same smell. I strip completely naked and enter the hot bath. Is there something of the corpse in me? I immediately wonder if they washed the wounded body before dressing it again.

A sense of the desert, of desolation, in the house.

Memories of an easy life.

His exquisite pleasure before my small Watteau, his Mandarin-like smile when I read him a concise image by a poet of the Far East.

Renata arrives. She is pale. She hasn't slept. She asks me questions, and I answer.

I must return to Sant'Anna by midday. I order a wreath and several bouquets of roses.

Renata wants to come with me.

We eat almost nothing. Death everywhere.

Seagulls flock in St. Mark's basin. Their quiet laughter, on the dark water's surface.

Renata is holding a bouquet of red roses bound with a light-blue ribbon.

Silence.

I advise her to control herself. She looks at me with courageous eyes.

We reach the pier. Step off the boat. There is no officer on guard.

Renata sets the roses at the feet of the corpse, kneels, and prays with her face buried in her closed hands. She does not cry.

After a few anguishing minutes, I nudge her and lead her away. She leaves by herself. I stay behind.

Twenty-four hours have passed since the moment of death.

I look at the face: it is more swollen, darker, and has blood in the nostrils and at the corners of the mouth.

Time passes. The guard changes. The same question lingers inside me: Why?

Luigi Bresciani comes in. He was one of Giuseppe Miraglia's most devoted friends, his flight instructor, despite being younger than he. We look at one another, unable to hold back our tears. We weep in each other's embrace.

Then the broken words, the explanation of the catastrophe, the technical discussion, new details, discoveries; and mute glances that touch the depths of our souls.

Two sailors bring in my wreath of white and red roses. I place it near his head. I also place Renata's bouquet near his right cheek (the one that was crushed).

Time passes, in unchanging horror. I go to look at Giorgio's face. He is waxen but serene. Blessed by profound peace.

It is night. I leave. I go home on foot, by way of the fondementa di Sant'Anna.

The moon is already high, behind the roof with ten chimneys. It is cold. A dry cold. Via Garibaldi is full of people. I hallucinate incessantly. I see Beppino walking ahead of me, with his short black cape, his quick step.

I walk along the Riva degli Schiavoni, the Piazzetta, and Piazza San Marco.

I walk by his house. I enter the alley that leads to Corte Michiel. The walls of the buildings close in on me like cliffs of ice.

Dim light in the vestibule. I climb the gloomy staircase, trembling. A woman's voice calls out: "Who is it?"

"Friends!"

At the top of the stairs stands the landlady. She says that the room is locked, having been locked by Gigi Bologna, who came to pick up Beppino's sword, two-pointed hat, and medals. I descend the stairs with a sorrow so heavy I wish I might never reach the bottom.

I flee. Chills run up and down my spine.

Santa Maria del Giglio: the bas-relief of Zara.

The bridges.

The narrow calle.

The Casa Rossa. Renata, anxious and pale.

We sit down at the table. Eat almost nothing. Our friend is there. The sweets he used to love, like a gluttonous child, are there. But there are no flowers. Two glass masks remain on the silver tray: Harlequin and Pantalone. I remove them, put them on the mantelpiece. We talk. About him. We drink our fill of despair.

I sleep for a few hours, with nightmares. I get up at three in the morning. I bring the thermos, full of hot coffee, that I used to take on flights.

I go out.

Moonlit night, diamondlike.

Venice dead, enclosed in an eternal diamond.

Deserted little streets and squares. The sound of my footsteps, almost frightening.

The hour chimes when I'm on the Ponte della Paglia. The sentries' cries multiply in the resonant glow.

Along the fondamenta di Sant'Anna, on the wall of a building lit up by the moon, I see the shadow of a soldier on watch, in the lookout, in arms.

This is the morning appointed for the great flight: a glorious morning. Not a breath of wind. Not a ripple on the lagoon. The sky is immaculate.

If only he were alive! At this hour we would be preparing

ourselves, donning our furs, testing our weapons, putting on our woolen skullcaps and leather gaiters. We would be cheerful, nimble, confident. Giorgio would be there getting everything ready in our seats. The message bag would already be there under the engine bonnet, as it was for Trieste.

I enter the death chamber.

Angelo Belloni is there. Triangular head, wide brow, big, intense eyes like a hawk's, unblinking.

We shake hands.

I notice at once that the pall has been moved, because the flowers I had earlier arranged around the body have been disarranged. The doctor has injected the body to preserve it a while longer.

There is no news from the relatives. We do not know whether the brother will come from Valona upon receiving the devastating news.

The two sailors are no longer standing at the head of the bed but at the foot. The room is already full of wreaths on stands.

Forms without beauty.

The pure form of the wreath is a perversion.

The stupidity of funeral wreaths assembled by vain florists. There is even an artificial one, made of porcelain and zinc.

The wreaths' shadows tremble on the wall. The candles' flames flicker, reflect off the bayonets.

I see the other two sailors standing guard through the doorway to the mechanic's room.

Angelo Belloni sits down beside me. He is slightly deaf. He talks and talks.

To answer him, I have to bring my mouth to his right ear.

He is a dear, true friend of the deceased. He talks about him. How well he knows him!

The tenderness of the friendships of youth.

He imitates a few of Beppino's mannerisms, remembers some of his little fixations.

Above all he praises his profound, hidden, humble goodness, giving one example after another.

He, too, tells me how much Beppino loved me, how he benefited from having met me.

We talk and talk. The friend has a lively, present, active spirit. We stand up almost at the same time, at once, with the same thought in mind.

I uncover the face of the deceased. Alas! The nose is swollen, bleeding, the nostrils stuffed with cotton. A horrific cotton bib hides the mouth. The bronze tint is darker still, without gold.

We feel stifled by the heavy atmosphere of flowers, candles, death. An atrocious taste on the tongue. We go out and see through the glass door that it is a bright, clear day outside! How many hours have passed?

This is the day, the day of the great flight. It is almost eight o'clock. At this hour we should already be airborne, flying towards Ancona. We should already be beyond the Punta Maestra, beyond all misery, beyond life, beyond ourselves.

I go out onto the pier.

Vermilion sunlight on the water's surface. Pure sky. The sun young and strong, dancing, aspiring to midday.

The lagoon is of iridescent silk, opaline. The leaning belfry of San Pietro looks made of mother-of-pearl.

The motor of a launch throbs energetically. Giorgio no longer hears it like the beating of his steely heart.

Dread, regret, the end of everything.

I go back into the room.

I feel offended by the idiotic shapes of the wreaths on their frames of cane, their fat, inert ribbons dangling, decked with golden letters. Only Renata's white roses look alive and sensate. Only the large bouquets of dark violets seem worthy of death.

I cannot stand it any longer. I leave and walk along the fondamenta. The red house with the ten chimneys is mirrored in the canal. Life is already unfolding, wretched and prattling. People look at my pale, survivor's face.

I go to the Arsenale. The Admiral receives me at once. I feel a pang in my heart. Our style of warfare dictated that the fallen should be replaced and the operation attempted, this very morning, on the appointed day. It was the best way to honor the dead hero.

To this lofty, severe mind, I briefly explain the need to carry on with the great flight. He understands and approves. He tells me he will support the expedition, as he had promised. He advises me to arrange things with the pilot I think most worthy to take the place of the fallen. He is plain, blunt, and to the point. I admired him already, but as of this moment I love him.

We talk about closing the body inside the coffin, and the funeral.

He tells me that Miraglia's father, who is old and unwell, will not be coming. Soon forty-eight hours will have passed. We decide that the corpse should be sealed inside today, at four o'clock in the afternoon.

I take my leave and go home.

It is such a beautiful day that I feel as if I have never seen one more beautiful. The twenty-third of December, our day!

Destiny has not only killed my companion in a single blow but dredged up a glorious morning from the bottom of the sea, to mock me. The sun rises with ineffable, unusual vigor, seeming so extraordinary perhaps because of my extreme fatigue.

I return home, back broken and bent. I have the shutters closed.

I take off my clothes, which are permeated with death. The handkerchief I remove from my pocket smells of wilted flowers and melted wax.

Renata prepares another bouquet of roses. She wants to return to Sant'Anna with me.

We hire a gondola.

Blue water, blissful, golden air, flocks of seagulls laughing their harsh laugh.

We dock at the Gardens so we can walk a little.

Hard, ringing ground. Naked, hopeless trees. If I look at the branches, they seem about to snap from my same sorrow.

Getting back into the gondola, we turn onto the canal, along the bank of dry trees. The captive balloon sways stupidly in the air, above its blackish cage.

The room is cluttered with new wreaths. The air is heavier than ever.

Renata kneels, sets down the roses, and prays. Then she steps out and leaves. She goes back in the gondola, alone with her secret.

Now begins the worst torture of all.

It is four o'clock, but the coffins still are not ready, and the welder has yet to arrive.

Between five and six o'clock, the smell of death in the room starts to become intolerable. I go out, come back, go out again.

I run into a close companion of ours, a young pilot who has already given ample demonstration of his prowess. I take him aside, lead him to the wooden pier, and talk to him. I ask him if he wants to take the fallen Beppino's place on the Dalmatian mission.

He hesitates. At last he says that he firmly believes that it has no chance of success, but that, as a good soldier, he will obey if so ordered.

He adds: "Only one engine. A treacherous aircraft. About nine hours in the air. We shall certainly fall and end up in the sea. And we can hardly count on the torpedo boats to rescue us. On the other hand, I am used to spending hours and hours in the water."

"And I get used to everything very quickly," I reply, finding my smile again for a brief moment.

My lost comrade's understated daring sweeps me up with it. I see his hands on the control column again, his green eyes behind the glass of the goggles. I sense that I shall never again find such a peer in my love of destiny.

We decide to discuss the matter with Commander Valli. Seeing my unchanging expression, the young man collects himself and assures me that he would be happy to attempt the flight with me if such an attempt is deemed necessary. But a friend of his, who has joined us in the meantime, rekindles the debate, opining that to go through with the mission would be a slight to the memory of the deceased . . .

The evening is opaline, golden, amber. The horizon is bejeweled, like a long succession of thrones.

Then the riches fade and turn cold. The sky and lagoon are two icy delicacies.

Can sweetness cut? This one does.

Man in his coffin adjusts to the horizon, ring of the universe.

I go back inside. I watch the wreaths being taken away. The sailors clear out the death room. I see the lidless coffin on the floor beside the small bed. The lid is propped up vertically against the wall.

My heart flutters so wildly, I lean on Luigi Bresciani's shoulder, though he, too, seems to be in need of support.

I regain my courage and push away those trying to drag me outside. I am resolved not to abandon my friend before the end. I remain standing, and silent.

The room is now empty. The sailors have cleared away all the wreaths. The candles have been moved. Of the flowers of mine that were on the pall, I let them take away the first and the most recent, except for the bouquet of white roses bound in a white ribbon.

The pall is removed. The frame of the cot appears, as do the wheels. Then I glimpse, in a flicker of flame, a dark stain under the bed, and I shudder.

The flag is removed from the headboard, the gauze from the unrecognizable face. Four sailors take the sheet by its four corners.

The open coffin lies on the floor, parallel to the bed. It is lined in lead, and rests on gilded feet.

I put my hand on my chin to prevent my teeth from chattering. The four sailors lift the sheet.

The corpse comes undone. I watch the joined hands come apart, the wrapped feet dangle, the head drop under its inert weight, the sailors' arms tense as the two men holding the coffin, the two mortuary workers, arrange the deposition from head to feet, indifferently, as if it were some sort of merchandise.

For a few seconds the soldiers' hunched bodies prevent me from seeing the corpse.

The two men guide the group, speaking softly. "This way. Now that way. That's it. Now down. That's it. It's the right size, a perfect fit!"

The right size: the body fits neatly inside the coffin. The bandaged feet rest on the bottom plank, while the head touches the top plank.

A kind of stony horror envelops me.

I feel, next to mine, Luigi Bresciani's soul, the pureset, tenderest, most devoted.

I alone come forward, kneel, look at the corpse, and lay the bouquet of roses on the poor, broken, bandaged feet.

The hands are yellow, the face almost black, like a mulatto's. The mouth is covered by the cotton bib.

I summon the courage to brush my lips lightly against the hand.

I rise again, choking; I turn, go towards Luigi, who is drained of color, his lips twitching like a child's. I lay my face on his shoulder, sobbing.

I hear the bed pass beside me on its wheels, as it is pushed towards the door at the back, open onto the cloister. The outside air enters, refreshing the irrespirable atmosphere of lingering smells, of flowers, wax, and decomposition.

I reopen my eyes.

The lead lid closes over the coffin. The welder grips the torch; the tongue of fire roars blue, yellow-tipped, filling the silence.

There are two men: one holds the live torch, the other holds a lamp, shedding light on their labor.

The door is left open onto the arcade. Cold air blows in, makes the dripping candles melt. Soot enters our nostrils.

The man maneuvering the flame is dark and young, with an impassive face, big and strong-limbed. His partner is about fifty, pensive, with a troubled face, moustache, and graying hair. They are bent over, one beside the other, with blowpipe, solderer, and rod of welding tin; together they work to fuse the lead.

The roar of the welder's flame fills the room.

All other sound has been banished.

There is only silence, and that voice.

At moments it becomes rhythmical, calling to mind the throbbing of a motor.

The jet of flame seals eternity. Time is infinite.

At each brief pause of the welder, one thinks: "There, it is done." But the roar does not stop.

The man wipes away the sweat with the back of his hand, then continues his work. The other examines the already soldered side, lowering his face to the seam, to look at it slantwise. He finds a flaw and alerts his partner, who approaches and rubs the spot.

This is the second stage of the parting.

The corpse is now separate from me, enclosed, alone; it already belongs to the grave. Soon it will belong to the church. Tomorrow it will be taken to the cemetery, laid in the depository, in a strange, unknown room. Thrice removed.

One day soon, it will be lowered into the earth, cast into the grave, buried. Four times removed.

He seemed still mine only a short while ago, however undone, however deformed. Now he's a prisoner.

The roses are with him, over his broken feet.

He could never rise again, even were Christ to call him.

The slab of lead weighs down upon him. The weld is complete, the seal perfect.

He is beyond us now. No longer in our air, the air we breathe, but in *his* air, the air of the tomb, the air of eternity, which the lungs between his fractured ribs do not consume.

The grizzled man examines the seam, making light for himself with the lamp, which practically burns his fingernails. He finds a few more flaws. And the roaring torch, which was sitting in a corner, is taken up again. The jet of flame is revived; the entire seal is rubbed and smoothed.

A voice, desolate and inhuman, says: "The sawdust."

I turn around. It's one of the hospital's doctors, a Navy doctor, small, hoary, diligent, precise. He repeats: "The sawdust."

I don't understand, and my eyes look all over the floor.

Not far from my feet, I see something white, which to my weary eyes looks like rose petals, from Renata's roses.

I bend down a little. They are wads of cotton.

Further away, in the middle of the room, I see again the dark stain I discovered under the bed.

It's blood. Blood and serum that seeped through the mattress . . . I feel my heart sink below my heels.

A sailor brings in the sawdust, and I watch the two welders sprinkle it over the lead coffin-lid. Why?

Because of the humidity. To protect the metal from the damp.

To coax the sawdust into the gap between the wooden box and the leaden one, the two men begin to slap the palms of their open hands rapidly against the wooden sides, the way masseurs slap muscles. I know that this technique, in that art, has a special name. The wood resounds. I close my eyes.

I imagine it is my supine friend waking up and making those thuds from the inside. I feel my exhausted mind on the verge of delirium and hallucination.

"Enough! Enough!" I cry in my head, but the cry does not come out.

The men meticulously continue their work until the gap is filled.

Then they sprinkle the remaining sawdust over the lid.

Then they take the wooden lid that is leaning against the wall.

The flame, meanwhile, roars, resting on the floor, near the window hidden by the unfurled flag.

The wooden lid is set in place, pressed down, and fitted. One of the men sticks in the screws and turns them.

On the lid is a gilded cross and a carved brass plaque.

Meanwhile a sailor wipes the floor clean of the bloodstain with a rag attached to a stick. When he has finished, he passes beside me, practically touching me, stick held high with the cloth dangling.

The coffin is finally ready. It is almost seven o'clock in the evening. I hear the cry of the sentry.

Four sailors lift the coffin with two straps of hemp. I draw near, put my hands underneath, and bear the weight.

I bump against the doorjamb when passing. We go out into the cloister and lay the coffin upon the wheeled bed. A long operation, because the coffin lurches, unable to find the proper position.

I lean forward to read the carved plaque: name and two dates. He was born on the *summer solstice*, June 21, 1883; he died on the *winter solstice*, December 21, 1915, at the age of thirty-two years and six months.

The little bed rolls on its wheels towards the Chapel.

The Chapel has no charm. The altar is in darkness.

I no longer know how to see, no longer know how to hear. I am enveloped in a horrible obtuseness.

The black and gold pall is laid over the coffin. A sailor beside me holds my flowers and waits for me to take them and arrange them again over the pall.

The two welders are working on Giorgio the mechanic's coffin.

The roar of the flame reaches my ears as I brush past the door of the first open room. I quicken my step.

I am nauseated by the smell of the flowers and wax. I go outside.

Darkness. Wandering shadows. Chatter. Smells of cooking, smells of poverty.

From time to time, I give a start. I keep seeing the small black cape fluttering before me. My knees buckle, broken by fatigue. I fear I shall never reach my refuge.

On the fondamenta di Sant'Anna a crowd of humble women throngs around the hospital gates.

Sorrowful faces of Mary, faces fraught with hardship and misfortune, faces of pity.

Emaciated children, all eyes, dirty and sad.

The sickly water of the canal.

The red house with ten funnel-shaped chimneys.

Gray sky, damp and cold.

When I cross the threshold of the Chapel, I no longer see anything but the two pall-covered biers between walls of wreaths.

The candles on the altar are lit.

Somebody says to me: "That's his brother." I see the brother, small like him, with a bony, energetic face and a short black beard. His jaw is moving continuously, convulsively moving, as if he were chewing something atrociously bitter.

He has come from Valona, from the command headquarters of a squadron of torpedo-boats. He left his night and day patrols to rush here. He finds the coffin sealed, draped with the pall. He brings the wind of war with him, the green smell of the lower Adriatic, something of the bridge of a torpedo-boat pursuing a target, something of the wake of a well-aimed torpedo. He is a man.

I have no wish to say anything. My teeth are clenched. I walk past a group of officers. I go and kneel down alone, beside the coffin, near to where the head is resting.

The head, unseen, lies two spans from me. There it is. I can see it through the pall and the wood. Yesterday evening it was darkened, smoky, swollen. Another night has passed. It is the third day. The decomposition continues.

I feel a horrible chill in my bones. To touch death, to leave one's mark on death, while one's heart is alive!

And yet we are alone again, the two of us, alone as in the cockpit in flight. Everyone else seems extraneous to me, even the brother. We are alone.

The priest says the funeral Mass. A prayer rises from the back of the Chapel, murmured by the sailors, a subdued, deep chorus.

My body feels immobilized. My knees hurt, I cannot move.

The priest now approaches the coffin, holding a book between two candles; he reads the prayer of the dead.

Yet my friend is here even now. When the ceremony ends, I feel that there are still several more degrees of separation to be crossed.

He is here, still mine. I smell his decayed flesh. I see the white roses over his bandaged feet.

Four sailors come forward to lift the coffin with broad straps. They take it away.

My heart aches and convulses. Death withdraws a bit further.

Moving instinctively, I approach and put my hands under the coffin: I feel its weight. The pall covers my arms up to the elbows.

As I walk I see nothing but the black and gold and the flowers.

Renata's flowers with the light-blue ribbon are there, together with mine.

We walk on and on. I feel the water nearby. We step onto a wooden planking. The other coffin is behind me, hard on my heels.

A shallop decked out in black and silver, its rudder covered with drapery, waits at the pier. I stand at the edge. The coffin lurches, escapes my grasp. I touch it no longer. I close my eyes.

The sailors lower it into the boat, set it down, feet pointed forward. The other coffin is laid beside it.

Then wreaths upon wreaths upon wreaths. As in a dream, a performance, a dance figure.

Under the gray sky, the yellow cries out, the red shrieks. Countless wreaths, carried by sailors, continue to pass by, one after the other.

They pass, they board, they fill the funeral boat, and two others as well.

It looks like the June festival when the *peate* come in from the islands, bearing their cargoes of flowers and fruit.[17]

Wreaths and more wreaths!

It is like a circular motion, a sort of dance figure, a sort of holy procession: something ancient, pagan. The wonderment stops the pain.

The boats are full. The motors crackle. The waterborne cortège sets out, passes under the wooden bridge thronged with people looking on and mourning.[18]

The people form their own wreath of sorrow on the arched bridge, in silence.

The shallop with the two coffins is towed by another boat.

A boat filled with flowers floats alongside it, on the left.

A black gondola, in whose cabin one glimpses the priest and his acolyte, is on the right.

Slowly the boats ply discolored lagoons cleft by their pale wake, death's wake, along a channel marked by poles.

The water is low, the shoals emerging.

And now the reddish walls encircling the island of the dead.

I turn to look at the Casino degli Spiriti in the distance, the gardens of Tomaso Contarini, the places of our delight. (Summer evenings, lunar evenings; gondolas full of women not ours; melancholy and disdain.)

We are at the quay, before a wall of corroded brick with cypresses rising above it.

We dock.

It is like a dream from beyond the sea, otherworldly.

I stand upon flagstones again.

And again I walk behind the coffin, again I touch it, take it in hand.

We enter the cloister, under the arcade. We head towards a door, towards the mortuary depository, where the two bodies will wait until Monday to be buried.

I do not stray from my casket. I enter a cold, whitewashed room.

The coffin is placed on two sawhorses. It is still covered by the pall and my flowers.

As I collect myself and bid my friend a last farewell (his body tossed about by the continual motion, the repeated attempts to set it down stably), here, again, come the wreaths.

They are enormous, some of them. The people carrying them arrange them against the walls, one on top of the other. There a hundred of them, or more.

The air is irrespirable. Flowers still alive, flowers already dead. The entire room is packed with them. To make room, one must press down the wreaths, squeeze them together, trample them . . . I feel faint. I am taken outside.

I fear I shall never love flowers again. I have been poisoned by the stench of the tomb.

My mind is absent. I am in a daze. I cannot remember the pause in the hospital courtyard.

As we are leaving the Chapel, the person in charge of the ceremony, Commander Valli, stops the two caskets in the middle of the courtyard.

I see some men standing in formation. Those in attendance draw up around them. I see admirals, generals, and officers with heads bared. The brother is beside me. There is deep silence. What are we waiting for?

I look around, and see many eyes looking at me. What is happening?

Commander Valli comes up to me and asks me if I would like to speak.

I think I must have turned even paler, because then he thoughtfully said: "No, no, if you can't, if you don't feel up to it . . ."

And all around was a frightening silence.

The gray sky bears down on my head like an iron cowl.

The silence seems eternal.

I have to wrench the words from my broken heart. The brother looks at me. Everyone's attention is on me. Their expectation is anguishing, and increases with each moment.

I take a step forward; then I turn towards the bier.

I don't see the other casket; and so I forget the other deceased.

I speak in a voice that makes every fiber in my body tremble, and which I almost do not recognize.

I see tears flowing down a face. And words suddenly fail me.

When the depository is finally stuffed full of flowers, the custodians close it. I hear it shut behind me.

We walk towards the quay, where the boats await.

Someone accosts me and shows me a message that a sandalo oarsman brought to him from the Casino degli Spiriti.[19]

Rosalinda is here.[20] She arrived this morning, unexpectedly. She went to the Casino to watch the funeral boat pass and then dock. She wishes to see me and talk to me. She asks me to come to her.

I can't. I have no strength left. I shall wait for her at the Casa Rossa, if she can come before her departure. She has to leave at two o'clock. It is already midday.

On the way back, my boat hugs the walls of San Michele, brick-red on a base of light-colored stone.

I recall a summer night, an August night. We had gone to Murano in a gondola. Rosalinda was with us. The lagoon was so phosphorescent that each stroke of the oar raised long, white flames. And we leaned out to watch. The women's chins were illuminated by it.

Along the cemetery walls we ceased our laughter and banter.

We heard only the measured thuds of the oars. And under the funereal walls the phosphorescence created rings and garlands of light.

A luminous melody encircled the isle of the dead.

And he heard it. He saw it. He already had his deep place there.

A respite. He is of the cemetery, but not yet of the earth. His grave has been dug but it will not be filled until after the sacred day.

The pain has dulled. I am now in a sort of dark torpor, dead tired.

Renata remains silent, enclosed in her secret, her unmoving eyes hollow under thick lashes, like the unblinking eyes of Roman eagles.

The house lies in tomblike stillness, surrounded by dead water like the island where I left my friend. The palazzo of the Lions is there, on the Canal, with its dried grasses, its look of wild abandonment, like a house of legend.[21] The white peacocks do not cry on the marble staircase green with mildew; but the seagulls weave and reweave their flights over the livid water, floating, then rising, more silent than snowflakes in windless air.

Someone rings at the door.

I can no longer hear the doorbell without giving a start.

It is Rosalinda, out of breath, veiled, with hands extended. I was no longer expecting her.

Evening falls quickly.

I have to take her back to the station.

I call for a gondola.

We enter its gloomy hull. The entire canal is dark. Inside the cabin, I cannot see her. The darkness is the same as that inside the coffin, out there, amidst all those withering wreaths.

Evening descends on the isle of the dead, the deserted cloister, the scattered tombstones, the grim well, a tomb among tombs, the closed door of the depository room, the grave dug into the muddy grass, the crosses dense and bristling like sticks in scrub, the underwater bells, the sirens of the vaporetti passing by . . .

I leave her abruptly on the darkened quay, where phantoms wander. I climb back inside the gondola's cabin.

My friend is out there inside his lead, just as I am inside this swaying prison that stinks of mildew and rot, at low tide.

All at once, I feel afraid. Someone is with me. I keep still, my eyes trained on the door.

As I write in the dark, my thought breaks off, my hand stops.

Then the strip of paper I have turned over floats upward and falls back down over my fingers, noiselessly.

I shudder in fear. And remain still, my entire body stiff, not daring to trace even one more sign in the darkness.

SECOND OFFERING

Tonight the bed sways and shakes like a double wing stretched between sea and sky. I open my mouth to drink the Adriatic's vigor, but no cool draught enters my throat.

Iodine turns my mouth to metal, my throat to steel. Steel heated red in the forge of my burning eye and tempered in the pool of my thick blood.

I cry out and do not hear my cry.

Alfredo Barbieri's pale face is at the edge of the bed as at the edge of the cockpit, but without goggles or leather aviator's cap. The pilot's gesture is imparted to my numbed arm but does not move it.

I see the blackened glove of Oreste Salamone in the act of shifting his heavy body, which had fallen onto the control column abandoned by Luigi Bàilo when he stood up to fire from the rear at the enemy circling round into his sights.

The body falls back to the right, head dangling. The leather cap fills like a round cup. The spraying begins, like sparks of a firebrand consumed in the wind's fury.

Luigi Bàilo returns to the fore by the footbridge between the two fuel tanks. He is no longer holding a weapon. With one hand he supports his mangled arm.

Only one able pilot remains at the helm. He must be protected, so he may lead the wings and their cargo back to the Fatherland.

The wounded one leans over his companion, to shield him, though disabled and unarmed.

I can see, through my mask, through the wool and skin, the sovereign transfiguration of a man's narrow face: the god in the ciborium.

And now the wounded man is wounded further within, from the third burst of gunfire. The magnanimous shield has been pierced. The will again glistens in the glistening crimson.

He staggers, bends backwards, leans against the fuel tank, tries to lock his knees, which are buckling beneath him. He does not want to give in. He can still act as a shield. He is needed.

From time to time, Oreste turns round to look at him. He takes a hand off of the control column to touch his brother and comfort him.

He turns around again and sees him lying on the footbridge, between copper tanks, on his back: a sack of blood.

The survivor used to be one life; now he is three lives, and all their indomitable love.

My breast is full of cries, but I do not hear my voice.

The bed sways, swerves, and then plummets. A desert of rocks, crumbling and porous, hurtles precipitously towards my unblinking eye. The moments are eternal. The fall never-ending.

Here is the Carso, pale. Here the forest of Tarnova, black. Here the Isonzo, cerulean.[1]

In my fall I now seem to see my bones shining white. My

mouth is open and parched as one of those crevices in the naked limestone.

I burn. The sweat drips like tears that can no longer fall by way of the lashes.

Midday. The streets of Pordenone are deserted and sad. Past a perspective of bare trees in the distance, I glimpse the sublime sapphire mountains. A stray dog darts in front of the car and the tires screech. I arrive at Headquarters. The door is ajar. I push it open and enter. I do not know why, but the sound of my footsteps on wood in the shadows frightens me. The house is deserted. Nobody appears. I call out.

A sandy-haired footsoldier appears behind a counter, mumbling with a mouthful of bread that he hasn't had a chance to swallow yet.

Paying no mind, I ask him: "Is Colonel Barbieri in the camp?"

He seems not to understand. He forces himself to swallow the troublesome mouthful.

"He's been expecting me," I add. "Where is he?"

He doesn't answer. He turns around and goes into the adjoining room.

The silence is so complete that from where I stand I can hear him muttering. A gust of wind rattles the windows, on which I can make out the snaillike trails of the raindrops. I notice the vertical lines of the wallpaper, the knots in the wood of the counter. There is something in the air that leads my mind to interpret the slightest signs.

The infantryman returns with a bundle of furs stained brown

and spattered with dried blood. He sets the grim package down on the counter the way a merchant lays down a bolt of fabric to be measured by the yard.

These are the remains of Alfredo Barbieri from the Ljubljana mission.

The air has turned to freezing crystal. It has the same quality as the spiritual mass of ice that surrounds the head of the corpse during the first hour. At my speed I slice through it the way a diamond cuts glass. And the howling cleaves my brain.

I arrive at La Comina. The massacre does not trouble the men's seasoned hearts. My comrades' welcome is not without smiles. I sense that youth is more troubled by midday hunger than by any other concern.

I climb another staircase of torment. I enter the small room in which Oreste Salomone is lying on a small field cot. At first all I see is the bandage wrapped around his head; then I see only his magnanimous eyes, immobile in the two recesses of his pallor.

He looks as if he, too, had lost all his blood in the wind and the roar, like the other two, even though the machine gun only tore a strip of scalp and a clump of hair from his head through the hard helmet.

He is made of veinless ivory, devoutly sculpted. Strength has abandoned him. The superhuman strength of his example has scattered into the universe and is no longer inside him. His fate stands like a timeless column atop him, as he lies there, patient.

All is completed. All is consummated. The room is inside four walls the way the coffin is inside four planks.

The reward for magnanimity is no larger than a coin. Near the head of the bed, amidst the vials of medication, shines a newly minted medal devoid of beauty.

The hero's hand is as weak as a young boy's. I hold it tightly in my own, as if to share in his glory, with a divine anguish aspiring to heroic sacrifice, the recompense for every misery and failing in me.

Before he speaks, fate's cruelty eats away at me inside. The forward position had been destined for me in the Ljubljana reprisal mission: the combat and control position, near the blue-black weapon.

"We waited for you till midnight," says the ivory ascetic.

I imagine their vain expectation in the dimly lit coffee shop on the deserted piazza. Destiny was about to cast so great a die onto a table of ignoble stone, between the dregs of liqueurs and the ash of cigars!

"He's not coming," Alfredo Barbieri had said at midnight. "I'm sorry. He was supposed to be the Signal for the squadrons."

And he had repeated a line of mine from the book of Electra.

After a brief silence, as if listening to the distant night, he had added: "All right, then. I'll take his place myself."

Luigi Bàilo had tried to dissuade him. "If he doesn't arrive in time, we can increase the bomb load with the equivalent of his weight."

"We need a Signal," the generous one replied. "Your Commander will come along with you."

The lights had gone out in the sad shop. Destiny had switched the dice in the dark. Death had struck my name from the tablet and promptly written the other's on it.

It is not true that death is the same for everyone.

The survivor speaks softly, not from deep in his bed but from the depths of his sacrifice, from the innermost recess of I know not what crypt overflowing with the powerful presence that emanates from venerated relics. His hand is still in mine, as I bend towards his strained breathing.

My chest deflates with every word that evokes my death to my living self, my glory to my disillusion. It is as if my chest were being emptied of the fleshly things that breathe and throb, and were filled instead with only an inexpressible feeling that is not regret or remorse, not rancor or sorrow or rage, not wonder or ecstasy or remembrance, but all of these inescapable emotions together.

"Tell me, tell me."

The colorless hero grows weaker and weaker. His pauses longer and longer. I show no pity. I prod his weariness.

"Tell me!"

He speaks not of the other, but of me: of me, the poet by my poetry, the fighter by my prowess. I am a shade returning from the bloody life of the heavens. I am a winged shade listening to his own myth.

The glorious head had two holes in it. Out of one, the blood sprayed and blessed my comrades, out of the other, it flew like sparks in the morning wind . . .

But suddenly the lids close over the large brown eyes, and tears fill the dark hollow circles beneath them.

Silence. I lay my cheek on a corner of the pillow, and I remain still, ecstatic, on the other side of my consciousness, with my sorrow, which is greater than the two of us, my sorrow, which has the shape and appearance of a victorious being.

And thus we are three again, as on the prow of the fighter plane.

For another departure? Into what other sky?

The air turns to cold crystal again, under the sharp diamond of speed. I resume my course. I feel only half-alive. Half of my soul has passed on; the other half is on its way, curious about the material world below, observing the mechanism of its tragedy.

I think of the instruments of the Passion, hung from wood no longer bearing the weight of the tortured body. I think of the great crosses erected at forks in the road, crosses without crucifixions, crowned by the watchful cock who did not crow the third time.

Four essences of wood made up the cross of the sacrifice: cedar, cypress, palm, and olive. Should we not, in our Western world, replace the palm and cedar with the ash and poplar of the heroic wing?

The airfield at Gonàrs is wretched as a flattened Calvary. "The Roman Eagle" is alone, apart, far from the row of light aeroplanes, a few steps from the little canal that was miraculously avoided in the deadly descent. Its two double, transverse wings, between prow and rudders, form the bloody cross.

It lies on the plain, on a rise. It looks like a solid structure of wood and canvas and metal, and yet it is a spiritual substance. It seems lifeless, and yet it is taut with life like a sail that swells with good fortune. It looks mute, and yet in one and the other wing-cell, between each rib, between one motor and another, between one fuselage and another, by way of the steel cables, in the cockpit full of instruments, and along the polished edge, the silence is such that to him who listens, it says unforgettable things. It is a testament of blood.

There is not one part that is not spattered with it. The blood is now congealed; and yet it drips onto my head when I bend down between the wheels of the undercarriage, not daring to kneel before unfamiliar witnesses. By the thousands, the droplets warm up, revive, redden anew, like the brown relic that turns quickly back into fiery liquid in its vial.[2]

I climb up the side near the prow, climb up by the force of my own shudder, barehanded, and the droplets press into my palms.

I relive my own death, suffer its ordeal anew. Here I am at my place, facing the blue-black machine gun, my back to the two control sticks. My heart beats in my throat, throbs in my palate, knocks against my teeth. Reality bursts through my dream; and my dream cuts through reality.

I hear the rumble of the light aircraft as they rise from the field to help adjust the aim of the artillery, then pass over the aerial transmitting station.

I glimpse, behind the barrel of the enemy's weapon firing its first burst at me, the horrific white on an eye.

I espy over a yellowish field a row of gray bombs all in a line, their vanes gleaming behind them.

I absorb the tremors of a sky shaken by waves bearing the messages of the distant battle of the Carso.

I see the cunning gesture of the encircling enemy, inviting me to descend and surrender.

I turn around with a start, as if someone had touched me. To the right of the control column abandoned by Luigi Bàilo, at the edge of the cockpit, along the line of the gun sight, I see the exact spot where my neck rests—like the spot on the chopping block the axe-wielding executioner indicates to the kneeling victim.

What imperious hand now pushes and bends me?

My head drops, stretches forward, dangles. My bones freeze.

The dark, perpendicular streak of blood looks as if it starts at my spellbound eye.

Faces, faces, faces, so many passions in so many faces flow through my wounded eye, countless as hot sand running through a fist. Not one stops. But I recognize them.

Is this not the Roman throng in May, on the evening of the Campidoglio?[3] Vast, undulant, howling?

I feel my pallor burning like a white-hot flame. There is nothing of myself left in me. I am like the demon of tumult, the genius of a free people.

My thirty years of constancy, my love and compassion for beautiful Italy, the courage of my solitude, my song in the desert, my contempt for incomprehension and insult, my patient waiting, the anxiety of my exile are transformed into a single mass of red-hot strength.[4] All the past converges towards all the future. At last I am living my *Credo*, in spirit and in blood. I am no longer drunk on myself alone but on my entire race.

Faces, faces, faces, forged in the embers of the flesh, stamped in the fire of blood.

The tumult breathes like a furnace, pants like a voracious crater, crackles like wildfire.

I enthrall and am enthralled. I rise to crown and be crowned.

An epic springtime uplifts and enchants me, as if all these ancient triumphal stones had been washed away by a crimson lifeblood.

Riotous swallows brush past Marcus Aurelius' green horse,

which at each cry of the birds looks about to throw the Emperor off its back and rear up before this latest destiny.[5]

The multitude's confused delirium becomes a clear voice in me.

I speak. My every word resounds in my skull as if reverberating in concave metal. Every breath strains the dome of my chest. It hurts and I feel proud that my joy is mixed with suffering.

It is like the pain of creation, the anguish of birth. The crowd howls in labor. The crowd howls and writhes to beget its fate.

Beyond the lead-covered railing I see thousands and thousands of faces and yet only one face: a face of passion and expectation, of will and insurrection, burning in my chest like a generous wound.

Like an improvised *chanson de geste*, my speech divides into broad laisses completed and transported by the roars of the crowd.

Overwhelmed by a cry louder than the rest, I lose my voice in the pause. The imperious cry seems to demand more than words.

An unknown hand lays a large sword, curved like a scimitar, on the leaden railing.

I pick it up and unsheathe it. That cry demanded this gesture. Its gleam is like a bolt of lightning flashing over the clamor.

It is the sword of Nino Bixio, the hero's sharp-edged weapon, with the names of all of his victories inscribed on the polished blade.[6]

I press my lips against the unsheathed sword. It does not feel cold to me, for there is no blood left in my lips. All my blood burns in my heart.

The throng's sudden silence is like a vortex drawing me in and spinning me round, a maelstrom sucking and destroying my life.

I cast my life aside, abandon my soul to the delirium. The last words are like the blows with which the smith boldly strikes the swage at the mouth of the furnace to make the molten metal flow into the mould.

The throng is like an incandescent melt. All of the mould's holes are open. A gigantic statue is cast.

I turn. I step down. I stagger, slightly dizzy. I am devoured by thirst. I ask for the kindess of a drink of water. The humble women gathered surround me with pity as I wait. A rough hand holds out a glass of lustral water. I quench my thirst and am purified. I drink, enact the libation that precedes the sacrifice.

I descend. I do not know who is carrying me. All around me is fervor and clamor, creation and exaltation, danger and victory, under a hazy sky of battle where the darting swallows cry.

It pains us to be unarmed. It pains us not to fight, not to be transformed into an onslaught of swift legions crossing the unjust border.

Disheveled youths with wild faces, dripping with sweat as after wrestling, throw themselves against the wheels as if to be crushed.

Laborers darkened by the cinders of toil, bent by attention, contorted by effort, laborers of every sort, who look to me as if they have all handled the hammer, struck the searing iron against the anvil, reach out to me with strong hands as if to grasp me and crush me with their sudden love.

Common women powerfully sculpted like the mother of the two Tribunes throw me flowers and give up their sons to war in one same gesture.[7]

The hem of a flag covers my eyes. It is the red flag of Trieste.[8] It forever flies over my head. At moments it flutters, falls, and blankets me. I fill its folds with my panting.

In the red shadow of its folds I hear the first toll of the Capitoline bell. My heart bursts. I rise. The wheels stop. The crowd falls silent. It is but a single column of vertebrae traversed by one same shudder.

The bell rings the tocsin. The peal of the brass penetrates all to the marrow. A vast cry drowns it out. War! War!

Does it toll from the depths of dead centuries? Or from the depths of centuries to come?

We are borne up by the twentieth wave of the centuries—ten and ten—by the second decuman surge.[9]

The bell of the people proclaims war. It is no longer bronze but red fire at the summit of the Latin sky. The entire Nation hears it and leaps.

War! War! The evening's splendor is overwhelmed by myriads of flaming eyes, by brandished flags and threats, by a free people glorified and taken back by their true god.

Faces faces faces, so many passions of so many faces flow through my wounded eye, countless as hot sand running through a fist.

If only I had a respite, as on that night after the throng!

I was almost as parched as I am now. Like one of those black-smiths who toil all day at the forge, negotiating the malleable fire, then come out seared and bronzed for the tavern.

Seeking myself, I found only my melancholy. Seeking silence, I found only my music.

On that night of triumph I set off alone towards the Aventine, towards Freedom's hill, alone as a lonely lover.[10] I was gripped by a sensual love of Rome, a voluptuous love of my Rome, like the love that consumed my strength in youth. I had breathed the scent of the multitude and was avid to breathe the secret breath of my Rome after so many years away, so many seasons of desire and regret.

Walking up Via di Santa Sabina, I paused at moments, under the burden of a life that had grown beyond the limits of my strength. The shade was like a veil covering beauty's forbidden flesh, and it lifted for me, though I was afraid to touch it. Every step brought me closer to excruciating happiness. The five years lost in a distant land weighed on my soul and ached in my heart; and yet my regret seemed to increase my power of possession manifold.

The deserted street belonged to me. I was lord of the hill. I did not raise my eyes to the heavens, not wanting to disperse my love of this world. All I wished to know of the night was the edge that was Rome's dark, starless dress.

Yet as I entered the small square in front of the Priory of Malta, at once a silent star flickered before me, flashing at eye-level.

My heart leapt in wonderment. Along the walls there was a palpable warmth which the twinkle of light mysteriously elicited with each flash, between each pause.

My heart beat as it does in childhood, when virgin sight first discovers the earth's mysterious grace. The closed door of the Garden of the Knights—the pierced door through which so many eyes fix their gaze upon the airy Dome through the palm trees— had I know not what clairvoyance about it, thanks perhaps to I know not what beloved eyelashes fluttering sweetly in memory.[11] And as it sparkled by the door, for a moment the earthly star brought back to life the gaze that had once revealed to me the image of that chaste garden, reflected in a nascent love.

My heart beat with desperate youth. I was alone in the silence and shadow, between walls that lived their pallor like a lunar memory, alone with that floating gleam which drew out the thread of my inner life. I seemed not to know what it was, not to remember, after five ambiguous summers in the extreme West (Italy! Italy!). I followed it like a beacon of my new season of life, forgetful, astonished, enraptured.[12]

It was the first firefly.

I touch another silence.

The evening of open accusation, against the treason of those who would repeat the dark maneuver, is dominated by a silence like no other.

I recapture the tone of my first words.

"Listen. Listen. I have some momentous things to say, things you don't know. Keep quiet. Listen to me. Afterwards, you will leap to your feet, all of you."

The theater is like a deep casting pit.

I see the metal cool. The molten statue of the crowd turns solid, stabilizes into a menacing relief, stands like a crushing mass.

They no longer shout. They listen. They no longer breathe. They listen. Every syllable penetrates the porous bone of their skulls and becomes embedded there.

It is a terrible labor of the hammer, against a resistant silence.

I strike once, strike again, strike yet again.

The formidable mass is on its feet. The molten colossus is made human again by its shout.

I believe that even then I suffered this same voluntary burning. It was as though I were being turned over and over in the fire I myself had lit. I was like the ember in the myth of Aetolia. When will my own mother put me back in her hearth to be consumed?[13]

Even then I had a terrible thirst. I wanted to kneel before the basins of Rome's fountains to drink my fill with my whole face.

Why won't you now let me drink a cool draught?

Back then, chance sometimes granted me surprising ways to quench my thirst.

That evening, when leaving the sweltering theater, I saw some red clouds in the sky, as if the people's bloody passion were reflected in them. The first barricade had been erected.

Light horsemen guarded the street corners and intersections. They saluted me when I passed. Under the wild forelocks of their Maremmano horses, I saw the whites of the animals' eyes, which evoked an indescribably tender memory in me. I touched a crupper, touched a mane in passing, with sudden, youthful delight. The soldiers smiled.

Smiles on weary twenty-year-old faces, vague as those that prelude sleep.

I recalled the smell of the stable at Faenza, the stall of my black Maremmano, who would try to nip me whenever I ran the brush under his belly, the forage I would slyly steal from other feeding troughs in order to fill his, the watering at dawn, when in the faint light the buglers' white horses looked to me as if they had descended from a moon of legend.

Thus my fever broke and abated.

Oh, bring me one of my dogs, put him on my bed beside my joined feet, let him spend this night with me!

Tonight the demon takes my glowing eye in the palm of his hand and blows on it with all the might of his swollen cheeks.

All the images catch fire.

Now the distant Battle of the Meuse enters my blaze. Battalions drunk on ether advance like those burning tracts of pine forest called "backfire" in the Lande of my exile, like the herds of animal flames I saw resin-tappers drive forward waving great green fronds.[14]

They approach on the run, growing larger and larger. I see them through the poles and spurs of barbed wire. I distinguish one by one the Bavarians' faces twisted in fury and terror. They burst into flame like bundles of kindling wood.

The killing fields become pyres. They do not burn up or turn to ash. They smolder a long time without flames, like peat.

I spend the whole night stretched against the barbed wire blocking the hill. I count the corpses.

They are caught in the iron brambles, trapped in the snarls of broken wire, dangling between one post and another like thieves poorly nailed to their crosses, twisting like beasts in snares.

They have no eyelids, no lips. I see their frozen, naked eyes; their frozen, naked teeth.

I see blood flow down onto the wood and iron, clotting, blackening, viscous as birdlime smeared on twigs.

There is no more dew, no more dawn over the world.

It is raining in torrents, on Ash Wednesday evening. A March downpour. I listen to the pelting.

I now have—I think—a more sensitive ear than when I composed "Rain in the Pine Grove."

I can see all the strings in the great harp of the air, and very nearly pluck them.

Would I could make two holes in the wall to the garden, and stick my dried-up hands outside!

Is the cloudburst not perhaps too violent for the downy new leaves?

Nerissa sends her maidservant out into the rain to bring me a bouquet of flowers she found in Padua this afternoon.

The dampness enters my room, the cool spreads into my bedclothes.

Speaking about the maidservant, the nurse tells me spiritedly:

"She came without an umbrella! She's dripping like a gutter. The flowers are all soaked. We'll have to wait for them to dry."

My incessant thirst smells the humid scent, which immediately saturates my darkness. My heart races. I ask the compassionate woman to approach, to let me touch the bouquet. I beg her. I threaten to tear off my blindfold and throw myself out of bed. I get my way.

The flowers are laid on the turndown. They lie under my seeing fingers. I touch them, separate them, recognize them.

There are hyacinths, tied into little bunches with string. The stems are unequal in length. Together they form a dense bundle. As I smell them the scent grows like the pain inside a deep scratch.

There are *zàgara*, as the Saracen Sicilians call orange blossoms, using the Arabic name. I learned this in adolescence, on my own shores, from the cabin boy on a schooner. I like the name so much that I need only say it to smell the fragrance.

There are hothouse zàgara: a bunch of leaves that make noise to the touch, with hard little buds in the middle. I feel them one by one. A few are closed, a few are split, a few are half open. A few are delicate and sensitive, like a nipple recoiling from a caress. The scent is pure, tart, childish. But the nostrils must seek it out amidst the gelid, dripping leaves, which moisten my chin and enter my mouth.

There are mignonettes. These are the most sodden with rain, imbued with water from the clouds. They smell strongest at the apex, like fingertips after applying makeup. Deep within their fragrance is a hint of milky figs, little green figs. There is also, if I think about it, a hint of ripe Reine-Claude plums. A smell of grass or fruit more than flowers.

I like the zàgara best, both the name and the flower. It is more slender, more rare. Not nuptial but virginal. I am still searching for it amidst the leaves. It turns the eye's fire white. It is hard and white like the sclera.

I remember the great orange plantations at Villacidro, on the island of Sardinia. I was lithe as an animal. My ankles were slender. I used to take off my shoes and socks to walk with bare young feet on the snowy flowers strewn all over the ground.

I remember a walled orange grove at Massa, near the Amalfi coast, if my memory does not deceive me. I was recovering badly from an evil potion. I was astonished, as if entering an unimaginable labyrinth. The tree trunks looked carved from the stone of secret grottoes. The flower was like the froth from which immortal flesh is born. The shade was almost watery, modulated by the dying song of I know not what siren banished from the sea.

The rain does not stop. I hear it pelting the garden, the quay, the campiello, the street.[15] The donor no doubt hasn't the courage of her maid to confront the deluge submerging shadowy Venice. The flowers themselves seemed to say this.

The boredom of immobility oppresses me. A dull rage stretches from the nape of my neck to my heels. I will get up, throw off my bandages, and go walk along the gutters.

My melancholy pleasure is already exhausted. My neck throbs. The hyacinths' stalks ooze an unpleasant fluid that has smeared onto my fingers.

But where is this scent of sweet violets coming from? Are there violets in the room? Who has hidden them from me?

I extend my hands carefully around me, searching. I find a bundle that had slipped from the covers to the edge of the bed. My heart races. It leaps at the slightest thing!

It's a bouquet of violets. When wet, it had no scent. The warmth of the bed brings it back to life. It is an exquisite surprise. I relish it as if I had picked them myself at the edge of an unknown field.

These are not the violets of Padua; for me they are the simple violets of golden Pisa.

I remember a March downpour in Pisa. We were in Piazza del Duomo. We took refuge under the architrave of the central portal and shook off the raindrops. And there we lingered, waiting for the rain to stop. *Imbres effugio*, said the speaking emblem on the door.

The rainfall watered the short grass with an even patter that sounded as intimate as the murmur of a seashell against the ear. Pressed up against the bronze of the doors, we slowly took possession of it, merging with it.

The dampness seemed to increase the preciousness of the material. Like curious children, we stuck our fingers into the metal foliage, caressed the garlanded little heads poking out between the olives and the branches. Above us the symbols spoke: *"Fons signatus, Hortus conclusus."*

To our astonishment, amidst the foliage we began to discover countless lizards, snails, frogs, birds, fruits. Our fingers felt the artist's pleasure in modeling the forms, his skill and his whimsy. The more we marveled at the bronze, the richer its patina became, the more powerful and profound. It was enhanced by our loving eyes, and returned our love in kind. Above us the symbols spoke: *"Onustior humilior, Tantummodo fulcimentum."*[16]

The hiss of the rain was slowly diminishing. It seemed to reach us and vanish inside us like the echoing harmony inside the Baptistry. The deserted lawn had an indescribable, neglected sweetness about it, along the walls of the old partisan city. Archbishop Ubaldo's Camposanto was closed, huddled in silence round its fifty-three ship-holds of soil from Calvary.[17]

And so we stepped down from the polished threshold. We quit the bronze and marble for the grass. Night was falling. We were alone. And life led us indulgently by the hand.

It was said that every day towards evening, a silent fever rose up from the ditches and canals beyond the Camposanto and floated over the holy lawn. But all we felt was the shudder of a soggy spring.

We walked between the outer wall of the Camposanto and the side of the cathedral, a magical space for our music. The frescoes within shone through the stone in our fantasy.

And our music had the face of the woman in a dress leaning forward, cheek resting on her psaltery.[18]

I was watchful, and attentive to my desire.

I was what I am when my nature and culture, my sensuality and intelligence cease to struggle and become fully reconciled.

I was a musical mystery, with the taste of the world in my mouth.

Every time I stopped and lingered, my companion, whom I called Ghìsola, would ask me: "What are you looking for?"[19]

Night was falling. The marble's shadow was cerulean. It was a stone that at dusk turned as blue as lapis lazuli. And it turned the grass blue too, as with a brushstroke of ultramarine.

The silence opened up before us, parting to the left and right, flowing on either side of us the way the river polishes a swimmer's body. Ours was simple, ineffable feeling. We were poor and light, we were rich and light. We were like two vagabonds without haversacks, two rulers without diadems.

"What are you looking for?" the beautiful Ghìsola asked me at intervals, as in a song.

Was I a magical seeker of treasures and springs? I had all my treasures and springs within me.

I was looking for my desire. And look what I found!

I paused, gently closing my eyes to hold my happiness under my eyelids. I was but a single sensation. My entire brain quivered with my keen nostrils.

I bent down in the damp shadow, nimbly felt around in the wet grass. Even my inclined face felt tinted with ultramarine; even my hands turned a pale blue.

"But what are you looking for? What are you looking for?"

I had found a tuft of violets.

All at once the face of love darkens and vanishes. A circle of solitude separates my woeful bed from the rest of the world.

Familiar voices seem to turn dry and alien.

All that remains of my soul is a dull rancor towards myself, hidden inside my desiccated body.

Shadow has the bleakness of abandonment.

I think back on the wounded man we found in a deserted stable, abandoned there for six days in the horrible stench of his gangrenous legs and the gases they emitted, a few strands of chewed hay in his mouth.

Watching over him was only a worn-out halter hanging from a ring on the empty feeding trough.

The horizons have closed in like four barriers, shut themselves up like a stockade. The city remains inside them, lifeless, breathless, soulless.

The house, full of cares, subdued voices, solicitude, secret sounds, little hidden idylls, has fallen silent, become almost nonexistent. Only the four walls of my room exist. Around them is the endless void.

Then only the four posts of my bed exist. I sense them in the darkness like the four stakes of a tent in the desert.

Then only my bones exist, only my skeleton wrapped in flesh. And inside the skeleton, a sort of sudden coagulation of life.

Life clots, curdles like blood no longer flowing. It is a terrible weight.

In my initial horror, I am tempted to rouse myself, to jump up and move about to prevent the weight from settling all in one spot and pressing against the left side of my chest.

It is as though, on the side of the heart, against the ribcage, one of those monstrous tumors that normally develop and feed on years of torment has formed and grown in a matter of seconds.

I remain immobile. I hear the ticking of the clock like a stabbing pain in the ear, then like a flickering star.

There is no fire in my eye. Only, from time to time, a fluttering ring that floats and fades westward.

My mind is seized by the same immobility as grips my bones. No life stirs within me. I have utterly lost the strength to move and shift the great, incoherent masses of lyric substance of which my melancholy consists.

I have a single illness, rooted in a single point of my being: a sort of abscess that arrived with my mature years, will not burst, and cannot be lanced by me or anyone else, nor removed or alleviated. *Vide cor meum.*[20]

This illness, which has devastated so much of my existence, squandered so much of my wealth, vitiated so much of my passion, diminished so much of my work, destroyed so many ideas, contaminated so much desire, degraded so much sorrow, my original illness, my hereditary illness, has now, perhaps for the first time, accumulated, isolated, concentrated inside me, and it hurts the way deadly infections hurt.

This is all I have, all I feel, all I suffer.

Were my hands not inert, I could touch it, measure it, come to know its shape, hardness, heat.

My torment is craven and powerless.

At once a sense of expectation seems to dissolve the torpor in my soul and almost revive my vital tension. Someone is approaching in the darkness without a word.

He draws near, bends over, touches me, removes the pain from my side, takes it upon himself like a burden, carries it away, and leaves.

Only a desolate weariness follows.

And, at the first hint of slumber, at once the injured eye comes horribly back to burning life. I cannot simply open the lids to escape the terrible apparition.

The bandage is too tight. The damp compress has dried out and burns me. The weight in my ribcage spreads over my whole stiff body.

Before sinking into the horror of the transformations, I feel my tongue turn metallic as my breath slows in sleep.

And the mother of King Lemuel says: "What, my son? What, child of my womb? What, child of my vows?"

And the mother of King Lemuel says: "Give not your strength to that which destroys kings."[21]

Why do I wish to recover?

Is this wish for recovery not unjust? In whose eyes might this long torment avail me? In whose eyes might this harsh suffering seem praiseworthy, and *let me regain what I have given?*[22]

If my flesh consents, my spirit resists. The body is trapped in deception, the soul is strengthened in truth.

The hesitation I felt on the evening of my return, before obeying the doctor's sentence, before taking to bed and letting myself be pinned down in this darkness, eaten away by the flame of infirmity, was but a warning, a foreboding of the soul.

I remained standing and smiled brightly. So I've lost an eye? "I have what I have given."

Such was the attitude, such were the words befitting the nature of the offering and the offerer.

Someone in the adjacent room is reading something aloud. I hear the pages rustle, but only grasp the words intermittently.

I lie with my head lower than my feet, ankles together, elbows against my sides, mouth open and parched, heart distressed. I begin to grow sluggish in my sweaty torment.

I hear the word "Fatherland," and a great shudder runs through me.

I hear the word "Fatherland" again, and the same shudder penetrates my marrow.

Out of my torpor, my sweat, my suffering, my tedium, my despair, a boon beyond expression is born.

"The right eye: Isn't that what we call one's most precious possession? You have given your right eye to the one you love: your seeing eye, your poet's light."

Pride is always ready to raise its head, alas. A sweet, severe hand humbles it.

Around my bed the same blind soldiers gather who surrounded my cot in the little field hospital where I made my first stop. Some have only one eye blindfolded; some have broad, bloodstained bandages around their heads. Some look at me with their un-covered eye and weep. Some, unable to see me, shyly touch me and tremble. They are my brothers. No one has ever been so close to me as these men.

It was a raw gray morning. The artillery's thunder shook the daylight around the sun the way the wind scatters the cinders of a burning tree stump. Shiny coals piled under bare trees on the banks of an Ausa black as the drainage canal of a fulling mill.[23] Nothing more.

On the threshold of the field hospital, the white of blood-soaked bandages, poor human flesh put out of action, the anxious mouth of one who cannot see, a tenacious smell of trenches and caves, the numbness of combat in darkness. Nothing more.

The wounded murmured my name and thronged in the cor-ridor, deeply moved. Instead of iron helmets they wore turbans of cotton and gauze on their heads. Some craned their necks, trying to catch a glimpse of me under the blindfold. I smiled, head held high, as in a trench of beaten earth, saying: "Chin up, lads!"

One of them, with both eyes blindfolded, called me by my Christian name. He was a soldier from my part of Abruzzi. He stammered, wanting to know what was wrong with me.

I was tired and famished, utterly drained of strength. Before admitting me into the dark room to examine me, the doctor had me lie down on a cot covered with a sheet of linen. I stretched out on my back. The violet wave throbbed in my lost eye, while the other was blinded by vertigo. I half shut my eyelids. With a thud of despair in my chest, I heard the rumble of an aerial battalion pass over the shelter. The sound sapped me of my remaining strength. It said to me: "No more! No more! No more!"

Then the shuffling and muttering outside made me realize that the wounded were forcing the door. Then those injured in one eye approached and stood beside my cot. Those wounded in both eyes also came and stood around the cot. They were silent. I could hear them breathing, sighing. I indistinctly saw those on my left, saw their linen turbans bow piously, saw their grim mouths, their resigned hands.

I felt compassion for them, just as they felt compassion for me. I was their comrade; they were my people. I was stripped of all privilege, without distinction, without importance, with no other glory than my humble sacrifice. I suffered not from my injury, but from no longer being able to fight, from being deprived of my wings, my weapons, my duties. I had been cast out of the war, removed from the fire, locked out of the forge in which the new substance was being smelted.

What did my face look like? At that moment I touched the bottom of sadness and sweetness. Nothing, in all my life, had ever done me so much harm and so much good. How did I look as a patient on that sheet, on that cot on which so many other simple soldiers had lain? I felt faint.

Then one of them, gently shaking his bandaged head, and in the sharp accent of his province, with wonderstruck pity, one of them said: "This is that man!"

I shall never forget his voice. And if I knew where to find that voice again, I would seek it out, wherever it might be.

A tremor deeper than the chasm of my ills, darker than all my substance, all my grief.

A terrible jolt that tears me away from myself and hurls me into an unfamiliar nightmare of blood and spirit where I do not know if I am being reborn or dying again.

A silent pang, without cries, like the bloody exertion of birthing, like a mother's retaliation against the child of her agony.

It's my mother! My mother! My mother, seizing my bones, tossing and turning in my darkness, returning to flesh in my flesh, burden of my torment.

She was in me, inside me, at the time of the struggle and fury. I carried her inside me, just as she carried me, alive in the pulse and the breath.

She bounded with my bravery, reigned with me from the heights, bowed with me over the ruin and fire, swelled with the veins in my neck when I shouted.

She shouted: "Me! Me! Here I am!" It was the voice of my very own offering. She offered herself to injury, exposed herself to mutilation and death.

She grew dark in my weary sleep, grew heavy on the hard ground, grew numb in the arm bent under my head, patiently waited for my night to fall.

I did not see her, did not call her. Her gaze was my gaze, her name was my name. No weapon in all the world's violence could sever the maternal bond.

With me she knew the trenches, with me she knew the burrow and the ditch, she knew the slavery of mud and the thrill of the sky, the smell of the votive pyre and the ineffable hour when soul and wing are a single cherub assumed into heaven by the breath of the Eternal.

She said: "Me! Me! Here I am!" She thirsted for the immortality of her son, who was poised to fulfill his destiny.

"Here I am!" And at the fountain of blood that gushed from her breast, all the soldiers quenched their thirst.

It was a love so full that I could not tell whether I was her creation or she mine.

It was a fire so resplendent that I could not distinguish whether it was I, unfulfilled, who burned with her fire, or she who burned with mine in fulfillment.

It was a sacrifice so vehement that I did not know whether she was my mother or my Nation, suspended as I was between cradle and grave.

Nor did I know whether I was giving her my youth reborn or she was reopening, between my windswept lashes, her dovelike eyes.

Ah, why do you suddenly want me to look at you? Why do you want me to gaze past my blindfold and into your pupil, which causes me such pain?

Why do you part from me, just as I once tore my bloodied self away from you on a rainy night in March, to cry the tears of mankind?

Take me away from this anguish. I cannot stand it any longer. Free me from this terror. I can no longer breathe.

Give me a little light. Open the windows. Lead me away from this frightening darkness, in which I have no peace.

Suspend, if only for an hour, the torture of these visions, the agony of these ghastly apparitions.

I cannot stand it any longer.

I want to tear off the bandages, tear out my eyes.

You bandage my forehead, blindfold my eyes, and leave me in the dark.

And yet I see, I see, I still see. In daylight and at night, I still see.

Here is what happens.

The doctor gives me a shot of sodium chloride in the sclera, injecting saltwater in the injured eye, where the yellow-crested sea wave darkens.

Before wrapping me again, with unwitting cruelty he shows me his little round mirror, by the light of the blue lamp.

I look at the pouch of water in the swollen eye, I see my wasted, wan face, my livid mouth twisted by sadness, the new white hairs in my neglected beard, my gaunt neck: an image of utter desolation, which settles in the retina and remains there.

The doctor places a damp compress over the injected spot, buries the funereal image under bothersome cloth, lowers my head back down onto the pillowless sheet, extinguishes the blue lamp, advises me to have patience, and discreetly leaves.

I am left in the dark, supine, immobile under a rain of fire, like the damned in the third circle. Little flames dart from my body and fall back down on me, burning and wounding me. And I cannot beat back the burning with a "dance of wretched hands," as down there in Hell.[24] My elbows are nailed to my sides. I can barely move the wrist joint. My back is shattered.

What is it, then?

Just now the doctor, after removing my bandages, held a flame before me and circled around me in every direction with it, to measure my field of vision.

That flame is now multiplying into painful shards of fire.

And my eye burns and waters; and bitterness fills my mouth.

And little by little the shards thin out and die down.

And I am left alone before the image of my misery.

And the transformation begins.

Human sadness becomes plastic. I know not what mysterious thumb incessantly shapes it.

The face is mine, as in the mirror, as in bright light, but burdened with an age the likes of which no mortal being has ever suffered. From what depths of sorrow and sin does it return to me? How many years of servitude have furrowed that brow? How many years of toil have shriveled that cheek? How many years of fatigue have withered those lips?

Then at once I am young again, my mien tyrannical and mad. My breath smokes and flashes between sharp teeth as though poisoned with phosphorus.

The material warps, quickly, monstrously, as in a series of concave and convex mirrors.

It is as if a putty knife were beating and working it like clay, to make it more malleable.

The lines come back together to form a figure of astonished, attentive spirituality.

It is the face of a boy. My face at sixteen. And all my despair now rekindles and sparks as under a great hammer-blow.

The brow is smooth under the dense mass of dark hair. The eyebrows trace such pure lines, they confer something ineffably virginal upon the melancholy, big eyes. The fine, half-open mouth exhales the anguish, as when the heart swells with a dream that threatens to break it.

Linger for another minute yet, O herald of Dawn! Console me.

Transformation's blind force is unstoppable.

Dull thuds shake my darkness. My heart throbs against the nape of my painful neck. Everything shifts, in my body and soul. I no longer feel the confines of my skeleton.

Are childhood and old age but a single calamity?

I see myself as a wrinkled baby; a little, decrepit monster hanging from a teat centuries old.

And yet I recognize myself. In the unnatural hideousness there is still a glimmer of resemblance, a mark of progeny, a sign of parenthood.

What is this terror that sunders my bones?

A thunder of cannons shakes my building to the foundations, and my eyes in their sockets.

Or is it perhaps the rumble of my agony?

I cannot flee. I have no eyelashes, no eyelids.

The blind man is condemned forever to see.

You know it, you know it. I have never spared myself. And I have never asked to be spared.

But this time I do ask; this time I plead.

Here she is! She is made of me, imbued with my same sadness, which has never quite risen to my heart because it was too heavy.

Yet now it rises to the rims of my eyes, to where the sea of tears washes over all men's faces.

She is sad with me, old with me, sick with me.

She is my mother.

My viaticum, my sendoff to war, was a goodbye more heart-rending than the final, wordless flash of a dying man's soul before death.

I had not seen her since the moment of my departure into voluntary exile.

It was the week in March that falls between my birthday and my name day, a week full of love, memories, regrets, and remorse.

I had begun to fret for her from afar, as if the Tronto was the hem of her dress.

I had begun to feel her from afar in the ground, the way one feels the season awaken underfoot.

The gravelly Tronto, a few trickles of blue water under a yellow-brick bridge, greeted me the way she used to do when she was happy.

The low hills, the yellow clay, the piles of rocks, were hers. And hers were the little trees in bloom. Hers the softness of the sea upon the narrow beach with its long rows of brown fishing boats pulled ashore in pairs. And when the women talked while mending the nets, they spoke of her, because they were smiling.

I see it all again.

And my heart leaps at the echo of Abruzzese speech, there, on a platform crowded with brutal railroad cars, in a station teeming with covetous life, within sight of the hillside covered with lean olive trees.

I see it all again.

A painted cart moves along the shore, drawn by a pair of white oxen. Is it not filled with my rustic childhood as with fragrant hay? The yoked animals stand out against the blue-green sea, glowing like the sirocco-filled sails in the distance.

The sand is tilled in furrows almost to the water's edge. I recognize the long green bands as fava beans and think they must be truly animal in nature. In one field scrawny hedge-maples look like gnarled, twisted hands bound by the dried-up rope of the vines. And has the spade left its polished blade in the sod it has cut? So brightly gleams the cut in the earth.

A rivulet glows white and foamy as milk fresh from the cow. A blackish straw stack is all golden where the straw was removed as needed. A hopeless heap of brown and twisted vines languishes on the blinding sand and looks as if it is breaking apart into writhing minutiae of snakes. A brick kiln stands beside a landslip of clay, with its red roof, its fuming smokestack, its clay-fisted men kneeling as they labor.

For you, for you, I love this frugality, this diligence, this resolve. For you is this humble, humbled land so dear to me.

And then, at Porto d'Ascoli, through an inlet in the modest hills, the great mountain appears. Pale blue, airy, snow-covered, blending with the radiant clouds, it bears me away to its reticent heights.

O final return to childhood, into your arms, which in your constant dream never stopped holding me!

I want to see it all again, I want to recognize it all.

You are everywhere, like air and water. You make everything good. You make everything simple.

The land is my initiation to your goodness.

Man's every mark on earth seems reconsecrated: the straightness of the street, the boundary of the field, the house of mud and reeds.

Sometimes at the solitary mouth of a rivulet is a flock that shines like the silt. I look towards the mountains where perhaps another flock drinks its fill at solitary springs.

A vast, dry riverbed coming down from the mountains is like an abandoned migration trail, like the barren sheep tracks of my forefathers. Inside me I hear the dead shepherds walking, their great flocks long gone.

And I am stung by a persistent regret, that of not returning to you barefoot, brother to the pilgrim on his way to the sanctuary of miracles, along the coastal road where people and things appear to me in profile as in the embroideries of your old blankets. And the gait of man, the pace of the ox, the form of the cart, and the donkey driver guiding his pack beast laden with sacks of flour, all forms are reduced to a primitive simplicity in my naïve emotion, as if I myself were a child interpreting them, like ocher spots on a white-washed wall.

You make my eyes virgin again, before they gaze deep into yours.

Now the beach becomes so narrow that the waves look about to wash over the land all the way to the foothills.

And something in me imitates my native beach. Everything is obedient and sweet to me, in my soul and in the air.

Do you remember? Do you remember the line of verse that made you smile and weep?

The way water falls into your cupped hand.

Am I not always the water that falls into your cupped hand for you?

You always catch my unsullied innocence.

Here is the house. Here the threshold. Here the staircase.

You stand at the top, supported by my sisters. The walls tremble, like my bones. My knees buckle. My heart swells and breaks over your happiness.

Why then did I choose yet again to take my broken heart far away? Why again let myself be carried off by a longing for "mad flight"?[25] Why again abandon the hearth of all troth for a tent exposed to every storm? Why did my love of destiny prevail over my filial love?

Né dolcezza di figlio . . . Nor a son's fondness . . .[26]

Light as a goddess she had taken my head, so heavy, into her lap, and made me a sleepy child again. I remained silent; she too. And all around us familiar things whispered. They made me feel so good, and so bad. Nothing in the world had ever made me feel so good, and so bad. And thus kneeling, I gazed at a hollow in the worn stone of the balcony's threshold, a space already dear to my childhood, which used to fill with rainwater during cloudbursts, and I would anxiously wait for the sparrows to come and quench their thirst as if at a watering trough free of danger. The hollow was dry, and this disturbed me. From time to time my mother's fingers lightly stroked my cheek. And I thought she was doing this to see if it was wet with tears. Perhaps she did not know that it was her gesture that moved me to tears, drawing them up from my depths.

Ah, why did I rouse myself instead of breaking down?

How many times, in that beloved home, had I heard a terrible cry ring out! How many times, between the breadbox and sideboard, between the coffer and dining table, had I heard, over my own anguish, that Aeschylean voice, as vivid as my own!

"I'm coming. Who's calling me?"

The Ulyssean wanderer with no oar or wing, but with a thousand souls, stood up to leave for exile, not as if heading for mournful privation, but as if towards greater power.

Another goodbye at the top of the stair.

If a mother's sorrow could turn to stone, the loveliest of holy statues would forever shine for mankind's devotion, at the top of that humble staircase.

"I'm coming. Who's calling me?"

Five years of exile in the extreme West, on the pine-covered ridge of an oceanside dune. A long succession of days and works, a long, patient wait.

Just as my mother's love could never see the lesions of time and life in my face, so my love preserved a spiritual, tutelary image of her, in which the light softened her features without blurring them.

Illness, too, seemed to me but a mystical process of refinement, an ascetic means to health. And from afar I did not guess what had been hidden from me out of compassion.

I have never feared suffering. My mother had set an example of great resolve for me from my very first years. And yet, as I prepared to take leave of her and go to war, my heart writhed and balked without cease, oppressed by a foreboding of unbearable sorrow.

O journey too long, race made no swifter by anguish, through the devastated land, the ruins of the Fùcino valley, through the Màrsica full of rubble and crops, full of widows and orphans, full of mourning and pallor and the toil of bruise-covered arms!

In my devotion, I had already made a pact with death, like any nameless sailor, foot soldier, or aviator. At daybreak on the 25th of May I had said to my gathered comrades: "None of you knew, of course, that you loved this Great Mother so much.[27] But who among us shall first know how to die for her? Is there one among us already marked, already chosen? Let me be he! Let the omen not deceive me! Let it not be a lie!"

I said: "We have no worth but our blood to spill, are measured only by the ground we have conquered. The day is rising, friends, behold the morning star; soon it will be dawn. Let us embrace and depart. What we have done is done. Now we must part; we shall meet again later. May God let us meet again, alive or dead, in a place of light."

But a man must part with his mortal mother before giving himself to the immortal mother.

I bade farewell to the little soldiers, volunteers aged sixteen, old men of fifty, there for the bitter campaign; and I imagined their mothers standing in the doorway or at the end of the street, tall in their draping brown aprons.

And fear never loosed its grip on my throat. And while the journey never seemed swift enough, every pause was an almost cowardly relief to me. And when I went into the shadow of the mountains, I closed my eyes as if I might never come back.

My wrist is broken, my hand dangling like some withered thing.

I am thirsty. I writhe with thirst. From the big toes, down there so far away, to the metal jaws that never moisten, my entire body craves water. In vain I ask for a sip.

The tears from my eyes and the sweat from my temples drip down to my lips. And I lap up the salty droplets. I feel as if I am licking them with my mother's mouth, that misshapen mouth that weighs heavy in me, suffers in my disfigured self.

Tell me if there is any agony crueler than this.

It is worse than the other. A pain that returns is like a viper. It turns round to bite me deeper within.

At that time I could, at moments, avert my burnt eyes. I bowed my face downward, to the ground. I laid my head on those poor feet wrapped in wool. I grasped my heart with all my shuddering ribs. I felt as if I was clutching it, stifling its beat, or squeezing a few drops of blood from it.

Now I cannot help but see, I cannot stop the unrelenting torture.

The image is not immobile. It moves, mutates. It is sad, and turns sadder. It is undone, and comes further undone. It opens its mouth, but cannot speak human speech; it can only chew its soul, mumble its desolation.

I think the torturer's twists of the rope are as nothing compared to what I suffer with every single movement I make.

But what have I done? What sin am I expiating?

The walls of Pescara, the brick arch, the crumbling church, the piazza with its sickly trees, the corner of my neglected house.

My little homeland. I feel it here and there like my own skin. It grows cold in me, grows hot in me. I am touched by what is old, repulsed by what is new. All its people, all its ages are contained in my anguish.

My door looks smaller to me. The entrance hall is damp and silent as a crypt without relics. I teeter on the stairway's first step. The silence terrifies me. I am afraid to see my sisters upstairs with their heads veiled. A spiderweb trembles in the grating that gives onto the courtyard. I hear clucking. I hear the squeaking pulley of the well. The past comes crashing down on me like an avalanche; it bows me, crowds me. I suffer my home all the way to the roof, to the attic, as if I had made the framework from my own bones, as if I had whitewashed it with my pallor.

There is no one at the top of the stair. I understand. The silence is piety, modesty. Misfortune waits in the second doorway, alone, and leads me by the hand.

The first room is empty. The happiness of yesteryear has left nothing but sharp knives to cut me to pieces.

The second room is empty. There are the books of my childhood and adolescence. There is the music stand of my brother who emigrated. There is the portrait of my father as a boy, with a goldfinch perched on his extended forefinger.

I have lived for so many years without remembering these things. How can they now come back to life so terribly inside me?

In the third room there is my white bed; there is the old painted armoire, with its murky, spotted mirrors; there is the walnut priedieu, where I used sit in anger and obstinate silence, wildly stubborn, refusing to admit I felt sick.

My knees buckle and the walls grab me, shackle me to them, and spin me round as on a wheel of torture.

In the fourth room there is the little wax Jesus inside a crystal globe; there is the Virgin of the Seven Swords; there are images of saints and relics collected by my father's sister, who died a saintly death. And there are my first prayers, the sweet morning ones, and the evening prayers, even sweeter, which to reenter my heart cleave my chest like the blades of the avenging angel.

Three stairs lead up to the fifth room, like three stairs to an altar.

It is blanketed in shadow, under the arched vault. It echoes. My heart beats against the walls with the blind force of destiny. The vast bed in which I was conceived and born fills the room. Inside me I think I hear my mother's cries, which did not penetrate my sealed ears when I was born. An indefinable odor of illness makes it hard to breathe. A hand touches me, making me start. A cold hand takes me and leads me towards the sixth room.

It is the sixth station: Veronica's shroud.

A calm voice says: "She is here." It makes my blood run cold. I recognize it. It belongs to the admirable maidservant, the faithful creature born of our soil, raised in our home, called Maria.

"She is here."

Is it my mother?

A poor little thing, hunched and formless, a thing of misery and pain, abased, humbled, lost.

Is it my mother?

I drag myself to her feet, crawl along the floor. I am emptied of all except terror. I raise my head, convulsing as if a vertebra in my neck were breaking. I raise my head and look.

I look at that face.

Fate should have blinded me first.

Did the Savior's face not look like this when he took all the sins of the world upon him?

Horrible and sublime, with eyes that do not see me, do not recognize me, eyes dark and fixed, in which love is but a nameless sadness, a sadness unto death and beyond death.

My mother!

A poor, dejected creature, shaken and misshapen; and a horrifying, ineffable greatness, which I enter as one enters a pious, awesome place, as if entering my own sacrifice.

I am like a terrified prisoner. Imprisoned inside her, my soul stares out at me from the depths of those unfamiliar pupils.

And the humble woman of the earth calls my name, repeats my name to that ever more inclined ear.

And then her two hands rise from her knees. All life stops, loses color, becomes nothing.

Is there anything that could hurt me more than those eyes without light?

There is her mouth, no longer possessed of beauty, or sweetness, or human form, or human sound.

Her two palms fall heavily upon my head, as if lifeless, soulless. The mouth wants to say my name, but can only manage a feeble moan.

And I am emptied, even of my terror. I have no more meaning. I know a death that perhaps no other son of woman shall ever know.

How can you, now, make me die again?
Today is the day of my birth.

I say to the doctor questioning me: "Imagine I have a living butterfly imprisoned in my cheek, whose brown wings extend beyond my lower eyelid and are continually beating along the rim of my eye."

He does not smile, but knits his brows.

I smile and add: "We must not kill it; we must free it."

I say to the doctor: "Imagine I have a small fern leaf in my eye, one of those dry ferns that look as though cut from a thin sheet of copper."

He replies: "Did you know that when you cut a fern stalk obliquely, you get the figure of the two-headed eagle?"

Sirenetta says: "The wisteria is already in bloom in all the windows."

I have something like a bright amethyst crystal in my sad eye. At moments it turns from mineral to vegetal and looks like closed wisteria flowers, like light, oscillating scales.

Sirenetta has a soothing, calming voice.

When she speaks, my heart finds peace, my pulse slows down.

Her voice reminds me of my mother's in her youth, when every evening she used to tell me a fairy tale as I lay in my little child-hood bed.

She reads me the poets, and a river of dreams leads me into the shade of the laurels.

When she stops reading, sorrow overcomes me at once.

She speaks in the Tuscan manner, pure Sienese. So must the young Saint Catherine have spoken as she tended her garden.

A bee left votive honey in her mouth.

On her tongue the sonnets of the *La Vita Nuova* touch me deeply, as they did when, at age sixteen, I read them on the grassy banks of the Affrico around Eastertime.

And being, to my bitter regret, "like those who cannot move," I too have had disheveled women's faces appear to me and say: "Your youth is dead!"

And, after these women, other faces have appeared to me, horrific to see, saying: "You are dead."[28]

Having a beautiful voice herself, my beloved child is sensitive to beautiful voices.

She tells me which voice she likes best among those of our family. She talks as if discussing the taste of the waters of different springs.

Then she tells me how once, when she was a pupil at Poggio Imperiale, she was taken on a night of the full moon to visit the observatory at Arcetri with some of her classmates.

In her memory she sees great white terraces of moon, great overlapping terraces close to the stars, as at the home of an imaginary astrologer in a chivalric romance.

And there she heard the most beautiful voice in the world.

It belonged to the humble assistant, who stood by the telescope and spoke of the mountains and valleys of the moon, the rings of Saturn, and the redness of Mars.

All the girls hung on his every word, under the spell of the full moon.

His pure voice was like a note of the celestial harmony.

And the corona of virgins fluttered, like a constellation made human, around the teacher of stars.

My daughter has two dark, Oriental eyes, the sort of Saracen eyes that bloomed in Sicily at the time of the Swabian sultan.[29]

Sometimes, when she leans towards me unexpectedly, her eyes look as if they were set in her temples, like those of the palfreys that stare out from Asian miniatures.

A white head, or rather, a head the color of peach-blossoms, with a dark brown, curly mane, hard to braid.

Sometimes, when she is seated on a low pillow and cutting strips of paper for me that hiss like dry palm fronds, I think of the "flower of Syria."[30]

She once gathered olive branches in the garden of Gethsemane and wove them with the same art, learned in our province, used on Palm Sunday.

With them she made a mat, as long as my body, for me to lie upon.

"The swallows are back," says Sirenetta, entering the shadow, the hint of a shout in her voice.

I think—I don't know why—of my old voice when, as a boy, I used to lift the iron lid of the well and, leaning over the stone wall furrowed by the rope, I would shout towards the bottom, where I could vaguely see my face reflected in the glistening water.

My eyes now see that sound of muffled silver, which trembled with the lightness of maidenhair fern.

I would then reclose the lid carefully, so that the thud of the iron might not stifle my secret cry.

I felt as if I had imprisoned a living thing inside that cool, dark well, like a bird that would continue fluttering and singing, flapping its wings against the damp brick.

Remembering how one evening I took her to see the Bovolo staircase[31] and how, to heighten the enchantment, I blindfolded her in a narrow street before we came out into the Corte Contarina, Sirenetta says: "Don't you think there are probably some nests in the Bovolo staircase? I want to go there again, to see if any swallows live there. That's what I would do if I were a swallow."

O child, unnail me from here, and take me with you.

I am pinned down, two nails in my armpits and two in my feet.

I remain silent. But the bounding instinct of my tired flesh imitates the swift swallow.

Its tiny, wild eyes open under my blindfold.

It enters the Corte Contarina. One cry, then another.

It soars above the Riva degli Schiavoni.

It passes over Chioggia.

It flies to San Francesco del Deserto.

It circles round the Oriental belfry on the island of San Lazzaro degli Armeni.

It lights a moment in the mouth of the Lion atop the column in the Piazzetta, where it is tempted to build its new nest.

It enters the Corte Contarina. A shrill, white cry.

It swoops down towards the dry wells behind the iron gates.

Then it brushes past the spiraling, superimposed arches with the musical speed of a hand plucking an arpeggio on the strings of a sculpted harp.

It shines and flits around the last balusters.

Then I see it disappear, I hear it screech under the vault.

Then I see it fly off like an arrow, over the roofs, and pierce the sky.

I hear it cry in pain, cry my pain to the sun.

As merciful hands wash and scent my body, part by part, like the bodies of the dead, a mild somnolence comes over me.

All the apparitions of my sleepless night have vanished in the morning light.

My left eye is allowed to see a little light.

The shutter is left ajar in such a way that the light does not enter, but still the old pink silk on the wall turns golden there.

The brightness falls on my naked eyelid, accompanied by a faint warmth that is only the softness of the light.

I feel my gaunt knees being rubbed. I feel them being polished like those of tomb statues.

The sleep the spring equinox brings me is like the sleep of Ilaria in her tomb at Lucca.[32] The light resembles that of the stained-glass window illuminating the gisant statue in the Tuscan cathedral.

The musical tone of my weariness attracts the most beautiful of my loving young greyhounds to my joined feet.

Very slowly I surrender to sleep, knowing I may never wake again.

The merciful hands cover me with a fresh sheet, giving my blind eye a vision of white.

I have escaped the night.

My unhappy soul seems whitened, as the Mystic would say.[33]

My sleep is no longer a blaze of terrible ghosts, but a tranquil, even glow.

The nurse said: "The façade of the house is already all dressed up in green *like Ornella.*"[34]

The wall dissolves without dust, and the tiny young leaves tremble almost directly over my face. My breath makes them move.

How long did I sleep? At once I feel my sick eye watering under the bandage. A tear reaches the corner of my mouth.

Are the tears my soul expresses and those my irritated eyelid sheds bitter with the same salt?

I guess that it's afternoon. In my wretched body a sort of golden glow remains of the sleep I enjoyed in the daylight.

I call out. It is three o'clock. I have slept a long time.

The nurse smiles and says the musicians have come to play.

From the adjacent room the first chords of the cello and violin reach my ears.

Sirenetta appears in the doorway. She is wearing a striped dress, her pretty brunette head rising up from a broad white collar, moving on her bare neck with a grace that only birds possess and which thus seems to obey the instinct for song.

She is a tunic-clad angel who has come detached from a Florentine chancel.

She precedes the music and announces it.

The first notes of the Flemish Beethoven's Trio truly touch my heart, bodily, the way the sticks strike the drums in Luca's living marble.[35]

It's the so-called Ghost Trio.

I listen to it as though after death.

The musicians are hidden, on the other side of the wall. The small, closed room acts like a resonance chamber.

The harpsichord, violin, and cello are three voices speaking as in a religious drama, a holy mystery play.

I have lowered the blindfold over the living eye as well.

When, after a pause, the instruments begin the Largo movement, I see a yellow area bleed into a violet one.

Then I see a violet sheet trimmed in yellow cover a carved relief of the crucifix.

The jutting, tortured knees lift the sheet at the center and, when the violin resumes the motif, the sheet turns purple in the middle.

At each moment I feel a deep sense of torment.

Each note pushes the chalice of life deeper into my veins, until it reaches my heart. I have not yet drunk from this cup, and begged that it be kept far from my lips.

Each note pushes it closer to the heart, and the heart does not open to receive it, but twists away and resists.

Now it is right here, at the edge. My heart stops, then is at once possessed, filled and fulfilled.

I glimpse my child's shadow, as she leans over my face.

Her light fingers touch my cheek, under the bandages, and become wet.

Above the cooled, smeared teardrops, a hot, liquid flow of tears gushes from the lost eye.

The life of the soul fills the bandages.

I have no illusions. I am certain that the water gushed from the blind eye before the other began to tear.

Now they both are living one same, sublime life. They are two living springs.

I know longer know where my affliction lies. My affliction is a boon unaware of itself.

My tears pour forth. My child has immersed her fingers in them but dares not wipe them away.

I feel her head near the pillow.

Then my daughter, flesh of my flesh, says a motherly word to me, who am on the threshold of old age, the loving word that mothers tell their children!

I feel that with that word, she takes me into her lap, as in an ancient Pietà, and suffers my wounds.

Make me drunk with music.

Make my soul shed more tears.

Touch the bottom of my wound with melody, and there awaken ineffable colors that exist only in the light-spectrum of stars.

I am now as though in the initial phase of decomposition. I am full of dissolving substances, fermenting juices. Inside me I hear gurglings I have heard before, deep in the night, when keeping vigil over corpses amidst funeral wreaths.

And yet I am marvelously alive. My spirit is the window of all mysteries. The vast lyric billow of creation passes through it, rising from the roots of the world to the triple furrow of my human brow.

Today I contemplate death dressed in I know not what heavenly modesty, of the sort I saw up north, in Gothic lands, in certain twelfth-century tomb sculptures.

My eyes are open like corollas at the first light of day, and my joined hands seem already to take part in eternal life.

I think of the art of the god who, on the new day, will refashion the faces of his chosen ones in the likeness of his own recondite beauty.

The ravages of time and life, on my supine face, will be erased in one stroke.

I shall become young again in the marble of my tomb, like the dead in the funerary stelae of the Greeks.

Sculpted standing, I shall hold by the bridle a great, wingèd horse unlike either the Hippogriff or Pegasus.

Death seems to me nothing but the form of my own perfection.

It will eternalize all the elements that life stirs and transforms in me in perpetual alchemy.

What "hymn with no lyre" will accompany my passing?

The days pass, the hours race by; and each day without dawn, each hour without change, finds me still nailed to the bed.

I do not want to recover. I need only the wound to mend. I want to get back on my feet, to rise again.

My friends call for me, my emulators await me. Out there, in the line of fire, in the sky of battle, it seems every day the summit of heroism is reached; and then, the following day, an unknown hero surpasses it.

I shall not rise but with the will to go beyond it.

I sense that, when back on my feet, I shall know better how to fight.

What skills, what wiles, what animal cunning won't I use to overcome my diminished sight! I shall keep the enemy always on my left or in front, so help me God. Like my wild Malatestino, I shall say: "*Io vedo pur con l'uno.*"[36] I can see just the same, even with one.

My fervor will be as before, but my daring shall be schooled by experience and whetted by patience.

Nothing today has any bounds. Man's bravery has no bounds. Heroism is limitless.

At the pinnacle of lyric power is the poet-hero.

Pindar cut his strings, mutilated his kithara, because he knew how much more beautiful it is to fight and take chances.

Danger has a lyrical effect on me. My poetry is sustained by my courage, not only in war but also—if I consider the great moments of my prior life—in peace, as in earlier times, during the cult of expectation, when I fashioned my wings and my arms.

Never have I felt myself so full of music as during the lulls in battle.

I think back on the air-raid on Canale d'Agordo, with Ermanno Beltramo; the pass through the sky of Gorizia, under domes of two-color explosions; the unintentional descent from three thousand to twelve hundred meters, as thrilling as the ascent; our mutual gesture of derision towards the enemy, who did not correct his aim; my indifference to the pain in my half-frozen right hand; my musical élan in contrast with the engine's weakened monotone; the wild frenzy of the song.

"Lyrical ignition, cold radiators," I said, jumping from the fuselage and onto the grass at Campoformido.

I was hungry.

On December 27, after the death of Giuseppe Miraglia, Giacomo Boni came to see me.

Having heard the news while traveling, he had hastened to Venice without stopping at Grado, where he was in fact to have met with Beppo (had we returned safely from the Zara excursion), so he could execute, from the air, some sketches of a land overrun in ancient times by barbarian invaders.

I see him again beside the flaming fireplace, seated in the armchair in which our late comrade used to sit. I see again his sweet yet frowning face, the ruddy complexion framed by gray hair, like some of Tintoretto's Procurators. I see again that unruly tuft over a brow full of wisdom and foresight.

He was returning from the Alps, where he had gone to deliver his white garments, leggings made to look like those that boar hunters wore in the time of Horace, when forced to spend the night gaitered in the snow.

He told me how, when he passed before them, the Alpini tried to stand up on their frozen legs and smiled. O gracious Italy! On a single day the surgeon lopped off the feet of two hundred and fifty men.

He told me how it was even worse in the Carso. The trenches filled with water, and the infantry stood in muddy water up to their knees for days and days. Their shoes were of the worst quality, cardboard shoes provided by swindlers who were shown every sort of indulgence instead of being shot en masse or forced to stand for three days in the stagnant muck of the trench with their own shoes on their feet. Three days—he said—are enough to finish a man off, even a thief.

Then, all of a sudden, interrupting his tale of horror and abomination, he told me that the previous September, when conversing with Giuseppe Miraglia, he happened to quote an Oriental invocation of the skylark: "O skylark, the day is not long enough for your trills!"

Whereupon the good pilot confided to him, with a certain shyness, that one morning, having set out for Pola before sunrise and finding himself in the middle of the sea, he saw the red-hot disk rising in the distant haze, and all the waters rejoicing "to that first stroke of the kettledrum." He let go the controls and crossed his arms. And, as the *Albatross*, left to itself, swayed in the tranquil air, he started singing, inventing the words and music of his song. Only then did he understand the rapture of Saint Francis in his *Canticle of the Creatures*. And he never remembered the words or music again.

"O skylark, the day is not long enough for your trills!"

The words of the Persian poet echo in my heart like a piercing melody. And I think of my buried friend's forgotten hymn.

I do not know whether I thirst more for water, music, or freedom.

I feel the sun behind the shutters. I feel that there is a March haze, clear and languid, over the canal. I feel that it is low tide.

The spring enters me like a new poison. My back hurts, my slumber is broken by starts and tremors.

I listen.

The lapping against the quay, after the boat has passed.

The dull thuds of the waves against the algae-covered stone.

The guttural cries of the seagulls, their raucous outbursts, shrill melées, floating pauses.

The throbbing of a seaborne motor.

The silly warble of a blackbird.

The grim buzz of a fly taking flight and alighting.

The tick-tock of the pendulum clock, connecting every interval.

The drip in the bathtub.

The groan of an oar in a rowlock.

Human voices on a traghetto.[37]

A rake passing over pebbles in the garden.

A small child weeping, unconsoled.

A woman's voice speaking, incomprehensibly.

Another woman's voice saying: "At what time? At what time?"

At moments the sounds and scraps of sounds and uneven pauses merge into a single harmony that bears away my sadness and something even sadder than my sadness.

At moments my attention separates them, singles them out, distinguishes them one by one.

And each in turn makes me suffer.

Now it's the endless dripping in the bathtub, as in some frightful cave! It is becoming unbearable. It eats away at me, bores a hole in me, passes through me.

I call the nurse and complain.

She spends a long time trying to tighten the knob of the spigot. Without success. The drip is obstinately against me.

The woman sighs and says: "It can't be helped."

She takes a wad of cotton and sticks it inside the spout. She believes she has silenced it.

The respite brings me great relief. I am so attentive to the silence in the bathroom that I no longer hear the other noises.

Then the drip resumes, alas! It passes through the cotton, like the troublesome watering of my bandaged eye.

Today the demon has put out the fires and invented a new torture.

The nurse comes in and says: "All the hyacinths have fallen in the rainstorm. They're all on the ground."

This grieves me.

She adds: "My fingers got all gooey when I picked up the prettiest ones. The broken stalks give off a fluid that sticks to your hands."

She further added: "But other buds are sprouting. A lot of them. And they'll be even prettier. I saw one blooming into a double flower, a purple so dark it looked black. And the bees were buzzing. They were chasing me just now. Why is it the darkest hyacinths have the strongest scent?"

The slightest thing bothers and upsets me. At certain moments all relationships and associations seem no longer to leave even the shadow of a trace in my mind. I become a material governed by no stable law, subject to sudden transmutations that exhaust or excite the body, which is almost transubstantiated, so to speak. I feel the most varied, discordant forces circulating in the sphere of my eye. The springtime's ebb and flow pass through me like an unnaturally accelerated sequence of tides laden with horrors and treasures.

The woman draws near. I smell the oozing garden.

I ask her if she has the sap of the hyacinths on her fingers.

"Oh, no," she replies promptly, in a tone as vivid as a blush.

And she delicately unwraps me and changes the now dry compress over the blister of saltwater.

Then she walks away. She closes the door behind her. I hear her descend the stairs.

A mysterious anguish swells inside me. Little by little, it changes shape and flows towards the eye, which seems to bear the brunt of the violent throbbing in the nape of my neck.

Where are the broken hyacinths she gathered?

The room fills with an ecstatic fragrance. My anguish flares up like madness.

With a sudden pang, the violet hyacinth bursts through the bulb of my eye.

I clench my teeth. I feel the root hairs intertwining in my brain. I distinctly feel each fleshy membrane and scale.

The stalk lengthens. The flower completes its growth, turns lush and heavy. It is dark, almost black. I can see it.

Who tore it from me?

My wild shout frightens me.

The viscous fluid gums up the compress, drips down my cheek.

The blackness sprouts again, with a sharper pain this time. It grows and breaks and smears its fluid on me. And I shout.

It sprouts again and breaks again.

Today I no longer have the dark hyacinth in my eye. Today I have I know not what furry flower there, between reddish and yellow, rather like the ear of a small puppy.

Now I have burning-hot clay in my eye, the kind that drinks up the water during a cloudburst. It is the blinding yellow clay that shines on the deserted shore of Versilia.

I feel its hot suction under the downpour.

And now I have the Etruscan bronze of a boy in my eye, touching the ground with his right hand.

He is dark red in color, as if just out of the oven, still glowing hot.

He never stands erect.

Tears from the enflamed eye drip down to the corner of my mouth. The bitterness blends with the metallic taste.

I think of the fishermen of Pescara setting out to sea in their fine, painted *paranze*, before daybreak, in a mistral wind, the taste of salt in their mouths.

A swallow cries desperately over a dark harmony of cannons and bells.

Evening approaches.

My nightly tormentor waits outside the door.

How can the March rain sound so silvery, so brilliant and clear?

Untie my feet.

How can the March rain have stolen the spirits of the dance from the sleeping Bacchante?

Untie my feet.

The March rain is playing castanets.

I shall grab her by the hair, her long, long hair.

Now the grace of my youth enters the room, without touching the floor, ever so gently raising a rainbow.

Is this magic my own?

Is illness thus magical in essence?

Everything is present. The past is present. The future is present.

This is my magic. In pain and in darkness, I grow not older, but younger and younger.

Echo of ancient and future times.

The eye is the magical point at which bodies and soul, times and eternity, mingle.

What must I finish?

What must I begin?

I am discovering a new physical quality in things. In everything I touch, in everything I hear, I sense a wondrous novelty.

What names shall I give to the constellations that glimmer in the remote distances of my pain?

The word I write in the dark loses its form and meaning. It is music.

"O skylark, the day is not long enough for your trills!"

I dream again of my lost friend's morning hymn. An indescribable urge to sing presses hard upon my racing heart.

The garden is full of noisy bees. If I prick my ear, I think I can hear the hum.

Like the sketch of a melody, a delightful memory of the "Diana of the Caucasus" comes back to me.

She owned great estates in the Kiel Government. Near a pond bejewelled with wild ducks was a large orchard, a beautiful cherry orchard.

It was tended by an old man with a florid beard à la Charlemagne. And this man alone looked after the apiary. The docile bees used to collect in his white beard. And his beard would sometimes turn into a long, golden swarm. Standing with his back against the trunk of a favorite cherry tree, he would not budge. He would breathe slowly. Closing his eyes, he would slowly sing a lullaby.

The memory of another song comes back to me.

I was at Ilse's, one night in the chimerical Paris winter.

The room was full of smoke, which the wind outside blew back through the flue of the burning fireplace. And our fairylike hostess, sensitive to cold, forbade us to open any windows.

Dressed in a gold-brocaded, blue tunic, Alistair danced his Gothic dances round a unicorn of gilded wood from a Burmese empire beloved of music. Amidst bronze stags and antelopes and other swift animals of the Far East that looked as if they were grazing on the rug, a poet officiated in rhyme, dressed as a violet bishop, his hair cut round in the fashion of Fra' Angelico's holy confraternity. Reclining on low cushions, the lady of the house looked like a wax figure with eyes of enamel; but she showed that she was alive by lightly moving her leg and the slenderest of ankles, just as the snake beats its tail in love or in anger.

It was one of those created moments when folly, fantasy, and nostalgia work together like three witches gathered round a suspicious brew.

But amidst all the falsity and delicacy two harsh forces were present: the smoke blown back in by the wind, and the Indian chanter Isnayat-Khan.

The smoke from the embers smothered the ghastly perfumes. And Isnayat's half-open mouth silenced the cackles and hoots of the nightbirds.

The unicorn looked in vain for a virgin's lap in which to rest its proud head and fall asleep in tender self-abnegation. Yet it seemed to take part in the perfection of the silence with its fabled mystery.

The chanter was sitting placidly, as if the smoke had come from his ancestral river and could not harm his voice. He was wearing a pinkish-yellow tunic and a large amber necklace. His brown hands rested on his knees. A short black beard completed the oval of his bronze face. The white of his eyes was purer than that of a turtle-dove eggshell. And he sang with his mouth always open, modulating the notes in his throat.

He knew more than five hundred modes.

He was a frail man, a fleshless human chest, and his chant seemed to rise up from the depths of a temple, from further down than the stone, further down than the underground hollows, and fuse within itself the aspirations of his entire stock, gather within itself the struggle of every root.

There were no more walls, no more narrow chimney, no more ghosts or masks or frauds.

There was the smoke of the pyre, and the sweat that bejeweled the holy singer's brow.

During the pause, no one dared to speak or cry out.

Isnayat looked at me at the start of each chant. He wanted me to know that he was singing for me alone.

For me alone he sang the antelucan, "predawn" chant, mysterious as the wind's message carried on the breath of the earth by Him "who strives to increase the light."

The four boards feel tighter round my body.

I feel them against my hips; I feel one against the soles of my feet, one against my cranium.

And the lid is nailed down.

No hallucination, no apparition.

All is black, as at the bottom of a vase when a liquid congeals into insubstantial little flakes, which then settle at the bottom.

If I sigh, my rising chest seems to raise that sediment up from the bottom, making it billow in the black oil. And each sigh increases the anguish.

I call and ask for the window to be opened, to let in some fresh air.

I feel the air enter my mouth like spring water.

I stretch all the way to the horizon, where the air must be already brightening with the dawn, to have a drink of it.

At once my body is vast.

My darkness is not limited by darkness, but is all darkness.

The four boards have fallen away. My entire body seems to breathe.

The circle of light re-forms and vanishes. Saturn has lost one of its rings, which journeys in the night, suspended.

It is a halo seeking a head to crown.

I hear the nurse near the window say: "Is that enough?"

"No. More."

"What a bright night!" she says. "The moon is high. You could read by its light!"

At once I lose my vastness. I become again a black body between four boards.

My boundaries are not those of the night, but of my misery.
I no longer taste the night air, but only my mouth of metal.
The window closes over me like a coffin lid.
I have the urge to tear off the bandages and leap to my feet.
The will rises from my desperate heart and nails me back down.
The effort quickens the heat of a sudden fever in me.
I burn. Sweat drips like tears that can no longer fall by way of the eyes.

So desperate is my desire to see the sky again, I am put beside the window out of pity.

The sun has set. Twilight too has faded. Nothing can harm me.

I am almost supine. I gaze at the sky with my uninjured eye, and the sky enters me as if I were transparent.

I am like quivering water, one of those pools of saltwater left behind on the sandy beach in front of my house in the faraway Lande.

Sirenetta crouches at my feet. I see a bouquet of dark irises behind her head.

It is as if her swollen, virgin's heart has entered my body. Certainly my own beats for two at this moment. It fills me from the nape of my neck to my big toe.

Agitation clouds the water, the sky recedes. I raise the bandage and look at it with my sick eye as well.

A gleam of stars flashes in my sick eye and breaks apart, as in a prism.

"Can you see the first star in the sky?" I ask Sirenetta.

"Not yet," she replies.

The stellar spectrum exists only in my ailing eye.

I ask: "Can we see the new moon from here?"

She rises to her feet. Her figure is etched against the window. She looks enlarged, as if by a repressed sigh.

"I can't find it," she replies. "Do you want me to go into the garden to look for it?"

I give her my yearning. My yearning gives her wings, which fill the room with shadow.

She goes downstairs. The shadow darkens. The sky is ashen. It turns opaque, inert.

Sirenetta reappears. Her lightness on the stairs sounds like a rising melody to me.

Is there a sickle moon under her feet?

Is she wearing the diadem of the moon on her brow?

She says: "The crescent moon is behind the house. You can't see it."

I am disappointed, like a child to whom a promise has not been kept.

I am put back in the hated bed.

All that remains of the sky in me is a desert of ash.

Giorgio plays me an air by Gerolamo Frescobaldi, a piece called "La Frescobalda."

The great sky of Ferrara arches over my melancholy.

I see the carts again, laden with linen, with all the world's white hair, passing through the broad, straight streets.

I see the ancient theater in Marfisa's palazzo again, piled full with linen, cluttered with Time's shorn white years.

I see the magical figure of a woman again, painted on a broken door with dusty spiderwebs hanging from it.

I am alone, and in the grips of a troubled melancholy. Magical eyes are watching me. And I dare not push the door open and cross the threshold again.

The creak of the rusty hinge would disrupt the music enthralling me.

In my sleeplessness Alexander Scriabin's prelude passes back and forth through my brow, which feels as light and transparent as a glass visor on an iron helmet.

My entire head weighs heavy, sunken deep in the pillow.

I am helmeted with what foot soldiers used to call a *cervelliera*. But the front part is made of glass, full of cracks and bubbles, and hot as a goblet just fashioned by a glassblower.

It is the only faintly luminous part of my sleepless body, just above the blindfold.

Scriabin's prelude is dark in color, violescent, like moiré unfurling in the evening wind.

It reminds me of the funereal veil that rippled in my lost eye and let me see nothing in the mirror but the pale crown of my bald head.

The hours pass. The music is like silence's dream.

I am not asleep, and yet life ebbs in me, little by little, like the tide. My pulse is weak. The hand on my chest cannot feel my heart.

The music recedes and then returns, changing in color like the surf in iridescent twilight.

Green, violet, and dark blue are the colors of this night.

At once I see the stars, the stars of the Equinox, plentiful as their reflection in the water.

Then I feel the dawn against the windowsill, leaning on it with both elbows, her long eyes stretching to where the hair sprouts from her temples.

I venture to turn my cheek slightly towards her. And all my despair begs to breathe.

But nobody is there to open the window. The house is asleep, the walls are asleep.

The sleep around me is dense, hard, unshakable.

Madness is sealed within my brow as in a vial. If I shout, my jawbone shakes the sickness in my eye.

My bowed head leans back, supine again. The silence no longer dreams of music. It is compact, immobile, inimical.

I await the toll of the Angelus bell like a salvation.

At once I hear something that sounds like a cock's crow, faint and faraway—more prisoner's groan than awakener's cry—over who knows what putrid canal, in what sordid courtyard still lit by a violet lantern.

There we were, fifty children,   *ALEXANDER*
fifty heirs of the mad flight,   *SCRIABIN*
sons of Icarus and the Sirens,
grandsons of the Labyrinth's Daedalus.
Spawned in the blue-green grottoes
of the Icarian Sea,
in the marine gynoecium
of the deepest sopranos,
by the pleasure of a feathered hero
turned demon of the depths.

Up through the violet whirlpool
we emerged into the dawn
at the craggy island's edge,
in a barren corrie of rocks.
Shaking the brine from our feathers,
we dried them in the midday sun,
spread them open to test them,
with arms raised
to the heavens' blue
as to a mother's teat.

Wing struck wing
in the quarry too tight.

At each wingbeat, brother
broke feathers against brother.
The heart swelled with height
like a light wing flapping.
Foot arched up on the big toe
we clung to the rock with our toes,
while the rest of the body,
blue with the cradle of sea,
became sky in anticipation of flight.

Then came the blast of the conch.
Our thrill was restrained.
We turned our ears to the rock,
that the hero might come
to release us,
moved by so much inexpert distress,
he who'd been forever submerged!
But a shadow loomed over us,
and we all turned and yelled
and saw the enemy against the sky.

Gigantic, all fist and jaw,
all wordless maw,
he brandished a great axe,
the axe invented by Daedalus,
who carved the first god in a tree trunk.
Descending into the thick of the fluttering wings,
he seized one of us, then another, then another still.

With repeated blows of the axe
he lopped the feathers from our shoulders.

Blood gushed from the cuts,
for not by Daedalean bonds
but by knots of living tendons
were our feathers attached to our dreams.
Fleeing and shrieking we trampled
our mangled harvest of feathers.
The cruel axe would not cease.
Downcast and writhing in pain,
we bled upon our feathers.

Only one escaped to the sky above.
Spurred on by his brothers' horror,
he used the space cleared by the axe
to spread his wings and take flight.
And his span appeared the greater to us.
We saw his shrunken feet
stained red with our bitter blood
as the beast, snarling, watched from above.
And all our eyes filled with sky
as we lay back on the tattered feathers.
And our race was unconquered in flight.

We had no dittany for our pain.
No one to dress our wounds
but the silent dew.

Our distress in the night
drank the Sirens' lament,
drank the Pleiades' song
with the silent dew.

The lame man with bronze feet
is slowed by his uneven step.
    And the ballerina
    dances round him
measured and airy as a child's voice
singing scales at matins in the choir.

Labored on the street of the world,
footstep follows footstep.
    And the ballerina
    dances round him
breezy and slender as cat straw flying
dustless and brilliant in a sudden whirlwind.

One thud after another
resounds in the earth of graves.
    And the ballerina
    dances round him
rhythmic and fluid as the water poured out by buckets
rising and falling round the waterwheel bathing the garden.

A handful of men
on the warship's bridge,
ram heading straight
to the terrible goal
in the moonless, starless night.
Machines and weapons, darkness and silence
from bow to stern.
And only one constellation
for the soul alone:
the Good Cause.

"I raise my arms
to let down my hair.
Under my arms
is the packet of myrrh
that makes my beloved feel drunk.
But I am far away."

A handful of men
devoted to night and to death.
Earmuffs on their heads,
sailors crouch by the cannons.
A great tremor shakes the hull.
The sky over the brave men's heads

is fate, smoke, and sparks.
And only one constellation
for the soul alone:
the Good Cause.

"I lie on my side
and I am a hill
that blocks the horizon
from the strength of the strong:
a hill that is only shadow."

A handful of men
made for victory and glory.
Long and tipped with bronze
the torpedoes lie in wait.
Mines in iron cages
rest in mounts jutting out
towards the black water.
And only one constellation
for the soul alone:
the Good Cause.

"I do not know if it is
sleep or languor, or
the gentle lamp
that lights me within.
Who shall hold me, so
transparent, in his arms?"

Lady, stay with me, for night is falling.

A great, silent event seems to be upon us, behind that narrow door. Now he enters.

The god of passion reappears to me in iron chains of adversity, which he breaks and drags with him. I do not follow him.

I remember you, that time you came. The entire beach was gold and soft as a cassie flower. A drowned man had washed ashore, swollen and white as a sodden wineskin. My bright room was fragrant with laurel. I can smell it still.

I know a dreaming demon who walks upon an unformed world, whose soft clay sticks to his heel. He calls me now.

I remember more remotely when you called at an Irish port, darkened with thousands and thousands of smoldering piles of coal, under the threat of a disastrous sun. Faceless expectation wafted a hint of whiteness through the smoke. I thought I saw you flutter up there, on the deck of the great ship, like the feather of an arrow buried in the flesh of a colossus who will not die. I did not know your name. But all at once I heard singing, from the mast of that sail-less ship, from Isolde's lookout: "Ah, alas, my child! Irish girl, you wild, adorable girl!"[38]

Again I take a form befitting melody and the unknown.

My mouth still smacks of metal. I have long had no taste but that of tempered steel in my thick blood.

Stay with me. Lock the door. Hide the key. Untie my blindfold, tear off my bandages. Open the window wide.

Let me drink the potion with you again, in a cup of air, tonight.

Tonight Scriabin dances,
strong as one of Igor's bowmen,
upon his own immortal heart
which sings a double melody
of sorrow and desire.

Each time it strikes,
his bloodied heel
breaks up the song, misshapes it.
Yet when his foot is raised
in the uneven rhythm,
desire and sorrow
find their timeless notes again
to be broken again underfoot.

He hears them, head thrown back,
pale with rapture; his face is
like a sublime lamp
lighting the dance but not leading it.
His entire soul unites and shines in it
like living, breathing alabaster.

And the shadow falls
from the laurel wood,

from the myrtle wood,
from the cypress wood.
And the face alone remains in light
above the frenzied, mysterious leaping.

His whole body
from the top of his chest to his heels
belongs to another god.
He wants that heart
naked and cast out
to mix with the earth,
to fold into the clods
like a cluster of grapes fallen at harvest
and restored to the thirsty soil.

He dances, dances
with desperate exuberance,
a light unto himself,
until he feels
under his hardening heel
his heart pressed into the earth,
become a thing of the earth,
until he hears the broken notes
of the black and vermilion
song of the future,
eternity's melody,
the deep and ever deeper hymn
of neverending sorrow.

I see musicians with keen, attentive faces lend their delicate ears to the slightest interval of sound, the slightest flutter in the resonant air.

They look extremely slender to me, with something gracefully animal about them that makes me think of ferrets, weasels, or ermines.

They change shape.

Now they are like beautiful angels consumed by the passions of the heavens. Their beauty seems made of sensitive nerves attached to an inner yoke and stretched from within to the breaking point.

From moment to moment, from note to note, from pause to pause, the unheard symphony makes their beauty grow sharper and sharper, unfleshing it.

All at once, as in a hot, humid gust, a crescendo bursts in my ears, accompanied by great booms of the kettledrum.

The booms resound in the nape of my neck and my chest, and I groan and scream in pain.

The sharp faces lean over me to hear my blood rumble and hiss.

They are so whetted by their attention that they cut me.

It is dark. A gloomy night.

The rings of Saturn, the rings of all ringed planets, turn in the vastness of my dead eye.

A living creature enters.

I don't know who it is.

The person stops at the edge of the bed. Says nothing.

From the breathing I can tell her head is bowed.

Is she waiting for one of my grim rings to crown her?

How heavy the halo is!

The green cloud now and then billowing up from the bottom of the eye, spreading into large, soft circles, reminds me of my garden in sandy Versilia.

Evening was falling from the Apuan Alps as I walked barefoot in the dust of sawn marble, leaving pale blue footprints.

I was tired, following a long day of difficult work. I lay down on my ascetic cot. A first flake of ash already covered the fire in my closed brain.

I never knew where the divine stillness came from that precedes the breeze as it rises over the Tyrrhenian; I tended to confuse it with my own relief.

I could no longer hear the virginal breath of the sea, nor that of my own poetry.

But, taking advantage of the silence, a tree toad took a blade of oat and climbed atop a spike of sorghum and there began to rehearse.

Between my half-closed lashes I saw the window turn slowly green, as if the garden below were reflected in it.

And the tree toad's voice gained assurance and strength, so that the sorghum bobbed with the cadence of his song.

And the sea drew nearer, sliding soundless onto the narrow beach.

And under heavy eyelids I saw the window turn as green as the waters at the bottom of the sea.

And with that blade of oat the tree toad drank in all the green of Versilia, turning it into song for my slumber.

And the sea rolled, foamless, onto the polished sand, drawing closer and closer. She was already under the hedge of reeds, penetrating through the interstices. And she let herself be combed by that comb of sharp reeds, like smooth, straight hair.

And the tree toad's song, reaching the highest note of green, broke into a twittering and suddenly stopped, without a quaver.

Then the window began to lose color.

A silent shape, indistinct, like a cuttlefish with sac and tentacles, appeared in the window's bay and released a great cloud of green that spread to the bottom of my weariness and put it to sleep.

I wrote down my returning dream as if with that ink.

Guido Pio has come. The streams of the great wake still seemed to trail behind him.

He came from Chioggia in his torpedo boat, at a speed of thirty knots. He was cruising abreast of a scirocco swell. The warship raised a froth a thousand times more splendid than the foam from which the Voluptas of mortals and immortals was born.[39] At every moment, between the stem and the cutwater parting the sea, something much younger and more beautiful was born: the heart of a seafaring hero.

"Four, three, zero!"

Who just spoke through the megaphone?

I recognize the Tuscan accent of Piero Orsini.

"A few degrees to starboard! One, zero, zero."

The living breath fills my ear. The commands echo in my skull as in the horn of the megaphone.

"We've got the *Fuciliere* straight ahead at naught seventy-four magnetic."

Let me breathe! Let me drink the wind, smell the danger, extinguish the sparks and the stars in my unrest! Let me relive the silence, the victory, the night!

I am not lying in my bed of misery, supine. I stand erect on the bridge of the *Impavido*; and the destroyer and the entire crew and I all have the same true name.[40]

The sea darkens; but in its quickening throb one already feels the night's phosphorescence.

The foam on the waves sparkles here and there with an inner light, like a batting eyelid granting a fugitive glimpse of a mysterious gaze.

The new moon is like a handful of burning sulfur. At moments a black cloud from the smokestack hides it, or appears to carry it off in its swirls like a fleeing star.

Life is not an abstraction of aspects and events, but a kind of diffuse sensuality, a consciousness available to all the senses, a substance to be smelled, touched, eaten.

I feel all things close to my senses, like the fisherman who walks barefoot on the beach uncovered by the ebb tide and bends down from time to time to examine and gather things he sees moving under the plants.

Nothing escapes the tirelessly attentive eyes that nature gave me. Everything nourishes and enriches me. Such thirst for life is similar to the need for death and immortality.

Indeed death is as present as life, as warm as life, as beautiful as life, as thrilling, promising, and transformative.

I stand erect, on two feet shod in light shoes that come easily unlaced; I stand erect on the bridge of the small warship, where there is room only for weapons and fighters.

The engines are already straining. The black cloud rises from the three smokestacks towards the gentle new moon shining yellow through the billows, burning like a handful of sulfur.

The sailors already have life jackets around their chests and have already inflated the collar, to keep the head above water in the agony of shipwreck.

I hear the second mate's voice ordering his men to put ship's-biscuit and tinned meat in the only two lifeboats.

A young officer, nervous and lithe as a leopard, with eyes that are fearlessness itself, treats his mates to champagne after completing an admirable maneuver, piloting the destroyer from the Arsenale to its berth.

We drink a cup in the wardroom, seated around a table with the sea chart on it, while the squadron commander, standing, dictates to the yeoman the order for the nighttime operation, to be sent to the other ships' captains.

Everyone's eyes sparkle with restrained good cheer. The operation is dangerous and most difficult; and this glass may be our last.

We are going to lay a blockade of sixty underwater mines around the bay of Panzano, between Punta Sdobba and Santa Croce. Each of the six torpedo boats is carrying ten mines calibrated to float three and a half meters below the surface. Each will go up against the enemy's searchlights and batteries, risk possible attacks from the enemy's ships, face the danger of running into mines or getting them tangled in the propellor, or perhaps run aground on a shoal.

A midshipman little more than a child, a Sicilian who looks like an Arab raised at the Court of Frederick of Swabia, rubs an aromatic leaf between his brown fingers, a leaf of one of those herbs

that grow in earthenware pots on windowsills in little solitary piaz-
zas. The scent is so strong that we all smell it, nostrils flaring.

That single leaf, on this fearsome warship where all is fire and
iron, that leaf of love seems infinitely precious to us, and calls to
mind the abandoned gardens of Giudecca and the Fondamente
Nuove.

The commander continues dictating the orders for the opera-
tion in his fine Tuscan accent, in the same crisp tongue as that
used in the missive Ramondo d'Amaretto Mannelli sent to Lio-
nardo Strozzi when the Genoese were broken by the Venetian and
Florentine fleets.

It is all a wondrous game that will last until dawn.

The midshipman puts the fragrant leaf between his white teeth
as he ties the black collar, to be later inflated with his breath,
around his neck.

We are ready. The ship weighs anchor.

The sky above our heads is full of smoke and sparks.

Along both sides of the deck, the huge mines in their iron cages
rest atop their mounts, jutting towards the water.

The long torpedoes are poised for attack, protected by their
tubes, bronze heads laden with TNT, like beasts lying in wait.

Sailors with ear muffs on their heads stand gathered round the
open-breeched cannons.

The entire deck is cluttered with weapons, machines, and vigi-
lant men. To go from stern to stem, one has to bend down, crawl
under an oily torpedo, climb over a prostrate sailor, knock one's

shins against the cabling of a mine, flatten oneself against a scalding-hot smokestack, get tangled up in line, receive a splash of seafoam in the face when leaning out over a railing.

I climb up to the bridge. We are already outside the harbor. It is night. The moon is setting over the sea. In an hour it will be gone.

The great rumbling of the engines shakes the whole ship. The smokestacks are still spewing too much smoke and too many sparks. All lights on board are extinguished, including cigarettes. The darkness is total, from stem to stern. Silence is imposed. The crew is quiet.

The last commands given through the megaphone resound in a sky speckled with sparks, and with stars that are inextinguishable sparks.

A light haze rises from the vast waters. The wake foams white, and the wave at the cutwater flows in two streams along the ship's sides, emitting strange gleams from time to time. Through the backwash one can make out the black form of the destroyer following behind us, and gradually all the others lined up behind it.

When the ship veers, oblique wakes break away from the central wake and create the impression of an immense silver rake.

Piero Orsini leans against the railing, out into the night, his entire soul in his searching eyes. Every so often he turns his ruddy face, the whites of his leonine eyes shot with blood, and issues a command in a precise, clipped accent.

The helmsman stands at the wheel, never taking his eye off the compass illuminated by a little light in its binnacle. He is clearly a man of pure Tyrrhenian stock, a true companion of Ulysses, with a face that looks carved by the winds of fortune.

Beside him are two engine-room telegraphs, with lighted dials that read: *Half throttle! Full throttle! Slow! Stop!*

The loudspeaker conveys the order to the machinists.

"Four, three, zero!"

We are traveling at twenty-three knots. The wash of the great wake sparkles under the stern lamps.

"A little to starboard!"

The navigator is bent over a chart—held in place by lead weights sheathed in canvas—entirely absorbed in measuring and calculating with protractor, slide rule, compass, and eraser, by the violet light of a small shaded lamp.

A great shooting star streaks across the August sky, burning out near Capella in Auriga.

Impatience eats away at me. I look keenly into the distant darkness for the prearranged signal from land. Nothing is visible yet.

I descend two small ladders and head astern, along the row of mines, climbing over the crouching sailors. From the poop deck one can see the dark shapes of the other destroyers lined up behind us.

Then, suddenly, the signal flashes, straight ahead. We are approaching the scene of the action. Every man steels his resolve. Luigi Rizzo must be at Mula di Muggia tonight.

"There's the beacon from Muggia ahead. See it?"

"Sì," the black megaphones answer in the dark.

And wherever the *sì* is heard, the whole sea belongs to Dante.[41]

"Follow the same courses as planned, at the same distances, at eight knots up to the canal, then six knots thereafter."

The ships' prows split my starry heart.

"One, two, zero!"

We slow down to a mere six knots.

The smokestacks are spewing too much smoke, too many sparks. Piero Orsini gets angry.

The orders are nevertheless given through the megaphone. Every shouted word seems to increase the feeling of danger in the air.

Our maneuver is executed with a sort of rhythmical precision. One by one, each ship passes ours to starboard, keeping its distance, black over the whitening wake that glows from time to time with unexpected phosphorescence.

"On course to mine barrage, east to starboard. Extinguish the stern light!"

We see the coast alight with the enemy's searchlights. We are navigating in shallow water, reducing our speed even more.

"One, zero, zero!"

We are practically scraping the bottom, feeling our way through the water. The ships seem to pant and wheeze, anguished like great cetaceans in danger of running aground.

"Reverse! Full throttle!"

The *Fuciliere* feels as if can no longer maneuver, as if it has grounded in the mire and is trying to come unstuck.

It is straight ahead of us, within call. The water gleams in the blue light of its aft lamps. Now they all seem to be in trouble and in danger. The sky is veiled. Long medusan tresses of cloud drag the constellations like nets dragging silvery fish. The ships' engines strain. We are almost aground; it could go either way.

Piero Orsini is there, watchful, all soul, an eye overcoming the night. What if, at that moment, the enemy were to sight us? What chance would we stand if we chose to fight?

"The *Fuciliere* is straight ahead, at naught seventy-four magnetic!"

Maneuver by maneuver, his clear commands lead the squadron back onto the right course, away from the shoals.

I see the enemy's searchlights crisscross in the distance, on dry land, long swords of white light. In the glow the coast looms so close that it looks as though we are about to drop anchor.

We are all tense, attentive and waiting. In a few minutes we shall reach the designated point of the barrage. The minutes seem like hours.

We have removed the rubber safety stoppers from the firing pins. The mines on their mounts are ready to be lowered into the sea. Standing, the sailors await the command.

The final minutes are eternal. We could be discovered at any moment. The coast is less than a mile away. The smokestacks are still cause for despair, spewing too much smoke, too many sparks.

At last, word comes from the bridge.

"Attention!"

The lieutenant looks at his watch, lighting the dial with a little lamp hidden in the palm of his hand, which emits a glow the color of blood.

Heads laden with destruction, gray as gigantic, solidified jellyfish, the huge mines await, silent, immobile. The double tooth of each mount juts into the stream of the forewave.

"Attention!"

"Let her go!"

The first mine rolls with the sound of a barrel coming apart, plunges into the foaming sea, and disappears.

"Attention!"

"Let her go!"

Eighteen seconds have passed, and then the next mine plunges as well, then the third, then the fourth, then all the rest, from all the ships lying obliquely in shrewd formation.

In three minutes the operation is over; the barrage is laid exactly where we had intended.

The sailors smile wildly, teeth gleaming. In his heart each one of them sees the enemy battleships blown to pieces.

"Four, three, zero!"

We resume our place at the head of the column, returning along the same route at our initial speed. The ships seem to quiver with martial delight.

Far away, on the mainland, the white shafts of the searchlights continue to crisscross. A few rockets explode. Our wake is so beautiful, it looks like a riotous Milky Way.

A sailor climbs to the command bridge, bringing me a cup of scalding hot coffee. The fragrance alone regales my nostrils and heartstrings. It is a naval nepenthe.

We light our cigarettes. The smoke seems to bring back the scent of the leaf the Saracen boy was rubbing between his brownish fingers.

A radiotelegram from Umberto Cagni comes in from the cruiser, the *Pisa*.

"Attention! Two submarines are lying in ambush along the security channel."

And again we breathe danger and death, at the first shudder of dawn.

Let me see the dawn! It will not harm me. Open the window wide! I'm suffocating.

The sun in the haze was orange in color, like a full moon rising. The six ships maneuvered, putting quickly about. In the water their wakes seemed to sketch vast instruments for my new music.

Gone was the night's mystery, vanished with the sparks and the stars. Now only the harsh warship was visible, with its three smoke-stacks, its four torpedoes, its empty, jutting mounts, its sailors lying down, at rest, eyes open.

We dropped anchor in Malamocco.

At Malamocco we encountered a convoy laden with wounded. Then Mass was celebrated for us. An invisible priest raised the host and chalice.

The entire morning had the color of wounds and the taste of blood.

Umberto Cagni has come.

From where? From the bridge of his sleek cruiser? From the balconied aft cabin where I went so many times with Giuseppe Miraglia to study convoy routes on sea charts while the Libyan hero's steely eye gleamed with the temptation of a "sneak attack" on the Dalmatian coast?[42]

Or has he come back to me from the depths of a song of Deeds performed across the sea? Or has he resurfaced from the bitterness of my distant, desperate envy?

How could I not give thanks to my god?

The hero celebrated in my terza rima is at my bedside. He is alive. He leans over me. He lightly touches me with the hand that lost a finger to frostbite in the arctic wilderness. He visits not the poet but the man of war, not the encomiast but the comrade.

The immortal eagle of song again bites my poisoned liver.

"Sit down, Cagni. Just think, here you'll find the same darkness you saw in the wells of Bu-Meliana, on that night in October. I was waiting for you. I, too, have lost my right eye, like your Lazaro Mocenigo in the battle against Pasha Kenaan in the waters off Chios. But if I can see your feral eyes flashing in the dark, surely you can see the glow of my blindfold. You bring me another kind of sight. I hope that, for me, too, the left eye will become 'the cold orb of all daring.'[43] I shall rise and fight again. Such is my wish. You took two hours to cut through your finger-bone with that

ghastly pair of scissors that allowed Simone Canepa to escape from
the tent. Well, here, under my pillow, I've got those same scissors
of yours."

 His presence is light. His step is light. His gestures are light. His
affectionate politeness is aimed at not disturbing the restful air
surrounding my restlessness. Even my nurse is not as circumspect
as this brusque man of war. I think of the way I handled the
wounded sailors on the Isola Morosina, who seemed not to feel
any pain when I moved them onto the muddy planks that served as
stretchers.
   Nevertheless, his politeness fortifies me, like certain mild drinks
that set the blood on fire.
   Inside me I am forging the steel that I wish I had hammered
when drawing my ten canzoni from the "fearless furnace."
   *Come, fire, do your work!/Glory, burst into flame! Come, singer
of peoples,/vie for victory!*
   The discontent and wrath of the unwarring years, the years of
shame, brighten for me as the necessary expectation of fulfillment.
   In an instant I relive the intense pain of the last canzone. In the
dream of the oceanside dune I hear again the baying of the Sardin-
ian dogs, the mastiffs of Fonni, the greyhounds of Monte Spada. I
see the "square formation" again, the battalion that buried its dead
at Tobras; I see them climb the impassable sand without me, I see
them go without me toward the "sure dawn," toward the sure
destiny without the one who believed he was the "herald of a new
life and the new glory's first-born."
   All is dream.

How and where did I join the battalion, become its leader, and lead it irresistibly to the "ultimate conquest"?

And is the long shadow of the first-born Hero now behind me or before me?

And is it not therefore true that on the threshold of old age I was reborn as the Prince of Youth, chosen by my comrades of the tribe of Mario Bianco?[44]

And is it not true that, in order to guide them, I rekindled myself "with a higher, purer fire"?

And is it not true that I have led them, and will lead them again, in the sky, on the sea and on land, and they shall obey in every greatest risk we face?

Hail, Youth. Glory to thee in the heavens,/glory o'er the seas, glory o'er the land!

All is dream, and occult fate, and predisposition of the will.

The urgency of my inner strength unbinds me. The throbs of my heart burst through my chest. The throbs in my nape stretch my blindfold.

With a sudden start I rise from the bed and tear off my bandages, gasping for breath as though sobbing.

"I cannot stay here any longer. I don't want to. Help me, Cagni. Take me away. Save me."

Alarmed, he supports me with his arm, holds up my head with his hand. He tries to persuade me, to calm me, to ease me back into my misery.

"I beg you! I beg you, my friend, my comrade! I'll never recover. I mustn't recover. Take me away from this pointless torture. Help me free myself from this trickery, this plot. Save me."

He is aghast. My anguish has entered him and confuses him.

I grope about and manage to light the blue lamp at the head of the bed. I see my brother, my exact coeval, turn livid in the lugubrious glow. And he sees me unbandaged, eye swollen and watering, face misshapen, as I saw it the other day in the doctor's small round mirror.

The nurse arrives. My will to revolt is broken by her compassionate, excessively trembling hands. All my strength melts into perfidious sweat. Sweat, tears, and the dampness of the compress soften my distress, weaken my sadness and my whole person. I no longer want anything, am no longer worth anything.

Where are fierce patience's scissors? Away, far away, irretrievably far, under the polar tent, among the remains of a poor, skinned dog.

The Admiral speaks to me of the Isola Morosina as if it were a great battleship anchored off the enemy coast. He knows what I did, with the sailors, in October 1915.

Once again everything becomes present and alive, everything pulsates and bleeds. The walkways of planks laid over the mud begin at my bed; the shaggy Maremma dogs of the two light cavalrymen guarding the telephone wires lay their muzzles on my pillow as on sacks of feed.

I see the young lieutenants devouring their coarse soup again, their feline eyes sparkling, as I enter the mess hut with the order to begin firing at noon.

Now I am walking with fervid good cheer down the little alleyway, on the bricks laid down to form a bridge in the mud.

Now I am climbing up the wooden tower that looks like a pagoda, hidden amidst the great boughs of an oak.

The sailors yell through their gleaming white teeth.

I see sky-blue Punta Sdobba and the Quaranta, the mountains' snowy crown, a corner of the Bosco Cappuccio, and Ronchi, and Doberdò, and the scrub of Monfalcone, and the smokestacks, and La Rocca, and Duino, and the reddish landslip of Sistiana, and Miramar, and Barcola, and Trieste in the distance like a form of light, as it appeared to me for the first time from above, between the tie-rods of the wing, weightless and huddled, almost chaste.

A transparent dragonfly lands on an oak leaf. A skylark soars in space, singing, never sated.[45]

I hear the voices of sailors and crows in trees already sick with autumn.

A seagull gleams in the air like a fighter plane.

The poplars in their fading shades of gold ravish me musically, like a harp's arpeggio.

"First gun, attention! Castagnola, fire!"

It is the first strike. The symphony begins. All the valleys rumble.

The Gazzola battery fires on the castle of Duino, where I once lived days of delight, in times of leisure and play.

Gazzola shoots from the end of a bridge on the left bank, hidden by brush and foliage.

I see the shell explode at the edge of the wood.

What is all this clamor?

All along the bank the megaphone transmits the orders of the day, from the Duke of Aosta to the sailors.

The symphony swells. Gazzola fires. Buraggi fires. The sun eats the yellowy smoke. The clamor spreads through all the batteries. Every pause is filled with the rapturous trill of the skylark. But little by little, the air itself turns metallic.

"Gun four, attention! Castagnola, fire! Gun four, fire!"

Small and blondish, with a toothbrush moustache over a jutting upper lip, the officer calculates the targeting coordinates in a notebook.

"Gun one, direction 1454, elevation 345."

A square-shouldered helmsman stands beside him, transmitter to his ear at all times. He has two large, bloodshot brown eyes like an Arab charger, a short, wild beard, and flared nostrils. He breathes forcefully. He looks cast from the ancient mould of our furious partisans, be their faction black or white. And he bends over that useless device, not hearing well.

He says: "Sdobba wants to know if it's B1 or B2."

He would do better to say: "Take them, God, for I hurl them at you!"[46]

The large metal horn, camouflaged green, hangs from a branch. We are all made green, men and objects, like the oak that conceals us.

"Gun two, direction 1402, elevation 230."

The shot lands short, in the sea. Beyond the water line, the houses of San Giovanni around the bell tower look placid in the October sun.

Buraggi fires at the houses of San Giovanni to adjust his aim. The fourth shot is also short. The round is over.

The lung of Uroni the sailor is punctured by a piece of shrapnel while reconnecting the telephone line. But he doesn't let himself fall backwards. He remains erect, on his feet, holding his vomit of blood inside with clenched teeth. When he finishes his task, he collapses, as the order passes through the reconnected wire.

A new round begins.

Sailors! Sailors!

My voice, my comrade voice, rings out in the shade of the low, dense trees where the fluvial evening caresses the wooden huts as if they were cabins of bliss.

This river has become more mysterious than the thunderstruck Timavo in the distance, where Castor's steaming horse once bathed. A band of red light stops the fleeing clouds. The cannons are hot, also camouflaged green, on pontoons covered with foliage. They burn my hand.

Tonight I shall sleep again with one eye open, inside this pontoon, between munitions and sacks, in a bunk as narrow as the dark carpenter's four planks.

Burn my hospital bed!

Call the sailors for me, so they can form lines in this place, which is like a lagoon-bog, one hundred thousand cubits above yesterday's life.

Sailors! Sailors!

The shade is all a coiled conch for amplifying my voice.

It is as if I am distributing a cordial palliative for fatigue and fever.

In my human skin I feel the cannons cool little by little.

In the shade the compact strength of these men is gray as new iron; but kindness displays their childish teeth through their smiles.

Is anyone tired here?

We are going to the munitions stores, my sons. The round is over. And the round begins again.

The pontoons lie low like a beaver, "which is both beast and fish."[47] In the watery silence, the cannons cool and breathe through open breeches.

The sailors file past, artillery shells on their shoulders, as beautiful in the beautiful evening as Attic bearers of sacred vases.

Whosoever does not fear death does not die. And death wants not him who seeks it.

I was leaning with my back against the parapet of Gun Three. I leave my post to get away from the battery and climb up to the lookout in the tree.

An Austrian shell explodes on the parapet of Gun Three. Four wounded.

Had my mother led me away by the hand?

I run to help. She seems not to let go of my hand. She knows she is about to hear the accent of her town, the accent of Ortona, in the blood.

We encounter a sailor whose sleeve, a second gunner's sleeve, is edged in red, the leather band of his wristwatch in shreds. A long roar streaks the blue over our heads. The walkway is spattered with blood. Is it a plank? It is a sparking ember.

But the stretchers are nothing but planks, nothing but muddy boards. And where will we get bandages? Where will we get medicine?

The naked hero rises again from the human clay. He is forged anew from the original mud.

"Why has the battery stopped firing?"

What anguish thus springs from the mangled body?

Here is a bloodied, convulsing body, and amidst all that throbbing agony there is yet a vigilant ear, an epitome of the soul, listening and gasping.

Giuseppe Maggiora can think only of his weapon. He wants to hear its thunder. Blood streams from his nose and into his restless mouth.

"Four years ago, October 18, Commander, we were in Benghazi. Do you remember?"

These are the first words he says to Buraggi when he sees him. A remembrance of war, a remembrance of victory, a heroic foreshortening of time and mind between two destinies.

And he begins to rave again about his silenced gun. He wants to return to the gun. Cut down, he wants to get back up and fight again. He tries to raise a blood-soaked hand, to threaten revenge.

"The battery has stopped firing!"

O my Maggiora, where are you now? Are you at La Mandria? Are you at royal Veneria? Have you begun living and burning again?

Why are you not at my bedside this evening, as I was at yours, on that October night, in hospital 71 on the Isola Morosina?

Do you remember?

You wouldn't stop thanking me—I, who had to make an effort not to fall to my knees and kiss your hands.

And there beside you was second gunner Corsani. Like you, he too kept thinking about his guns. And he had just had his right eye removed from its socket. And was blindfolded as I am now. He was so serene, so gentle that it now makes me ashamed.

Do you remember?

Uroni was also there, the one who fixed the telephone wire. And he was in danger. But all he could think of was the battery, and he begged and pleaded to go back there; he wept with regret, promised to do better, and did not know he was sublime.

And you did not know it either, O my Maggiora.

And when I left that little field hospital on the Ausa, having lost my right eye, in my wild sadness I thought of those few who would have wept. I thought of Corsani, who would have wept. I thought of you, who would have wept.

How sweet it would be to have you both here, this evening, at my bedside, one on either side of me!

Another would have wept as well, perhaps even more: Giovanni Federico, the sailor from my mother's land, the sailor from Ortona.

But all that remain of his eyes are the sockets of bone, as he lies in the island's small cemetery, where I had promised to lay a carved stone in his memory. I have not yet done so.

This evening I pick him up again, I lay him down again on that rough plank covered with my cavalryman's cape. And this evening as well, my mother is with me, and helps me.

The most beautiful human smile is the smile that shines over the mangled shreds of inhuman pain.

What Mary ever had the face of her who bows before our suffering?

Giovanni is wounded in the stomach, kidneys, and ribcage. On what side shall we lay him down?

If we put him face down, he does not cry. If we lay him on his back, he does not cry. And yet his agony splits even the dead plank. I am kneeling in the mud. In a silent spasm he points his feet against my thigh. And I clench my jaw.

He is barefoot. Half naked. He is returning to the cradle. Returning to his race.

I am of his race. And I suffer his pain with a boundless immensity that I cannot express, which spans all of childhood to all of old age, all rivers from source to mouth, all mountains from foot to summit.

His wretched flesh is my wretched flesh. His constancy in suffering is the constancy of my mother and my people.

There he lies, face down. Cut down. He is twenty years old.

He lies there like the animals the butcher quarters on his block. His soul is as divine as his body is gross. He is covered only by the tatters of his coarse shirt; and his exposed private parts, the signs of his sex, augment the horror and misery and innocence and compassion and sacred procreation cut short.

His hairless face is turned towards me, and he does not take his eyes off me. He drinks me in. Drinks from me a pity come back to him from the altar of the church where he was baptized and confirmed.

Through my mouth my mother speaks to him as his mother once spoke to him.

And the gentlest of childhood smiles appears on his face at the final moment of his torment.

Peerless music of godly war!

Heroism, blood, death, kindness, and hope had put me in a state of grace in which to receive and prolong an unheard-of melody.

How could the musical sentiment of Titian's painting, in which the pipes of the portative organ recede in symmetrical distances with the garden's noble trees amidst the fountains, ever compare to this?[48]

No great cathedral organ ever filled a nave with its thunder the way that broad avenue of silent poplars filled my soul.

Other nerves and tendons and fibers were torn to separate me from the wounded, and from the dying man. I had washed myself poorly and still had blood under my fingernails and on my clothes.

O Isola Morosina, all tawny with grasses and azure with ponds like the fairest of Saint Mark's daughters, recumbent in the October evening, in you I have left my passion's innermost mystery, my music's most secret pulse.

I envy the humble twenty-year-old hero of my same stock who finds peace in you, beneath his little cross of rough-hewn wood. He may not hear, but were I lying in that mound of fresh earth I made him with a nameless sexton's shovel, I should hear indeed your poplars' golden melody resonate forever in my eternity.

Was not an angel counting them? Was not an angel tempering them? Was not an angel harmonizing them?

For my love, all three had the face of the smiling, dying youth.

So much life, so much red life is still inside me!

My pain is full of blood. My dreams are full of blood. My every thought has the weight of blood.

Sometimes my past, to my revulsion, bleeds inside me like a slaughterhouse cluttered with quartered animals hung from hooks.

I write my passion in blood. And as the sculptor has clay under his fingernails, I have dried blood under mine.

There, on the little medicine table, between a yellow vial of atropine and a roll of gauze, is a little washbasin glowing red; and amidst the redness gleams a slender steel instrument.

The shutters of the last window, in the corner, are ajar.

The bell strikes one o'clock in the afternoon. I am alone. My people are at table. The hour transpierces my feet with a sharper nail.

Now and then a breath of air reaches my blindfold.

I am thirsty. Just now the whites of Renata's eyes quivered like rivulets.

My people are eating. Taking comfort.

An illicit shaft of light enters through the half-closed shutters. It makes the washbasin shimmer. The fresh blood inside the porcelain rim is as bright as a scarlet rose.

A faint shadow passes back and forth. A fleeting shadow brushes past the basin, disappears, returns.

I follow it intently. It is enough to stir my melancholy and exasperate my distress.

It is the shadow of a butterfly.

The darkness thickens, as the crater in my eye erupts again.

It is like a sudden uprising of fiery clouds, roused and entranced by an epic rhythm.

It is a solid, rich material that takes shape as pain, a frenzy of crags in metamorphosis.

It is a background for some great deed unknown to me.

Everything is burning again. The dawn no longer has dewdrops but sparks.

The matins of the birds begin.

At first they crackle like green firebrands.

The fire catches, spreads, blazes.

The fire trills, warbles, twitters.

In the flaming chorus I discern another sound.

The extraneous sound grows louder. The song seems to give way.

I recognize rain.

The rain washes over the song as over a low fire of vine shoots.

The song breaks up into narrow tongues of flame.

Little by little the rain crushes it, wearies it, puts it out.

The steady patter prevails.

Night returns; she leans her elbows on the bedstead, brings a black finger to her lips, and stares at me.

I am always thirsty. My torturers forbid me to drink, and continue to steel my mouth with iodine.

Today a word in my empty brain, the insistent sound of a word, whets the torment with images of liquid and cold: *aloscia*.

I think it was a summer drink of lemon, honey, and spices.

The demon has rekindled all the fires deep inside my eye; and he blows with all his madness on the wretched pyre, as during the most desperate hours of this unrelenting martyrdom.

The burning reduces my whole hapless body to a bundle of brushwood at the edge of the blaze.

The fern leaf inside my eye multiplies; it grows, thickens.

Soon I am like the thicket of ferns, copper and gold, which I saw at the edge of a burning forest in the Lande, untouched by the blaze.

The flames had grazed it without burning it. And I felt amazed and superstitious to see a thing so light and flammable at the perimeter of the fire, intact. It was ready to burst into flame in an instant, to turn to ash in an instant; yet the voracity of the blaze had miraculously spared it.

Who has wrapped me in hot ash? The peak of my heart begins to spark, breaking through the ash.

I am my ash, and I am my phoenix. I am opaque, and I blaze anew.

I survive the pyre, drunk with immortality.

Who has hoisted me upon my horse with so imperious a hand?

The spirit of attention enters me like a god armed with a thousand eyes.

Attention creates what it contemplates.

I create heat.

This is my secret fate.

O forest of the Extreme West! O forest of myriad wounds! O exile of my virtue wept in tears like resin!

I ride on horseback through pine woods already scorched.

I wander through young pine woods with no future, sacrificed like the prime-choice children fed to the hot bronze idol.

The ground is hot and smoky in spots, blackish and streaked with pale ash.

The pines are grim and dark, burnt all the way to the top, with no needles, only naked branches; but all still standing, like martyrs unbowed.

A few, though charred, have fire still consuming the mutilated trunk, seeking the roots, devouring them underground.

A few have light flakes of ash covering the blackness for the entire length of their barren shafts.

My horse risks sinking his hoof into every hollow trunk as into a red-hot sheath. I never let up my vigilance. I am all eyes, all acumen. The black shards threaten to puncture the sole of the hoof like the iron wedges once used to stop enemy cavalcades.

The ash is hot, strewn with embers. I smell an odor of burnt horn, as outside the blacksmith's door. I inhale the heat. I alternately hear sounds of blowing, crackling, crunching. I am sweating, panting.

Who is that man with singed face, clothing afire, rolling in the sand of the garde-feu and screaming?

I advance through the ashen wasteland.

I ride through the grim forest, between ash and sand.

From time to time a quiet whirlwind lifts the ash high in the air.

I see the long, slender funnel rise into the silent sky and undulate.

I am spellbound.

I spur the horse towards it, to observe it more closely.

As I draw near, it vanishes.

And another rises up farther away; and yet another; and another still.

They silently sway in the burning air; they beckon, dissolve, disperse.

They are like the ghosts of holocausts.

I cross over the ditches and broad, sandy roads called *gardes-feu* in the Lande, which failed to save the adjacent forests. The sand has mingled with the ash and powdered charcoal.

Under a mass of fallen earth, a tangle of roots burns and smokes, groaning, hissing, crackling.

Here and there, amidst the charring and incineration, I glimpse an intact blade of dry grass, an intact fern leaf.

Here and there, on the banks of ditches scorched by the blaze, I discover a clump of green grass, a stalk full of little pink and violet flowers.

The astonished soul sees itself in them.

No longer specters of ash, but columns of grim smoke.

And a sinister rumbling, which seems to rise up from the bowels of the earth.

I spur my horse on, through the burnt pines, as if towards an expiatory chasm.[49]

The fascination of danger girds my chest like a snake.

The ground fumes and crackles under his hooves.

Dense clouds of smoke swallow up flames in the distance.

A bitterness of resin stings my throat.

The rumbling increases, shakes and deafens me.

A song bursts forth deep inside me whenever bright flames appear suddenly between one trunk and another.

Beauty of fire, newer than springtime to me, always.

A multitude of flames is arrayed in the field before me like an impenetrable army.

Over the crackling of pitch, the hissing of resin, the crunchings and poppings, they sing.

They advance in a single line, voracious.

They devour my eyes, devour my face.

They are orange in color, flickering blue and green and gray by turns.

At times they darken like embers or flash like lightning.

Every little change in them disturbs me, like spellbinding glances.

They have left behind a charred, fuming forest. They advance in a great long chain, deployed in a battle line that recedes into the distance, vanishing in a cloud of black smoke.

Their violence is such that it seems not to rise from the surface of the ground, where the underbrush is rooted, but to burst up from the depths, spew forth from the abyss, like the magma in open craters.

They are violent and tenacious, impetuous and constant.

They teach how to fight.

These are the ways of the art of fire.

They storm the trunks, attacking first the outer roots above ground.

Then they creep upwards, along the bark.

They look as if they are feeling about, searching where best to bite.

They catch where a branch was pruned, where there is a resinous scab, a fragrant wound; and they persist.

When there is a lull in the wind, they abate.

But the flame has sunk its teeth into the quick of the trunk and will not let up. It remains alone, suspended, intent on devouring, detached from the rest, alone with its hunger and fury, unrelenting and obstinate.

I think—I know not why—of those naval battles, those desperate raids and attacks when the ships' sides are gripped by fists and jaws, and enemy axes chop wrists and cleave skulls; yet the terrible hands never let go of the wood, the teeth remain lodged in the wood, even as the bodies plunge below and sink.

Thus do the flame's red talons, the flame's red maw, remain clasped to the trunk, separate from the receding body.

O inert combatant, remember Aeschylus' brother.[50]

Some trunks burn only on one side, as if the fire erupted from within, along the vertical incision made by the resin tapper.

The fire is like a tattered flag, hoisted up the mast.

And now the wind grows stronger.

All the victorious flags flutter and flap, tear into tatters that fly away.

A great briny gust arrives from the open sea.

The fire leaps and spreads, leaps higher than the treetops, engulfing whole pines, turning them red from root to crest with the roar of a cyclone.

Scales of flaming bark and burning cones are cast afar like lapilli from a volcano.

Countless nests woven by caterpillar larvae catch fire and fly even farther, spreading the blaze into the sheltered forest.

The resin crackles, fries, sizzles. The clay pots glow red hot, boil and overflow, fly up and fall back down, explode like hand grenades. Every burst ejects thousands of red needles.

Then, through the din, a mysterious melody begins to emerge, surging and flowing.

Are the Salamanders singing?[51]

The flames and smoke fly away to the heavens. An eddy of dark smoke fills the air and assails the sun.

I can see the sun through it, looking like a red-hot disk starting to cool.

Now I no longer see it. It has been swallowed up.

The wind relents, the smoke thins out.

I see the disk again. Little by little, it turns from red to tawny, then tawny to blond.

But in the shadow the blaze is more splendid than the sun.

And now the whole perimeter of the smoky cloud itself turns a resplendent blond.

Will the sun triumph?

For a moment it shines bright again in the sky, as the great flame falls back and creeps along the ground.

But up inside the trunks' higher knots, the little flame thrives, gnawing away.

And up inside the wasted trunks already bound for death, the little flame persists, seeking the last bead of sap.

And in the lull in the assault, the mysterious melody grows more distinct. It is clear as a soprano's song. It carries me beyond all burning.

Are the Salamanders singing?

The Ocean blows its lusty blasts again from dune to dune.

The crash and thunder overwhelm the enchanted voice that delivers from harm what burns.

The crash and thunder become a lowing of buffalo, a roaring of lionesses.

Enraged again, the flames advance in battle array, taller and denser.

"This way, forest!" cries the implacable field general wearing my war face. "All the forest and all its scents, follow me!"

He is the first to attack, the first to seize the bristling beast by the mane with his red hand.

"This way, men! This way, people of the forest!" cries the daring enemy wearing my war face.

Fire shall smite fire, flame shall kill flame, and with their clashing ashes the world shall be refecundated.

Who is that man with scorched face and clothing afire, throwing himself onto the sand and burrowing into it as if to bury himself?

He does not put out the fire.

"This way, men! Elders, women, children, this way! All the people of the Lande who have hands and breath, follow me!"

I lead the backfire.

The chain of flames is countered by a human chain. The blaze's front is countered by an opposing front.

The backfire spreads.

With long fresh pine boughs the young, the old, the women, the children beat the red beast, force it to advance towards the other advancing beast.

Help! Help!

The flames fall back under the thrashing. The gusting wind blows smoke onto the thrashers. The growing radiance singes eyebrows, beards, clothes. The throat goes dry, the eyes tear.

Help! Help!

The backfire advances. The enemy approaches. It goes from yellow to red by turns; breaks up into myriad parts; then comes back together; dissolves and disperses. It sputters, groans, crackles, creaks, hisses, snaps.

Help! Help!

From what entrails rises this soul-splitting cry of pain and terror?

It is no longer the voice of the element. It is the voice of the creature.

Caught between fire and backfire, crazed animals seek a path of escape.

The fire pursues them, the backfire hems them in.

Blinded by the glare, they butt against the crackling trunks in the growing haze.

They dash through the long, torrid corridor of a labyrinth without exit, howling, and their doleful howl bursts through the stifling soot in a whirlwind of fiery scales and flaming pinecones.

Help! Help!

We stamp on the embers, tread on the firebrands, swallow the sparks.

Are these obstinate thrashers a phalanx of martyrs forced to combat the fires of the Lord?

Each is up against a flaming angel and a thousand tortuous swords.

The children cry; the old fall to their knees; the women wail as in the throes of childbirth.

Who is Lord of this fiery battle?

And what deep century reddens this struggle of flames?

I see the great goddess Cybele without towers or lions.[52]

I see her multicolored dress of air, water, earth, fire.

I see her tree carriers, the bristly ranks of dendrophores who resemble the sacred tree.

Who wails? Who roars? Who calls from chasm and summit?

The sun goes dark.

Is what drowns out the clash between the two raging adversaries the New Gods' thunder?

Where they fight, all is already devoured. All is black char and ember and hot ash. There is nothing left to burn.

The fire dies.

The fire is dead!

The pain dulls, the terror falls silent.

But again a whirlwind takes the still-sparking ash and lifts it up to the grim, now dispersing cloud.

I see the long, slender funnel rise, undulate, recede.

It is the holocaust's ghost.

Holocaust, fresh victim
dressed in white, high-waisted,
toward your splendor extends
a hand filled with dew
like the bearbine's lone calyx,
which the dawn fills to the brim.

Holocaust, Holocaust,
you were robbed of a man's heart
in which the blood struggled, boiling
like the golden resin oozing
into a hanging pot.
But the robber's hand
was burnt to the wristbone;
the offense was atoned,
and the future was glimpsed.
Holocaust, Holocaust,
smother not in your ashes
immortality's star,
the spark at the apex of the heart.

Does the grim whirlwind
again stir the dead ashes?
It is what does not die.

Do silent specters rise again
in the stillness of a cleansed sky?
Silence awaits.
From what waters blows the spirit
who moves the lifeless desert?
The waters are calm.
What is this flutter of wings?
What is this flash of feathers?
The species of the Sun.
What is this golden miracle
more beautiful than all flames?
The hymn reborn, O king Lemuel.

I hear the Phoenixes singing!
Ecstasy courses in me
like a heavenly river in spate.
I feel my god in me.

I hear the Phoenixes singing
a chant that has the scent of myrrh
and the joy of bitterness.
I feel my god in me.

All ash is seed,
all stumps are saplings,
the whole desert is springtime.
I feel my god in me.

The whole forest is reborn with palms,
the whole forest rises high into the ether,
free of the burden of weight.
I feel my god in me.

Atop the Idumean palms
sing the Phoenixes reborn,
neither bending nor breaking them.
I feel my god in me.

O Phoenixes of Holocausts,
I'll not speak of your purple Orient,
nor of your crest of unknown orbs.
I see my god in me.

O Phoenixes of Holocausts,
I'll not reveal the votive word
that opens and closes each round of the hymn.
I serve my god in me.

THIRD OFFERING

Sleepy calends of April. The midday rain upon the foliage subsides and then stops.

My slumber puts me in tune with the garden, which I cannot see.

I can hear that the tide is high, the quay submerged.

A melody of birds resounds all through my chest, as if my assuaged spirits were singing.

Divine respite. A slumber similar to ecstasy, transparent and lithe like a brook on a plain.

Watching over me is not Sirenetta, but our sister Water, "*humble, precious, chaste*" creature of the Canticle.[1]

With long, silvery hands she seeks the veins in my gaunt body, disentangles and divides them, lengthens and guides them towards the earth, towards peace.

I seem to feel one of them descend from my shoulder and down my arm with virginal clarity, flowing beyond my fingers, lengthening in my hand like a crystal bow for playing an instrument whose strings are the spring rain.

I hear the rain resume, after the lull.

My hearing floats upon the somnolence, like those birthing leaves shaped like attentive ears.

The melody of birds and spirits begins to fade.

At once I feel my mouth go dry. The sheet of steel covers my tongue and palate again.

I raise a hand towards the one watching over me.

"Sister Water!" murmurs the drooping wisteria. "Sister Water!" cry the rosebushes anxious to bloom. And the mind's violets, inclining their teary faces, sigh: "Sister Water!"

I am like one of those conical hills depicted in the backgrounds of Umbrian paintings, with a crest of sun-baked Calvary and slopes furrowed by streams.

To be a fine Italian pine
atop a Roman hill
when the moon is full;
to feel the night wind
move the tender treetops
born amidst old needles
at the tips of old branches,
rosy as the fingers of infants.

To be the tallest, darkest cypress
at the Villa d'Este
after twilight,
when the fountain
removes the veil of maidenhair
from its dripping ear
to listen to the distant sound
of Tivoli's waterfall;
to caress the evening's grace
with the delicate pale green
that frames the boughs of grief.

To be the spirit of a blind blade
of grass in the Forum
and struggle patiently

to find a fissure in the august stone
on which the hooves of Triumphs strode;
and to discover one at last
and labor with slender tip
and emerge green and joyous into a sun
that never saw anything greater than Rome.

Brief respite. Unrest again strains my heart, distress empties my chest.

Luigi Bresciani and Roberto Prunas come to see me. They announce that tomorrow morning they will undertake their long test flight, and that this test will be considered the definitive trial of the large marine craft in which all of us Adriatic fighters had placed our hopes of predominance and victory.

My heart beats so fast that I think I am dying. The throbbing prevents me from hearing their words. I feel Gino lean over me and place his hand on my heart. I lose all sense of time and place. It is like the time when we leaned against each other for support, as the four sailors took the funeral shroud by its four corners and carried our Miraglia's body to the coffin lying open on the floor, parallel to the bed.

A sudden horror imprisons my body as if inside a block of ice; and my friend, too, seems imprisoned in the same block.

How much time has passed?

My heart has calmed down,, but I am dying of sadness.

Gino and Roberto have left into the night. Tomorrow morning they will be one beside the other in the great winged vessel, as I was with my pilot, whom I shall meet again, face to face, one day.

I have violated the prohibition. I raised myself up on my elbows to send them a last salute and my last best wishes.

Never have I felt a more violent urge to get up.

"Take me with you! Save me! And I shall save you! Whoever takes me away will take my good luck with him."

They can no longer hear me. They are walking away down the calle, away to their camp, away and over the bridge.

They have compassion for me, of course. But they cannot help but feel elated, as we always felt on the eve of a test flight.

It is the night of the second of April. A new moon. Over the roof I see the starry sky. The spring stars look as new as the almond blossoms. The wind and the yearning of youth scent the azure.

I want to breathe the April stars.

Why did you leave me so soon? Why, Gino, did you go away so soon?

Just now you seemed united with me, as on the evening of December 23 when I stood up after brushing my lips against the three-day-old corpse and saw you drained of color, saw your lips quivering like a child's, and buried my face in your shoulder and wept with you.

Had you stayed longer, had you let Roberto Prunas leave and stayed a while longer, alone with me, we would certainly have seen again the man for whom we vied in love. He would have been standing between my pillow and your chair.

Why were you in such a hurry?

Was your girlfriend, whom I have never met, waiting for you at home under the Barbarigo portico, which I have never visited?

Were your dogs waiting for you, the same who one December evening announced your arrival to me and Beppino, as we lingered in front of the bas-relief of Zara at Santa Maria del Giglio?

Were you anxious to return to your music, which seems to help you free your precise machines from the law of gravity?

I do not know why you left me feeling such regret this evening. It is as if I have your handprint on my breathless chest.

You sometimes have the face of a little boy. And you spoke to me as if to a little boy when you promised me you would wait for me to fly your aircraft for the first time over the enemy.

You seemed as if you were trying to deceive me.

But I will get back on my feet. In a few days, I will. And I shall start again. And I tell you, no daring mission can be carried out without my good luck.

I have felt ashamed for wanting to recover. But now I know that I let myself be tortured for nothing. My eye is lost. The imprisoned butterfly is gone; the fern is gone. A terrible black spider has settled, with its solid abdomen, right in the middle. And no one will ever chase it away.

My doctors seemed to fear a miracle. Now they are no longer afraid. A sinister fate has been fulfilled. I want you to know this.

You shall have a very watchful cyclops as your comrade.

Where are you? Are you at home, with your woman and your dog? Or did you go back to the Arsenale, to your Sea Eagle's hangar, where your mechanics are perhaps working at night on the finishing touches?

I write this in the dark, on strips of paper not unlike those with which I used to communicate observations and orders under the deafening roar of the engine, and I should like to send this to you tonight. I should like you to know tonight, on the eve of your flight, that I am thinking of you and have great confidence in you.

But perhaps you would not be able to read these signs.

Tonight, too, the bed sways and vibrates like a double wing extended between sea and sky.

I shall not sleep tonight. I cannot sleep at night.

Will you sleep?

You must. Tomorrow morning your hand must be infallible, your eyes sharp, your mind alert.

You are about to give the Fatherland a new weapon.

With you we shall destroy Pola. We shall spare nothing but the Colosseum, the Roman relics, and the vestiges of Italy.

With you we shall dominate the entire Dalmatian coast. We shall threaten Cattaro and Durazzo.

I so yearn to see you again, to talk to you again.

Do you not hear me calling you?

Why not come back, if you cannot sleep?

My heart is throbbing in my throat again. What a terrible motor I have in my chest!

I don't know if I'm dying of waiting, of sadness, or of thirst.

You know something? My tormentors will not let me drink.

They are harsh with me, as you were harsh with Luigi Bologna when the two of you plunged your aeroplane into the sea, in enemy waters, and after resisting for hours and hours, he could no longer stand the torment of thirst and wanted to quench it with the water in your radiator, and you pointed your pistol at his temple and said: "If you touch a single drop, I will shoot you."

How I loved this heroic act of yours, towards a heroic comrade, to save your weapon and two soldiers! From you, who smile so shyly, who always carry your boyish, blond, beardless head tilted towards your left shoulder.

Tonight, my friend, let me drink a sip of water from your radiator.

I am not sleeping. I cannot sleep. At night even less than during the day.

Now that my left eye can see a bit of light, a troubling anguish assails me when the twilight behind the panes of the half-open window turns livid.

It is the hour when darkness falls upon the city, and I beg that the window not be closed. I drink the last light with the craving of a dying man.

When the shutters are bolted, the room becomes a coffin. The four walls close in on the body like four planks of wood. The errant glimmers in my bandaged eye form a spectral figure of sleeplessness.

Is Gino Bresciani asleep?

I hear the Largo movement of the Ghost Trio again. The little room next door, sonorous as a resonance chamber, has preserved it, the way an old coffer preserves a fragrance.

Tonight the dialogue between violin and cello is but a plea rising up from the depths of death.

I remember the December evening when I sank my lips into the fullness of death, into the pinewood full of decaying flesh, like a weary beast of burden at the trough.

I did not drift off to sleep until it was broad daylight, when I could see the sunlight shining through the slats of the shutters and hear the canal reawaken with familiar voices and sounds.

In my slumber I kept feeling the bed sway, and my sick motor throbbing inside me.

It is late. The sleep grants me no relief. I feel tired, broken. My mouth is so parched that I cannot even form words. My unruly heart leaps and races in wild fits. The nurse changes my compresses and bandages. Her hands tremble.

"Who is landing at the quay?" I ask her.

A motorboat growls while maneuvering into the berth. The roar is deafening. The window panes rattle, the walls vibrate.

"I'll go see," she replies.

She leaves, then returns.

"Two Navy officers have stepped out of a motorboat and are walking towards San Maurizio."

The rumbling continues. I suffer it in my every fibre. I am full of screams that do not pass the threshold of my teeth.

I listen. I hear a sound of footsteps in the calle.

"What now?"

The nurse goes out. Looks through the window of the adjacent room. She returns.

"The two officers are accompanying a lady wearing a veil. They're taking her aboard. They're leaving."

Two hours have passed.

A motorboat pulls up to the quay again and shakes the whole house with its rumbling.

I question the nurse.

She goes out and returns.

"The two officers are accompanying the veiled lady again. She looks faint. They're supporting her."

I seem no longer to have a room, no longer a bed.

I am lying in the calle, near the little quay, which smells of rot at low tide.

I lie here like a disabled mendicant.

My head has been bandaged for I know not how long. I have a wound that nobody uncovers or dresses anymore.

There is nothing sadder in the world than this little quay where the deceased's poor companion boarded the boat to go see the body, and where she disembarked after seeing it for the last time.

She had to leave the rooms in which she lived with him and his dogs. She became an intruder, and is now staying somewhere unknown to me in Campo di San Maurizio not far from here. She is poor, alone, with nothing left.

What is she doing at this hour? She cannot keep vigil over her friend. The body is at Sant'Anna, in the same mortuary chamber where I kept vigil over Giuseppe Miraglia for three nights.

The sailors stand guard as then.

The large naval flag covers the wall.

Who told me his face is not visible because it was completely burnt up when the fuel tanks exploded?

Like Giuseppe Miraglia, like me, his right eye was injured.

His entire right side is bruised, broken.

The candles flicker and melt in my brain, as then.

I see the poor widowed creature slip repeatedly on the little quay, along the garden's corroded wall.

She is never done walking away.

She is a tatter fluttering against brickwork dark as clotted blood.

I have always sensed something sinister in this small, greenish quay, ever since the evening an old gondola kept endlessly bumping against the stairs uncovered by the low tide, putrid as the edge of a sewer. The stair had become so high that the foot could not reach far enough to descend.

One gray, humid morning in late January, when coming out of the house I heard women's voices. They were leaning over the canal. I asked them what they were doing.

They were drowning five kittens born during the night. They carried them in their aprons, and threw them one by one into the water. The narrow calle, the little deserted square with its walled well, smacked of murder.

The grieving woman's shadow will never again leave that wall. The stone is wet with tears, a tide of tears.

Where is Roberto Prunas in the dead of night? How far away will the current roll his corpse?

The current now comes towards me, and brings him to me between tides.

I see his olive face, aged by two deep furrows around his thin mouth.

He had the face of a Sardinian herdsman, etched with boredom and reflection. He spoke with irony, and sometimes wit, but his mask was like those countrysides furrowed by dry torrents awaiting sudden spates. The tears had carved furrows down his cheeks, down to the chin. And they looked as if they might fill up again at any moment.

He is alone in the sea tonight, lost in the silent immensity.

Perhaps a torpedo boat is passing over him with lights off.

He is bloated. His burns steep in the brine.

I see the wretched specter along the wall, the cold body turned over and over by the current.

Luigi Bresciani rests in his funeral bed, under the pall.

My bundle of flowers rests on his joined feet.

He no longer hears the swashing against the wharf, which filled our ears as we kept vigil over our lamented comrade.

I have awakened to the thuds of my bursting heart and feel a hard board against my right elbow.

Who brought my friend's coffin in here? I move the other elbow and feel the same obstruction. It can only be the coffin of my other friend, who is always on the side of my heart.

I lie between the two, with no lid over me. And when the heart's thunder abates, I hear a cock crow. A shudder girds my chest.

I listen. It is not a modulated, four-note crowing. It is a lament of only one note, now long, now short. The ear strains to recognize it.

The cock of the canal is sadder than the cock of the Lande that Desiderio Moriar heard on the sands of the Extreme West.

I hear a dull thudding that is no longer my heart.

It is a body bumping into the stair of the quay, at almost the same level as the cobblestones of the calle.

High tide.

Yesterday evening, the man who brought the funeral wreath to Sant'Anna hospital saw the boat return to the Arsenale with a diver who had failed to find the corpse.

And now Roberto Prunas's body comes to bump against the quay.

My body turns to ice.

He wants to be here with the three of us. He wants me to love him as I love the other two.

The window is open. There is something muted in the air.

Through the bandages I see a faint glow with dark shadows passing over it like women in cloaks on all fours.

The images are tiny, yet have an ineffable greatness about them.

I think of the Suppliants in the atrium of a palace from some heroic age.

I have a pain deep within me that follows the rhythm of this bowed procession, bent right to left.

I feel as if my chest is caving in, painfully, little by little, and I haven't the strength to make it rise with my breath.

I place a hand over my heart and do not feel it beating. My pulse is slow, almost imperceptible.

A bell peals across the sky, wrapped in a violet cloud.

The sound colors my vision, which seems to descend as though falling to the level of tears.

A light step pauses in the doorway, as if my silence meant I was asleep.

I ask: "Is it low tide?"

Sirenetta approaches the window and looks perhaps at the stone stairs that lead up to Corè's garden.[2] Surely the last five are green.

"Yes," she replies.

And a greenish smell of the grave passes over her head before reaching my unbeating heart.

How many days till Holy Thursday?
When will these pitiless bells be silent?

They ring not for me except to chime goodbyes, farewells, separations, abandonments, condemnations.

They take from me everything sweet that might still be born in me, everything that might still resemble a secret good in me.

If I linger in a dream, the toll of the bells snatches it away and dispels it.

If I linger in a hope, the toll of the bells takes it from me and dashes it.

"I will do this."

"No you won't."

"I can do this."

"No you can't."

"I will regain my strength, my will, my courage."

"You are deluded, mistaken. Your fairy tale is over."

"Then I wish to die."

"You shall die by living."

Thus does the monotonous, endless sound flatten and lengthen my unhappiness the way the rolling-pin does the dough, the way the mould does the brick.

Now I lie flattened, body and soul, in this bed. I have no more depth. I have no more shape. I have no yesterday, no tomorrow. I die by living.

I dreamt I was folding my flesh like a colorless cape.

Then I dreamt I unfolded it and hung it from a nail jutting out from a colorless wall.

At the point of dozing off this morning, I felt pass through my fingers the golden threads that Titian wove into the skin of Sacred Love and the clothing of Profane Love.

I had at the tips of my fingers I know not what flash of clairvoyance.

Renata and Venier lie down on the rug beside my bed, face up.[3]

Each puts an arm behind his head, imitating my habitual position when sleeping.

They remain silent; but I am listening to them.

I hear Sirenetta repress a sigh.

The window is ajar. The lull fills all space, all creatures.

My life overflows. It spills into the two of them, one on each side of me, like the water in a fountain falling from statue to statue.

I see the convolutions of my brain as clearly as on a physiological chart for students.

I can make out all the ramifications of the vascular tree.

My body is diaphanous. The skeleton appears to me as precisely as in a macabre drawing by Albrecht Dürer. I count the ribs and vertebrae. The delicate network of nerves is the color of rust.

My blood grows thicker and thicker. I feel like beating it, the way one beats milk in a churn, with a dasher, or with the wasted bones of my own hands.

The violet apparitions return.

There is a forest of amethyst in my eye. Birds come from all sides in great flocks and light on the stiff branches.

The first are yellow like canaries. Then the species and colors multiply without end.

I remember a charming episode recounted to me, on the eve of the Battle of the Marne, by the wife of the guard commander, Thévenin, as I was nailing flags to the fence posts of my kennel.

A number of steamships had come into the port of Marseille carrying a great many birds from the islands, to be sold in the markets of Europe.

Abandoning hope of keeping them alive, the importers opened all the cages. And for a few days the city was festooned with a variegated multitude of flying gems. With each new ship that landed at port from the colonies, the disembarked troops could be seen crossing the streets with their heads in the air, their dark faces made childlike again by the wondrous spectacle.

Infantrymen from the Alps to the Carso send me wildflowers gathered in the trenches and dolines, laurel leaves gathered when passing through gardens laid to waste.

Superstitious women from my land in the Abruzzi send me packets of medicinal herbs and jars of unguents.

Veterans of the Marne and Verdun send me crude words of brotherhood in the jargon of war. They are more comforting than any false balm.

Talismans of every form and substance accumulate at my bedside; and each contains an occult miracle that can be revealed only by faith.

At dawn I dreamt that my mother was leaning over me, her face rejuvenated, and removing my bandages, uncovering my eyelid, and soothing it first with her breath, and then by pressing her lips to it.

I was healed. I had regained my sight in full. My injured eye had become fresh and clear again, as in a reawakening of adolescence.

So lifelike was the illusion that I raised myself up on my elbow, trembling. I raised the slack bandage and the compress, now dry. I closed my left eye. And there was the spider again, black and motionless.

My mother does not know, does not understand. She, too, is inside her own darkness.

Yet for several days now, during her visits, she has worn a face less false, the face I saw before my exile.

She brings me fragments of a faraway life so vivid that I can touch them. Sometimes she brings one of our relatives.

She has brought me Rafaele, a farmer who can imitate the calls of migratory birds and create all kinds of decoys out of bone, reeds, and skin.

Rafaele brings me a live quail, which stirs a memory of the pity I used to feel for the quails imprisoned in certain low, slatted cages, who would rub their heads bare against the sides and wear the skin down to the bone from the repeated blows.

I hear that ceaseless agitation again. I see the tiny, bare skulls again, the bleeding beaks. My four walls, my four boards, fill with the same sadness that used to fill our old house and make me suddenly want to run away or kill myself.

I also used to want to kill myself whenever the whole house resounded with the screams the fatted pigs emitted in the court-yard as their throats were being slit, filling the basins beneath them with blood. The horror would chase me from room to room. Life filled me with terror, pursuing me as though with a pig-sticker in hand. I would take refuge in a corner, face to the wall, one hand in my convulsing mouth. Sobs would shake me all through the night. The following morning I would feel drained, as if someone had opened a vein in my neck.

Why has this temptation to flee beyond the reach of all cruelty and horror now returned to me from so far away?

Equipped with his perforated disk and his little lamp-mirror, was the oculist just now reading inside my spent eye or inside my flaming brain? He had a grim look on his face.

It is windy today.

I hear the gondolas bumping against the ferry's pier and creaking. I hear the long howl of the canal. I hear voices shredded and carried away in tatters.

The blast penetrates all the way into my closed room. The door is continually groaning.

"I'm coming. Who's calling me?"

In the small room where yesterday my war quintet played music old and new, today a quintet of doctors is arguing.

There are five of them, like the fingers on a groping hand.

I hear their voices through the door, where my destiny listens with bated breath.

I have never experienced so much suffering at the sound of the human voice as during this hour. Their confused wrangling is like an instrument of torture that functions from a distance. My living body is twisted and pierced in a variety of ways, slowly or violently, depending on the intonation.

But one voice, more shrill and pitiless than the others, saws my ribs one by one and cuts out my sternum.

And another, every time it insinuates itself into the terrible concert, is like a sharp instrument that begins the "enucleation" of the eye and then abandons it.

When will this torture end?

Now I hear the funereal quintet laugh a raucous laugh, practically in unison.

My unhappy eye is there, on their little table, next to an ashtray, like one of those artificial, painted anatomical parts which the janitor has been dusting off for years and which the doctor handles while lecturing indolent students.

A furtive ray of sunlight passes through the vial of atropine, brightens the big cocoonlike roll of cotton, the rolls of bandages, and a glass in which Sirenetta put this morning's finest rose.

A blackbird chortles so loudly it sounds as if it is on the windowsill.

How that silly blackbird annoys me!

It sings all day long without ever varying its graceless song.

It sounds like one of my countless judges.

Who in the world has ever been more judged and condemned than I?

I see a council of worms passing judgment on my abandoned corpse.

One day last October, on a footbridge over the Isonzo at Gradisca, a bitter war comrade of mine said to me: "May fate let me die in such a way that men can no longer judge me."

The other night I dreamt that an exploding grenade had blown off my legs, my arms, and my other eye. I was a bloody trunk watering a few rocks of the Carso with myself.

"Judge me."

A beautiful soul has no joy but in giving itself utterly.

But when will love cease to cause me pain?

On a forgotten day of my childhood, down in my land of Pescara, I once saw, at the edge of I forget which field, a piece of bread placed atop a boundary stone.

No passerby would take it.

Nor did I.

I am immobile again, with something dank inside me and around me, as though I were lying in muck at the bottom of a pond.

The dampness of the compress over my eye slowly seeps into the bandages wrapped around my head.

The east wind must be blowing. I hear the unvarying patter of the rain on the skylight in the bathroom and, every so often, a drip that cadences the monotony.

It is as if I can see the raindrops on the surface of the stagnant water in which I am freezing.

Everything is gray, cold, late.

There is boredom in the pillow, the sheets, my bones, the sounds I hear, the glimmers I faintly see.

My thoughts, sadness, patience, disgust, dejection, expectation, have all become like my damp bandage, which grows tepid with my warmth.

My eye's terrible life is spent. The demon of fire no longer inhabits the optic cup. My brain sees nothing but the pale-blue blister produced by the needle, which the doctor actually showed me yesterday in his little round mirror.

The blister swells around the discolored iris in which the insensate pupil dilates. A thin stream of blood and tears flows from the corner of my weakened eyelids.

The soul wishes it could blow on the wound the way one blows on a firebrand to rekindle it.

I mourn my flaming, sparkling blindness.

I turn my attention to my supine body. I survey it from neck to feet, look for some remaining, vital sap, some still vigorous node from which a burgeon might yet emerge.

My feet are far away, extraneous, like those of someone maimed by frostbite, like those we saw bound together in Alpine field hospitals, when the surgeon's knife worked without rest.

Now it is as though my will cannot convey movement to the tendons of my big toes, where they lie one beside the other.

The nurse tells me that all the rose bushes in the garden have come to leaf and budded.

Rain washes the tender verdure.

Hyacinths bend earthwards, some stalks break, the sap oozing out.

I can feel it between my fingers, sticky as a thread of fresh birdlime.

After the torture of that evening, the image of that flower strangely unfolds to my senses.

The rain carries the soil away from the plant, and the bulb emerges, pearly as the white of an eye.

I hear footsteps ascending the staircase. I hear Sirenetta's voice.

I feel her draw near, the way water feels the flight of a brown bird reflected in it, towards evening.

She has brought me a young aviator from Sant'Andrea, a gracious friend, the one I used to call my squire because he helped me put on my furs, leggings, gloves, and leather cap before flying.

He approaches my bed with infinite caution.

Perhaps, coming in from the light, his eyes cannot see me.

He is near the head of the bed. I can feel him trembling. He kneels down.

I turn the unbandaged eye slightly towards him.

His face is at almost the same level as mine.

I can make out the golden crown and stars on his shoulder.

I can make out the cropped hair over his pale brow.

He is emotional. The first thing he saw must have been my white bandages.

He takes my hand and murmurs a few words.

I can smell the sea on him, the wind of the heights, the odor one breathes over the engine-bonnet when the propellor is turning.

Is he back from a flight? Have his long hands just now let go of the controls?

He tells me that yesterday he tried to fly over Pola. About thirty miles from the coast, a malfunction in one cylinder forced him to set the airplane down in the sea. Unable to repair it so that he could take flight again, he tried to approach the coast by driving on the surface of the water.

The sea was barely rippling. The horizon on all sides appeared deserted.

Suddenly, in the wake of the pontoons, something black and shiny leapt up. Other flashes appeared here and there in the vicinity of the wings. An arched back cut in front of the nose. A marine dance accompanied the crawling aircraft.

It was a school of dolphins. Darting and leaping, they not only followed the wake but every so often scraped the rudders and wings, threatening to damage the fragile structure.

The young man bows his head towards me to see my smile, bringing his fresh smile close to mine, which cleaves the arid metal of my mouth.

A new myth is created. Man's friends, the dolphins, no longer dance around Arion's ship or Icarus's dead body, kept afloat by his structure of featherless wings.[4] Icarus streaks over the water with a skimming flight, like a seagull pursuing a swimming prey.

"We had to resort to the machine gun to protect ourselves," the aviator adds, laughing. "Then suddenly the propellor broke. A splash of water hit me in the face. A leaping dolphin had struck one of the blades. We couldn't advance any further, but the coast was in sight. Another dolphin, with another leap, broke the tip of the left wing. A torpedo boat came to our rescue. It towed us through the Malamocco pass."

In my dream the bed sways to and fro, like the aircraft on the swell.

I recall the sudden horror I felt, one day during my youth, when I was swimming in the Adriatic and saw a dolphin's dark back emerge from the water a few arm's lengths from my naked chest.

My eyes burn as when the spray of a choppy sea splashes against my face.

I have a salty taste in my mouth, stronger than the metallic taste.

I am left alone.

The compress has dried up and the dressing no longer holds. My eye waters, the injured eyelid burns.

A flameless heat spreads over my whole head. A dull rage against my body, from throat to heels.

I raise my hand to tear away the bandages, to throw off the sheet. Patience writhes like a chastised animal.

My eyebrow is made of thorns. Soulless tears fall onto my dry lips.

I feel my will not inside me but above me, like a sharp blade the exact length of my subdued body.

With ineffable malaise, I think of the pinkish well of Verona marble that stands in the middle of my campiello. The water at the bottom was foul, the wooden lid rotten and falling apart. The authorities plugged the opening with lime. Now the campiello no longer breathes. The lips of its silence are no longer half closed but sealed. I can feel it suffer from here.

Sirenetta reminds me of an image of the Far East dear to my dead.

A woman steps out of her house one morning to draw water and sees that during the night a bearbine shoot has nimbly twisted itself around the damp rope of the bucket and blossomed. She goes back into the house and says, "The bearbine has taken the rope. Who will give me water?"

I am there, in a corner, sitting on a reed mat, when she comes back inside.

I hear the sound the empty pitcher makes when set down on the floor.

Then the delicate voice of the servant girl, who is still bending down, refreshes my throat like water drawn from the most mysterious shadow.

I was still there, near the threshold, in the limpid evening, when the woman went out of the house to throw away the water in which she had washed some clothes. Although the bucket was heavy, she walked lightly and barefoot onto the grass, and her skirt did not rustle as it billowed.

In the middle of the lawn, she stopped. A raucous melody of insects rose up from the ground. All the grass was alive with sounds and glimmers.

I glimpsed the heel of one of her bare feet, by the light of a small night fire.

The woman kept perfectly still, listening, her pail on her head.

She turned and walked back towards the threshold with an even lighter, more cautious step.

She went back inside, and set down the bucket, unemptied, in silence.

For weeks and weeks they condemned my body to sweat and anguish, dried it up, deprived it of water, vein by vein, fiber by fiber.

I suffered the dryness like certain stretches of the Roman campagna when the ground splits apart and exhales fever.

Always open, my mouth was like one of those cracks, hard and dry like volcanic land. Made bitter by the metallic taste of iodine, no longer human, the very maw of desolation, it seemed to fissure painfully every time my throat contracted in an effort to wet it.

My thick blood, laden with toxins, burdened the heart, which in deadly dismay struggled to repel it.

I saw my bones shine white as a skeleton abandoned on the desert sand.

I thought of those little plants in the Arabian desert that drink the night's dew and briefly flower at dawn before the murderous sun cuts them down. I had noticed them when taking the fetters off my horse, El-Nar, who nibbled at them with delicate lips.

I now enjoy only the brief sensual pleasure of those plants, a predawn bliss.

I have drunk. I have been allowed to drink.

The water penetrates every fiber of my being, invades my whole body the way new sap invades a withered tree.

I am irrigated.

The cool descends to my roots.

Everything revives deep within me.
I raise my head as though my neck were a stem come back to life.
But then a sweet, despotic hand lowers it again.

El-Nar, lithe fervor of the desert, companion of my uncharted freedom!
He thrusts his sensitive nostrils towards my pillow and sniffs me.
He seeks out the palm of my hand with lips so fine, they could drink from a table glass.
He asks me, as was his wont, for a handful of pearl barley.
In the shadow I see the glow of the whites of his big eyes, which look as though elongated by kohl, like those of a Fatimid princess.

Lithe and wondrously attuned to my own litheness. At every pace we were one single animal. Whenever, at a walk or at rest, I playfully rubbed his flank ever so lightly with my spur, he would bend his fine neck, turning his great forelock towards the stirrup, and raise his hind leg up to it, trying to rid himself of the annoyance with the same movement as a greyhound scratching himself. And he defended himself with such childish grace that I could not refrain from repeating the game.

If only I could hear his whinny again, and feel that supple vigor flow miraculously again through this wretched, wasted body!

When I used to tie him to the door of some carpet storehouse, using his lovely woven fetters of red, blue, and silver, he would whinny in a sort of minor key to let me know he was annoyed and it was time for me to get back in the saddle. How to describe the silvery neigh he would emit when we were heading back to Cairo from the desert at a final gallop, and we saw in the distance, in the pearlescent night, the lights of the Bayram?[5]

He was a burnt sorrel of that fiery color our elders used to call "metallic." When he was spotted with sweat and would emerge from shadow into sunlight, he looked as though cast from hot bronze rich in copper. But his restless, nervous vitality and visibly throbbing veins were unlike any metal.

O El-Nar, docile lightning of my fantasy, bearer of my solitary happiness, are you now only dust? Hot, fine dust like that which swirls in the blasts of the Khamsin?[6]

When it came time to leave, I had the courage to abandon you because, having loved your perfection in the roadless desert, I did not want you to end up hobbled by the harshness of the West and shut up in some dismal stable.

I kissed you on your starred brow and between your nostrils warm with your spirits.

You bent your fine neck; and your mane did not touch the ground like the mane of Achilles's steed.

Yet if the deity had given you, too, the voice of man, perhaps you would have revealed your sorrow to me and foretold my fate.

O rose gardens of Aziyeh, bloom again for me![7]

I am still young, and I do not fear the desert.

I tear off my bandages, untie my knees, unbind my feet.

The dawn loves me. I drink the dew to purge my blood of all toxins.

The sunrise loves me. I chew the sprouting wheatgrass, that my heart may beat at full strength again.

I myself have combed my horse's forelock, mane, and tail. I myself have given him barley and bran to eat and water to drink.

I bound into the saddle. El-Nar neighs at the sun.

He would be the envy of Alexander himself, for whom I went looking immediately upon arrival, down along the strip of land that lies between Lake Mareotis and the Mediterranean Sea.

Now my faithful steed and I form a single creature. And my heart shouts to me that we are bound for extraordinary joy.

I pass the Qasr-en-Nil bridge, cross the island of Gezireh, pass over the second arm of the Nile, turn left, and follow the riverbank along the gardens of Gizeh. Reaching the end of the Roda Bridge, I turn right and take the Pyramid Road along the great, tree-lined bank. I begin to breathe the wind of the desert.

To go towards the desert is to go towards temptation.

Past Aziyeh, from the top of the scarp, I see a field of roses to my left. As in a dream, I see a vast garden of tall bushes, fleshly and flaming, like that in which Saint Francis had rolled about in the thorns in mortification.

I smile to myself at the image of the Seraph of Assisi suddenly appearing in an Egyptian street at the head of a rosy procession of evangelized ibises.

I lean over my horse's mane and say: "What shall we do, El-Nar?"

Gardeners in long light-blue tunics are cutting the roses and laying them in esparto baskets.

My heart races in the freshest of poetry; and it knows not, nor wants to know, if it is about to obey the spirit of temptation or the spirit of mortification.

"El-Nar, gentle companion, if I don't give you free rein now, I doubt you will ever have another chance to gallop through a rose garden at the edge of the desert."

No sooner said than done. I coax the horse down the escarpment. We jump over the brook and enter the thicket. I hear the men shouting furiously. I see them abandon their cutting, gather up their long staffs, and come racing after me, yelling.

Clearly they are counting on El-Nar being slowed by the first obstacles he encounters. Already bleeding from the forceful thorns, my steed hesitates for a moment before cleaving the bushes with his breast, unable to jump over them.

He need only hear my voice through his mane, urging him on. He no longer feels the pain, pays no more mind to the tangles of brush. A boyish, heroic madness takes hold of him and carries him away. He rediscovers the winged gallop of the Bayram evenings, lengthens his stride as over the sandy plain, leaving a trail of divine devastation in his wake.

But up ahead lies the canal, and stagnant pools left behind by the flood. The furious men do not rest. I turn round in the saddle and see them brandishing their long, menacing staffs. If I do not take to my heels, they will kill me or leave me battered on the ground.

"El-Nar! El-Nar! We've reached the water. Fly! My heart is in yours!"

We measure the canal with courage alone.

As in a dream, and hoisted by the power of dream, we are on the other side; we are at the edge of the desert, in the region of gods and kings.

"El-Nar! El-Nar! Let me worship you. You carry not my heart in yours, but the heart of immortal Rakush."[8]

I see the great pyramid of Cheops. I do not look back. The pools of water dazzle me like fragments of a falling sky. The wind is splendor's heartbeat. Poetry is my airy substance. My breath is a chant immune to mere syllables.

I see the snub-nosed face of the crouching Sphinx rise up from the solar sands.

I halt the gallop before the inaccessible figure on the horizon. The language of enigma fills my happiness, which seems about to spring forth from the earth when the horse, upon stopping, rears up.

I am thrown from the saddle. I feel my human feet sink into hot sand, while my happiness flies off into the limitless radiance.

"El-Nar, El-Nar, how cruelly the roses have spurred you!"

I throw my arms around my bleeding, foaming brother's neck. His parted mane cascades over me. I feel all his veins and muscles trembling from the lacerations in his fine, leonine coat.

"Dear sweet brother, I could weep for you."

I lead him into the shade. I wet my fingers in his blood and sweat. From his breast and crupper I extract the thorns still embedded. To remove the thorns from his legs, I bend down and kneel, in an act of worship.

He inclines his head towards me, following every movement of my brotherly hands with the great eyes of his burning, generous soul.

Hallucination takes the shape of a reality so vivid that present, speaking people are, by comparison, bodiless phantoms. Nor can I make it stop.

Just now, as I reclined in the nearly scalding bath, my head supported by a taut band, horses came as if to the drinking trough. I could hear the water hiss between their soft lips. When they raised their muzzles, I saw the water drip from the corners of their mouths. In the small, marble bathroom, their snorts resounded like crashing cymbals.

A bristling Maremman hound that had torn off the ear of a pockfaced corporal from Girgenti when I was a light cavalryman is back and looking at me askance.

And I am greatly saddened by the gaze of Malatesta, my fine Irish steeplechaser, dapple-gray and dock-tailed, who died on a bridge over the Arno, eviscerated by the broken shaft of the cart to which my persecutors had condemned him in his old age.

Horses, countless horses, as at Versailles on the first August holiday of the French war.

They are tied to a rope extended from trunk to trunk, under trees that to this day display the art of the pruning-hook. Hay, straw, and manure mar the elegance of the noble avenues.

But one has a great bouquet of roses on his shattered shoulder, while another, who was showing his gangrenous legs, black with blood and flies, is covered with a mantilla of Flemish lace.

The royal city is transformed into an equine city.

I see horses round neglected basins green with floating rot. The palace is dead, unspeakably dead. An object. The perspective of the Grand Canal recedes, like a Styx not allowed to bend, into the melancholy of an endless Hades.[9]

I see other horses around an even gloomier pond. They neigh at the dark, grim water, which reminds me of the surface of my Lake Nemi under an overcast sky. Their temporary watering troughs, shaped like black boats, are shaded by elms. A nauseating smell of stables colors the king's delights.

Now they are all dead, slaughtered, butchered en masse.

The Battle of the Marne leaves them behind, lying on the grass strewn with empty bottles and unexploded shells. They are all in the same pose, all making the same lugubrious gesture, as far as the horizon, bellies swollen, hind legs stiff in air.

Over sweet meadows of Spanish clover, bloated bellies, legs raised, yellowed gums, milky eyes, swarms of crows, whirlwinds of flies.

And in the villages and camps, on the roads, everywhere, slaughtered horses; and that horrific gesture, always the same; and the gleams of their horseshoes in the charred forest, under a splash of heartrending sun.

In a beet field, behind some wreckage of gun carriages and ammunition wagons, I discover a horse still alive.

It is alone. It cannot walk. It has a broken fetlock, a deep wound in the buttock, and another in the withers.

But it is calm. Its eye is serene. The clamor has ceased. The pandemonium has ended. All is silence. The birds do not sing. A few men pass, below, along the path, in the drizzle, canvas sacks folded over their heads. Near a house in ruins, a threshing-machine lies upside down, legs in the air like the carrion. The grassy hill slopes so gently it seems to express an ineffable tenderness of the land. The cock on the belfry reigns over a silence softened by the fine rain. At rare moments the wind blows a humid gust. The smell of death takes its breath away.

The surviving horse tries to graze around itself, stretching its neck. It is alone. Soon night will fall. A stray swallow brushes past its crupper without a cry.

> O melancholy, melancholy,
> why bring back from so far away
> what once weighed on you so heavily?

Now you also bring back my childhood favorite, from the time when, in the comfort of home, my mother was a thoughtful flower of the fittest youth in my land of Pescara.

He comes to me through an undergrowth of memories, as when he used to part the tall hay, still uncut, with his breast.

He cleaves a path through my life, which falls away to either side, touching the good earth with the bent tips of the stalks.

He was a small Sardinian horse. A bay with tawny markings, one white stocking, and a white nose and mouth. He had a long bushy mane and tail. His name was Aquilino.

In the stable, between his stall and that of a pair of large draught horses, there was an empty stall in which I would have liked to put my small iron-framed bed. When I could elude supervision, I would go downstairs, heart racing, and enter the stable through the courtyard door. Recognizing my childish step, Aquilino would whinny faintly, as if to avoid letting others hear and realize where I was. My pleasure was always so great that I would let the straps of my overalls fall.

Then his whinny would quaver with impatience; and as I gathered together the bread, apples, sugar and everything else that made up my snack, as well as everything I had managed to grab from the pantry for my gluttonous friend, I would satisfy my hunger with my smile alone, which possessed I know not what species of nutrient, the likes of which I have never tasted since.

A door in the stable led into the carriage shed. The shed was almost always in shadow, illuminated only by the light that shone down, as in a chapel, through the tinted panes of a fan window. The large wedding coach was here, upholstered in blue cloth, with silk curtains over the windows and silver handles on the doors. There was also a gig with a bellows-top and a two-wheeled wicker wine cart. And, hanging from the rafters, the harnesses and trappings I never tired of looking at: collars, breast bands, crupper straps, girths, traces, reins, buckles, breechings, perpetually shiny rings, and the long whips I yearned to use.

But let us leave that little boy crouched on the floor, gathering together in shadow the bread and fruit he had taken from his own mouth for love, that boy already thirsting for an unusual life and mysterious communions, enchanted by that whinny as if by a spellbinding voice, illuminated by his own smile as if by an underground lamp. Let me leave him here, within my reach. Let me recognize in his act, and in his delight, an image of fleeting happiness that is my own, and which from time to time sheds its light on me, even here, in this bed of pain.

Was I already inhabited by the lyric demon that exalts and transfigures everything for me?

Was the magical sense of life already awakening in me?

Just as Aquilino whinnied softly to me, I, too, spoke to him in a low voice. Just as he understood me, I, too, understood him, content to stand on my own two feet in the straw, like he on his four hooves.

From the palm of my hand he would take the pieces of bread, slices of apple, and lumps of sugar with an expert lightness that felt ticklish to me and sometimes made me burst into convulsive, suppressed laughter or uncontrollable giggles. But I felt uneasy about the two big draught horses beside us, who kept rattling the wooden balls attached to the ropes of their halters, for I was keen not to be discovered there.

And that fear, that caution, that understanding, created an indescribable, fantastical remoteness in the enclosed stall. The black, immobile gaze that Aquilino kept fixed on me as he masticated; his impudent face, with its white-and-pink patch over lips that moved like the muzzle of a little hare; his way of entreating me, with a desirous quiver of the nostrils, when he had finished; his mischievous way of nipping me on the shoulder when, to goad him, I would hide the rest behind my back; all his gestures of twofold grace gradually confused my own species with his in my mind, and left me enchanted.

"I'll give you this, too, if you let me pull one hair from you—if you let me pull two—if you let me pull three . . ."

I remember I had to overcome a slight sense of shame and remorse at the moment of plucking the hair from his mane. Did it hurt him? Did he know that I needed them to make a slipknot for the swallows under the eaves?

It was my sister Ernesta who had put me up to tearing out his hair. And thus my heart ached, perhaps for having given on the condition of receiving, perhaps for thinking I would bring sorrow to the little nest of mud.

When I pulled, I came away with far more than three hairs in my hand.

Then the stable boy, who was an accomplice to my secret forays, entered. And he hoisted me up and placed me astride the "*sardignolo.*"

I loved to ride horseback at a standstill, as in a dream. But I did not like to be watched.

"Go away, and come back later," I would say to the stable boy.

I would close my eyes. I was under a spell. A door would open at the edge of the forest. It was getting dark. I could never see the end of the trail.

That time, however, the feeding trough remained there, against the wall, and the wall did not break open; and the horse would not walk, even though I spoke to him in a soft voice.

But I had those hairs in my hand and a vague sense of torment in my heart.

A sudden screech, a white flash.

Had a swallow entered through the broken glass of the skylight?

Was there a nest in the stable's vault?

How long had it been there?

I trembled, dumbfounded.

A light feather fluttered down through the enchanted air; just what I needed for the bird-trap.

I didn't wait for the stable boy to take me down from the horse. I lifted a leg to one side and slid down into the straw below.

"I'll be back, Aquilino. I'll be back before evening."

And I headed straight for the hearth, my brow already bearing the first vertical furrow of the will.

And I cast that handful of horsehair into the enchanted fire.

> O melancholy, melancholy,
> why bring back from so far away
> what once weighed on you so heavily?

I, my brother, and my three sisters had gone down to the carriage shed and climbed into the wedding coach, whose blue upholstery smelled of dried rain. A cushion was still warm from the cat that had been sleeping on it.

The door to the stable was open. Aquilino was lying in agony on the straw. My father knelt beside the dying animal, between the coachman and stable boy, who was holding a medicine cup and a boxwood spoon and crying softly.

Huddled together in dread, we looked on from the carriage door without weeping, our sinking hearts not letting a single drop of blood or tear of sorrow pass. We were looking at death for the first time, we who had never given it a thought except, perhaps, on the night after All Saints' Day, when we would wait for it to bring us presents.[10]

I could see the horse's legs move convulsively. The stockinged one hurt me most, and the twitching of his poor white muzzle hurt me even more.

But I did not cry; I alone, of the five of us, controlled my sorrow. The stable boy broke into sobs. I stuffed mine back into my throat with I know not what scorn. I noticed that the poor animal's legs had gone stiff.

We huddled even more tightly together, chilled to the bone under the dark sky of the carriage, in the dim light of the fan window. For the first time, with our ten unswerving eyes, we were looking at death. But I preserved the impression for all of us.

Then my father stood up, came back out, stopped, and turned to face us in our dismay. In the icy silence within my breast, and in a tone that still rings bright and clear in my ear and my soul, he said: "Gabriele."

O melancholy, melancholy,
why bring back from so far away
what once weighed on you so heavily?

O cessate di piagarmi . . .

Who has sent me this interpreter of the responses my blind-folded sibyl has neglected to write upon the errant leaves?

She sings; and the song takes my sorrow and gives it fluidity, clarity, makes it a full, sweet current that transports me to a place whence I wish never to return.

Her sweet voice hits the low contralto notes when she sings the second lament:

O lasciatemi morir . . .[11]

The current is like a slow eddy no longer following the horizon line but descending towards blue-violet depths.

It turns briny.

It sets me down in the aquatic darkness of my Icarian sepulcher.

Non so più cosa son cosa faccio . . .[12]

She looks like a boy but is not dressed like Cherubino. She is dressed in the Italian manner, in traditional two-color clothing, and wearing a large velvet beret that makes me think of Pisanello. All she lacks is a fine dirk behind her curved loins, and the skill to do harm.

Evening approaches. The light softens. A weightless pity that goes by the name of Aelis has opened the window farthest from me, and granted me a glass of water with a golden rim.

In my eye I have an oval-shaped blister, a sort of other eye with an unsteady focus. But, in the distance, reflected in the mirror, I can see the great wall of wisteria; and in the depths of my brain, my own abject wisteria is beginning to blossom again.

The air enters the room. I imagine it brings a young sickle moon, just as the hay is most fragrant when cut. It touches me all over my wasted body, the way embalming fingers do.

Every pleasure of mine is a torment.

I am now thirstier than before I drank.

I feel the fibrils throb in every muscle, as if I were full of chrysalides about to burst.

I am suffering. The smell of roses increases. I imagine that the tide is rising.

I am suffering. Give me a cure that will stun me, numb me, annihilate me.

Silence that singing.

And now another mine adrift explodes, around Chioggia. It shakes the pain in my eye socket.

Can the cruelty of my springtime be trilling in Cherubino's throat?

Take one of my thrice-wrapped bandages and strangle him!

The crescent moon is at the summit of the sky. The songs have left an indescribable languor in the silent room. Cherubino's sigh lingers between the folds of the discolored curtains.

I have had the shutters opened. I am lying near the window. The glow rains down on my hands and makes them look even more bloodless.

I raise the blindfold and glimpse the moon's face through the hairy legs of the spider lurking at the center of my right eye.

The evening wind has dropped. The garden is still, but the light is so bright that one can tell the more recent greenery from that which has already darkened.

Against the iron of the windowsill I see the young leaves gleam as though spread with wax.

The balustrade, the vases, the stone putti shine white as snow.

On the other side of the canal the palazzi of beautiful, famous women loom silent, abandoned. All the windows of Palazzo Da Mula are shuttered; Corè's truncated house looks more than ever like a haunted ruin. The cypresses rise higher than the great, rusticated ashlar from which carpets of Virginia creeper hang.

Down that staircase, which is now a velvet shadow, came a masquerade led by a Harlequin in white, on a night of the full moon in a summer that now seems long past. She had a blue parrot on her shoulder and was leading by a leash one of those small panthers which, in a nocturnal orgy on the Cithaeron, once sucked on the breasts of the Maenads, which had swelled suddenly with milk.

O Fantasy, who play your impudent games with time and distances!

I can see the white Harlequin on the staircase of the truncated palazzo, drawn in Longhi's hand, perverted and sharpened, as she raises the edge of her mask to eat three seeds of Persephone's pomegranate in Hades.

A confused din rises from St. Mark's basin.

Is the masquerade of capes, tricorns, and dominos returning? Are the bewigged servants about to appear at the top of the stairs with their gilt oil-lamps?

I listen and wait.

I raise the blindfold, and the eye staring at the moon seems sicker to me.

My heart leaps. The din approaches. I recognize a war song.

Now the whole canal echoes with it. I close my eyes. In my veiled sight the chorus is red.

I get up and lean towards the window pane.

I see three large *peate* being towed by a steamboat. They are full of recruits yelling and singing their way to faraway trenches.

They are the Fatherland's cargo, a cargo of flesh and blood more beautiful than the fruits of the shores and islands unloaded at the Rialto bridge in deep baskets.

The new soldiers' cry makes the house shake as if from artillery blasts.

A sudden strength makes my nerves contract. I stand up, lean

against the shutters, rest my head against the cold pane. A deep
shudder runs through me.

I raise the blindfold and watch with both eyes, especially the
wounded one, the cargo of blood passing by and leaving a lumi-
nous wake in the dead water.

The nurse has caught me in the act. She eases me back down
onto the pillows.

The moon shines in the crystal visor created by my tears
from the irritation, perhaps, of my enflamed eyelids, or from
an emotion similar, perhaps, to what I have known from sublime
music.

The din has faded. The silence and glow become a single sense
of gloom.

The scent of irises someone picked for me in the gardens of
Giudecca suddenly becomes unbearable.

To escape the horrifying image, I call to mind Tuscan walls,
along white roads, crowned by beautiful violet flowers, as the car-
ter passes, dozing in an April sleep.

The smell is suffocating me. I see the rotten wreaths atop my
lost friend's mound of earth.

I see his sweet blond hair gleam in there, where everything is
perhaps already formless.

Near the mound I see the Roman cippus planted atop the skull
of my other beloved friend. The gold of Icarus's wing glimmers in
the hollow, under an arm extended by the immortal will.

The corpse of Roberto Prunas, bloated and waxen, has stopped against a barrage of mines. Trapped, it swings to and fro, wasting away in its smock as in a loose sack.

None shall write his name over that watery grave.

The tide rises, the tide ebbs. The moon waxes and then withers.

Sleep is an implacable god again tonight, like his dark brother.

Although the rigor of my horizontal discipline has been eased, the bothersome treatments continue. With index and middle fingers joined, the doctor touches my closed eyelids, examining the tension. Every so often his frown relaxes or hardens. There is still the risk that, to save my other endangered eye in time, he will have to cut this one out.

He continues, meanwhile, to inject it with saltwater, as though feeding an aquarium. He is unaware of the wonders he creates.

Today, in the depths, the marine life is splendid. An oceanic abyss opens up in my retinal cup, an indescribable maelstrom of starry seas in which I see shapes of unknown form and colors not to be found in any spectrum.

What are sirens, tritons, Nereids and all the inventions of Neptunian myth compared to these ineffable creatures peopling my vast gardens of coral, the arcades of my gigantic, stony polyparies?

What are the meandering palaces and tortuous labyrinths of legend compared to these crags of amber and beryl rounded into corries, in which living constellations of sea anemones blossom by the thousands?

"The plastic of the first man was fashioned from the elemental virgin earth, created of Himself by God, the first protoplast."[13]

I smell the damp, oily clay in these words, which return to my memory from I know not what dusty tome.

At the back of my eye there is a protoplast god, and an inexhaustible plastic mass: the elemental earth.

With one same invisible thumb, the Almighty shapes and obliterates, forms and transforms, creates from the unknown and annihilates into the unknown.

The nameless, numberless craftsmen of Egypt and India, the guilds of potters who adorned vases and brick walls, the choral artisans of Gothic edifices never invented or perpetuated over the centuries as many images as the small sphere of my infirm eye collects in a single night.

The plastic mass is illuminated from time to time by flashes of divination, polished from time to time by a sinuous, fluvial melody.

What does the doctor discover through his pierced disk when he stares into my pupil, opened by the powers of a drop of liquid?

Sublime revelations lie hidden in the human eye, like the expressive forms of sensitive crystal in an unexplored mine.

The eye of the Indian, the Egyptian, the Chaldean, the Persian, the Etruscan, the Hellene, the eye of Moses himself, believed it could read, in the signs of the universe, the origins of the universe itself.

But the eye shall read the new cosmogony in the eye itself, which is the mystical spiracle of the creating brain.

Et remotissima prope.[14]

What are these titanic apparitions in architectural settings of quadrangular, superimposed crags?

Is Aeschylus returning to me with his lost tragedy of Prometheus the Fire-Bearer?[15]

He had wanted it to be staged at early nightfall, to the honor and delight of the torch-waving ephebes.

Distant imaginings and meditations on the lost tragedies of Aeschylus return to me in events and catastrophes portrayed with a grandeur that wrests cries of wonder and rapture from my breast.

Here is Glaucus Marinus.

Here is the Niobean trilogy.

Here is the Theban trilogy.

Here is the Shepherd of souls.

Here is the fate of Ixion, here the fate of Sisyphus.[16]

Aeschylus was unknown to Dante. If the singer of Capaneus had known the tragedian of the "fierce Erinyes," where would he have put him in his Inferno?[17]

The scaffold of rafters, planks, and wheels that Michelangelo climbed to paint the vault of the Sistine Chapel reassembled itself for me in a dream.

I brushed the marvel with my eyelashes, touched the marvel with my hand.

"This is beautiful material," said Francesco Francia, caressing the statue of Pope Julius. And Buonarroti became indignant.

The titanic work of art is as beautiful as a butterfly's wing.

Seen from up close, it has, in each part and in the whole, the compact perfection of an eggshell, a continuity similar to the sheen of an elephant's tusk. It is one of the most beautiful materials in the world, born whole from a masculine brain the way the ancient lapidaries believed certain miraculous gemstones were generated in the heads of certain solitary animals.

O flowing hair of potent sibyls!

The slowness of the centuries alone is not enough, it seems, to grant even a single fragment of this *intonaco* its proper worth; for this intonaco was prepared by Michelangelo himself, who then had to paint it within a couple of hours, after having ground the pigments and prepared everything himself.[18]

The strokes of the palette knife are visible. I find them deeply moving. They are like traces of a battle won by dint of mental lightning bolts.

The vault was poorly lit. We know from his crude sonnet to Giovanni da Pistoia in what painful position the artist painted. He had no cartoons to guide him. What sort of help did he have, then?

Take the hand of God the Father. Gigantic. How did he manage to make the size of the rest in proportion to it, when the paintbrush was dripping onto his face and his belly was hanging just under his chin?[19]

When he was painting Adam's head, the figure's feet were down below, as far away as my own when, under the effect of medications, I lose all sense of my body and become misshapen beyond measure.

I do not believe that in all the dramas of the mind we have ever seen a brain more aflame than this.

The instinct of divination continually accompanied the work. If it is true that in the Sistine Chapel he was not "in the right place," it is also true that he was not a painter, as he himself confessed in rhyme to his Giovanni.[20]

He had the breath of his prophets and sibyls in his "harpylike breast," and the lightning of Mount Tabor forever in his furrowed brow, did this desperate laborer, this breathless grinder and plasterer.[21] He worked only by inspiration and miracle. And the handle of his paintbrush was nothing if not a divining rod.

Using my fingernails, I stole a fragment of the precious material, a chip of the eggshell; and now I want to mount it on iron ring and make it a heroic gift to my sleepless spirit.

What cut gem could ever equal it?

Never have I felt such regret upon awakening.

Clearly this dream was sent to me by the archangel whose my name I bear.

Does ecstasy descend into the blessed from above, or does it rise up into them from below?

I cannot compare what I felt to anything, nor assign it any meaning, not even by imagining a dawn suddenly rising from the waters of the spirit and illuminating the summit of the flesh.

I was the young boy of Prato, I was the friend of the Bisenzio.

It was April, as now; it was Eastertime.

I was walking along the grassy bank of the Affrico, holding the hand of the *compiuta donzella*,[22] who was sixteen years old, like me, and wore her fine Tuscan name like a light crown of flowers, though I never revealed it in the *Canto novo*'s silvery Alcaic strophe of the willows.[23]

Our silent bliss grew with every step we took.

But from afar she spotted her mother walking towards us, looking for us; and she told me.

So we lingered, and we trembled both like the willows. And it felt as if the sudden flame of a blush had risen to our faces from our heels, and from even further below: from the modesty of springtime itself.

How can a dream now bring the blush back from so far away and turn it into so glorious a jubilation of the blood?

And why did I wake up?

I ask one of the musicians to let me see his cello. He brings it delicately to me, with a modest smile.

This Alberghini is a keen hunter of instruments and seeks them far and wide. When he gets wind of a violin or viola hidden away somewhere, he sets out like others in search of a boar or a hare, and does not rest until he has found it.

This cello of his was made by Andrea Guarneri. He had the good luck to find it in Egypt, in Cairo. I smile at the thought that I have in my hand a thoroughbred like El-Nar, one that resembles my sorrel down to its coat.

The finish is rich and intact, a fine reddish-brown that lets the gold underneath shine through. On the back the gold is more visible, showing through in bands and spots, and here and there on the sides, suggesting amber. The neck is pale, polished by the sliding hand. But the true marvel is in the middle of the back, where a bird of paradise cast a fleeting image of the treasure of its throat, and the reflection remained, captured in the time-less finish.

The musician tells me he obtained it from a short-fingered friend of his in Cairo, giving him a small Gagliano in exchange.

The latter had bought it in Cremona province. A rustic cellist used to play it in the choir gallery of a country church. During a solemn ceremony the gallery collapsed, along with the organ, cello, musicians, and singers. The cellist broke his leg. The instrument was damaged in back but not in its soul. After a few days, it was taken away from an unskilled restorer.

"With its bridge and its round-ended F-holes, doesn't it look like a beautiful face with a beautiful voice? It's alive. It needs no bow. It plays itself, sings by itself. In Mexico City, women would come up to me, fascinated by the angelic timbre, and touch its skin, which was more precious and sensitive than their own."

Thus speaks the Emilian gunner in his gray-green uniform.

"Women's skin corrodes the finish. In Nice I saw a Stradivarius whose varnish had been stripped in large part by the naked arm and decolletée of a female violinist.

"On the other hand, in Ferrara I saw another Stradivarius inside a bell jar. One of the first, in the Amati style. Most of its wood has turned to dust, but the strength of the varnish holds it together. I remember I was afraid even to breathe in front of that relic.

"Who can really say anything certain about the varnishes? The red? The yellow? To have remained so intact, that one must have diamond dust in it."

I have my hand on the cello's shoulder, while the gunner, seated, holds it by the fingerboard. His words seem to pass through the sensitive strings and wood before reaching my ears.

"There is a mysterious communion between the structure of a man and that of the instrument. There is a definite relationship between the wholeness of the musician and the quality of the sound.

"It used to be played without the end pin, resting the cello on one's crossed ankles. The play of the legs would temper any vibrations that were too strong before they reached the soundboard.

"Bone is musical. It's as if the bones of a good musician are filled with air instead of marrow. The tibia and femur are continually influencing the sound. Every note can be corrected by skillful pressure. For example, an E-flat in the fourth position quavers. A clever cellist can make up for this with his leg.

"The bow is also very important. Depending on the kind of bow, the richness of the sound can vary. There must be a vital correspondence between the wood of the bow and the wood of the instrument. The fiber of wood that has not been bent under heat immediately conveys the hand's intention. Here is a taut 'Tourte' bow, with an octagonal bowstick, an ebony frog, and an eye of mother-of-pearl. Here's another, with a round bowstick with a black leather grip inlaid with little iron studs, a frog of dark tortoiseshell and a golden eye.

"Here is a 'Dodd,' an English bow, which has another charm, or perhaps not, with its whalebone grip and ivory frog, and its octagonal pommel of ivory and silver.

"And here's still another, unadorned and nameless, poor, in fact, a real Franciscan bow fit for the Canticle of the Creatures, which has little to recommend it other than the reddish-brown color of its wood, which perfectly matches my Guarneri.

"And this, for reasons unknown, is the only one that works with my cello. It is the only one that can coax the full voice out of its soul.

"They understand each other. If you look at their wood, you could almost believe that this bow was extracted from the instrument's side, like Eve from Adam's ribcage."

The gunner starts laughing a full, childish laugh, plucking the chanterelle. "Could be," I say to him. "Instruments are demonic in nature. Sometimes at the top of the neck, instead of a scroll, the old masters used to put a likeness of the beautiful Enemy. I once saw a bass viol whose neck ended in a horned head. In my town in Abruzzi I saw a viola d'amore whose pegbox ended in a sort of long-necked ghoul arching back towards the player, to tempt him and penetrate his heart with its treacherous charm."

"There's no doubt about it," adds the gunner, no longer jesting. "A great luthier is a sorcerer. When choosing the wood, he is illuminated by magic alone. Why does a Testore choose a soft, plain wood through which sound flows continuously like airy sap? And why, on the other hand, does a Guarneri del Gesù not give much importance to the choice, but feels he can transform any wood with his mysterious touch? There you have a true occult poet. He only works by inspiration. He'll cut two imperious F-holes for you in the violin's face, two powerful sound holes; and the face is alive, expressive—it speaks to you, impatient to sing.

"What, then, is the influence of the F-holes on the soundboard? Gesù's Fs do not look like Amati's, or Stradivario's, or any others. How did he come up with them?

"And Gennaro Gagliano, 'the Transparent,' who hurls his striped little tigers at the throat of Music, isn't he a sorcerer too?"

I like the passion of this exquisite cellist trained in heavy artillery, who feels and expresses the life of living things with almost lyric intensity.

He says: "There was no such thing as a muted cello, for practice. So I decided to make one, with a very narrow resonance chamber extending the length of the tailpiece. By chance, a new instrument was born, with the delightful sound of an English horn, perfect for dance melodies."

"Let's call it the *alberghina*," I say.

He goes to fetch his alberghina. He returns. And he plays me a gigue, a courante, and a galliard.

Halfway through the galliard, we hear the grim howl of the siren, followed by cannon fire.

Sirenetta brings me a strange book of music and does not want to tell me where she got it.

It is written by hand, in a light, swift hand, and bound in a yellowish parchment that looks like pressed pulp. But I am not supposed to read.

On the back cover is the following handwritten statement: *Ignavia est iacere ubi possis surgere.* "Sloth is lying down when one could get up."

Is this a reproach to the bedridden, in the voice of a compassionate tongue?

I caress the pages. The paper is thin and soft, like a dry leaf beginning to deteriorate around the edges.

Sirenetta tells me it is a tablature for lute, a collection of airs. And she reads me the titles: *Passomezo*, by Vincenzio Galilei, *Intrada anglicana*, *Volta ursina*, *Pavana lacrimata*, *Gagliarda passionata*, *Gagliarda di Diomede* . . .

Arnold Dolmetsch reappears to me, with his petite companion, a Dutch woman of Spanish origin, a Haarlem hyacinth dark as the rosary of Felipe II painted by Juan Pantoja. Her name is Melodia.

In Zurich we used to go walking in a secluded pine wood illuminated like a Gothic nave. Arnold would bring his lute with him, made in Venice by Magno Steger. It looked like the keel of a galley, striped with alternating bright and dark staves, and was extraordinarily light. He played accompaniment to his lovely companion's singing, after saying: "She doesn't know how to sing. It's her greatest merit."

He placed the instrument's case in front of him as a music stand, with the tablatures on top. Leaning against a moss-covered trunk of pine, Melodia sang, lightly swaying, tracing vague, dreamy gestures in the air, occasionally stopping to search for the forgotten words of an old song.

She used to sing the old songs of the troubadours, like the one by Thibaut de Champagne, king of Navarre, which begins: "Amors me fait commencier"; and another, "L'autrier par la mati-née"; and "J'aloie l'autrier errant sans compagnon."[24]

She would sing old English songs from the time of the Trage-dians, such as Desdemona's lament "O willow, willow, willow shall be my garland," and the beautiful "Have you seen but a whyte Lillie," set to the words of Ben Jonson.

Between the tree trunks and in the alabaster glow, her small, naïve gestures wove the spidery threads of loves long dead.

Sleep came over me as I let the music book's soft pages slide between my fingers.

I had a delightful dream, like the one about redness. I drank the most beautiful song in the world.

I was in the hall of a great castle in Scotland. Or in what earldom without name or climate?

The hall was an indescribable marvel of color, adorned by human art as the bird of paradise is adorned by godly art. In the damasks, brocades, and velvets, the emerald green, the raven black, the gold-tinged greenish black created unheard-of harmonies with the same living intelligence found in the plumage of birds of paradise. And the complexions of the women and youths glowed far more than in the finest pictures of Sir Joshua and Gainsborough. And some of the women and youths on sofas caressed the soft fur of spaniels with great ears dappled gray and chestnut, white and orange.

And a voice sang as though the bird of paradise had stolen the nocturnal art of the nightingale in June and succeeded in making it solar, or sublimating it and coloring it with the colors of its feathers.

And all this joy for the eyes was modulated by that singing, submerged one minute, reemerging the next, ebbing and flowing by turns.

Ah, what could these notes I seek to evoke ever be, O visible song of the unseen bird of paradise?

Every time I wake, I lose a promised land.

Sensuality troubles my waking hours and menaces my sleep. *Accessus morbi.*[25] Again I suffer the attacks and travails of the hereditary illness that so tormented the broken, humiliated Giorgio Aurispa.[26]

The mother of King Lemuel says sorrowfully: "What, my son?"

Another voice comes in and says indulgently: "Why flee the defenseless young woman and the rose gardens deeper within her than that of Aziyeh, which you have already known? Why flee her large eyes as pitiful as those of your thorn-ravaged Arabian, why turn away from the supernatural succession of tragic faces that mask her skull when she is delirious? What good does it do you to shun these things, O too vigilant ascetic, when they alone can help you explore a mystery your virtues and renunciations could never illuminate?

"How could they ever harm your will to devotion and perfection? And even if your scorn is painful, how could it ever diminish you? And if your melancholy once drew continual strength and took wing from the continual clash between your sensuality and your intelligence, how can you think of suppressing the most active, lyric leavening of your inner life?"

Who has spoken thus?

I remove my blindfold, sit up in bed, and cruelly watch the band of sunlight stretching away, little by little, over the miniatures on the wall, over the sofa's faded cushions, over the delicate harpsichord.

Has Melodia, in a broad taffeta skirt, returned to the ebony keyboard to sing me "O My Clarissa," the old song of William Lawes?

And so the sun set, righteous and strong, into the doline surrounded by scrubby pines stunted by the bora of Trieste.

There was a hut, with reed matting for a roof, for the battery officers.

One barrage of fire had massacred our men.

The bloody pile was far away but seemed to be approaching, with a slithering of entrails. I could hear it the way one hears, ears pricked, a brigade advancing on hands and knees through rocks and brush.

The men were there, before their frowning commander.

The commander's voice roared. The sun, at that moment, was setting, begilding the men's pallor.

They were fighting for Christian flesh, the nation's flesh, this poor flesh of ours.

The sunlight fell on the tables, which looked almost like animals, each different from the rest, with their stains, cracks, knots, nails, and marks.

The wan-faced captain could not control the miserable quivering of his lips. His fingers sparkled with too many rings.

The sunlight fell on the soldiers' shirts and stockings hanging from the line.

The talk was of the constant mistakes, the number of dead, the base attempts at excuses.

The sunlight fell on a row of shiny mess tins.

Tired pots hung over the doline, creaking like old train carriages on unsteady rails.

The sunlight fell on a shovel, an iron club, a pistol, a barrel, a trough of lime.

The commander's voice, implacable, did not cease its condemnations. A callow second lieutenant broke down into sobs. As a pot screeched, a stray bird passed overhead, white belly flashing.

The sunlight fell on a stock of red-tipped artillery shells enclosed in their cages of rough-hewn wood.

All of a sudden the captain fell to the ground and rolled to the bottom of the doline, overcome by convulsions like a woman.

Had the carnage arrived on the march?

I saw the karstic doline redden all around the edge with shredded flesh, like an eyelid turned inside out.

I am lying in front of the window. The moon is full. There is not a breath of wind.

Corè's house is inhabited by white peacocks. I see nothing but the vast foundation of white stone and the trees of the hidden garden and a strip of luminous water.

A solitary, mystical grandeur, as in a dead city of Persia or India.

The canal is like a sacred river in which the ashes of pyres have been scattered at sunset.

No voices are heard, no thudding oars, no sound at all. It is as if life expired centuries ago.

The indifferent moon contemplates an exanimate beauty like that of Angkor and Anuradhapura.

Suddenly the wail of the alarm siren rends the silence.

A cannon blast booms from the Lido to San Giorgio, and from San Giorgio down to the Fondamente Nuove, announcing a nocturnal raid of winged destroyers.

Thus threatened, the entire city wondrously revives in my flesh, in my bones, in every one of my veins.

The domes, belfries, arcades, loggias, and statues are my limbs, my pain.

And I shrink into my pillows, face turned to the sky of light, not knowing which part of me will be maimed.

My human life disperses. Inside me is the life of the marble and the power of sculpted history, awaiting the nameless ravage.

Beauty of the night, how often I have missed you!

How avid I was always to see, to look, to know, how insatiable! And yet, O errant eyes of mine, you have not seen enough, you have not looked enough, you have not been able to embrace every face of the manifest deity.

And one of you is now spent, while the other grows dim and tired and is perhaps destined to darken.

"Look! Look!"

The full moon's glow resounds with the voice that could harmonize with every note of misfortune and every note of happiness: Ghìsola's voice.

"Look! Look!"

She was rousing me from sleep. I was drowning in sleep as in a river of blackness. I felt as if she was holding me by the armpits and struggling to pull me up, out of the sluggish whirlpool.

"Look! Look!"

Thus she dragged me to the window, and I raised my leaden eyelids and saw great peaks of sapphire, supernatural summits of a planet without people.

"Look!"

The Apuan Alps were transfigured on a lunar night risen up from the depths of the age-old memory of who knows what ecstatic god.

I closed my eyes again, pressed by sleep's inertia.

"Look!"

I reopened them and closed them again. The divine spectacle was washed away by the waters of the immemorial river.

And why, that day in Athens, did I not run fast enough to reach the Acropolis before the August sunset's sudden orgiastic frenzy waned?

And why, that day near Thebes of the hundred gates, under the great acacia trees, did I not take off my shoes and walk barefoot on the golden carpet of yellow flowers, but decided to go back aboard the lazy boat?

"Look! Look!"

Who knows how beautiful the night is, down in the Valley of Blood, between one hut and another, one tent and another!

Who knows how white the enchanted rocks gleam at Campolongo as the fog rises from the Val d'Astico! Who knows how large the cyclopean cliffs and towers of rock loom at Bosco Agro, in that battery where, as evening fell, I saw, peering out between two cannons red-hot from firing, a deer!

"Look! Look!"

Will I spend the whole night enumerating my regrets?

It is Holy Thursday.

A day of gloom. I follow the light's vicissitudes in the mirror before me.

A cloud passes. A cloud breaks up into tufts like fleece in a carder's hands.

The sun disappears, and everything seems to turn cold. The mirror freezes like a quadrangular puddle.

My skin shudders under the blankets.

The silence resembles the silence before dawn.

The belfries have no more voice. Weary of vibrating, the bells rest, mouths turned downwards, full of shadow. The ropes dangle, smooth and greasy in two spots from the bell-ringer's hands.

What sadness they cast upon each hour of my days past!

And yet this unwonted silence gives me no rest. Sadness no longer comes to me through the air, no longer comes from above. Today it crouches at my feet, wingless. It sleeps, and in its sleep, it thrashes.

The violet glimmers in my bandaged eye form nuclei and then vanish, then re-form. Faint spots of the same color appear and disappear in the field of the healthy eye. It is the color of Holy Thursday.

Wisteria in bloom adorns all the windows, adorns the wall to the left, the trellis to the right. Corè's house is crowned with wisteria, all along the truncated stone. The sky must be like the bishops' amethyst.

The motif that dominates the Largo of the first Trio comes back to me, with the image associated with it. The holy knees bleed. The patella gleams white amidst the blood.

I have one leg atop the other, a position that calls to mind a pose of Judas I know.

When, during the Supper of the Last Passover, as the disciples were eating, Jesus said: "Verily I say unto you, One of you which eateth with me shall betray me," Judas Iscariot was sitting with one leg crossed over the other. Upon hearing the Master's words, *he removed the leg that was atop the other*, as if to stand up . . .

"Judas was seated, with legs crossed . . . "

An important moment, and movement. He was still seated, but about to stand up. He was about to say: "Master, am I he?"

Near him, at table, was James, son of Zebedee, the Galilean fisherman. And he realized that Judas had removed the leg that was atop the other at that moment. And he turned to look at him.

There is no Angelus this evening. Grace has quit the Lady of Heaven. The Mother weeps, one hand over her brow, the other under her chin, as in the crypt at Aquileia, where perhaps today the soldiers are looking upon her with sorrow in their hearts.[27]

Renata returns from a tour of the tombs. She enters my room with a sigh of fatigue and collapses into an armchair. Arching her arms over her head, she removes her hat, Thessalian in shape and adorned with two small round roses. She is tired. She has been walking over calli, fondamente, campi, and campielli, going from church to church.

The room is filled with violet twilight. Her bare face is very white, almost phosphorescent. On her brown dress I think I smell a scent of candles, a scent of faded grass and gillyflowers.

Which was the seventh church? San Giovanni e Paolo, near the marble ospedale where my doctors are.

What is Colleoni doing on his pedestal? He is covered with sacks.[28] But the swallows above the lonely piazza scream for him, persistent as in merciless combat.

"I'm so tired!" says Sirenetta.

And her girlish voice, drunk on brackish air and broken by the effort of swimming, her Bocca d'Arno voice, touches my heart as it once did.

She slides onto the cushion at my feet. She rests her face on my knees.

Her face is narrower, her chin sharper. Touching her, my hands see her, as if I were totally blind.

She is small this evening. She is a poor, tired little girl, exhausted by the shadows and funereal scents, and in need of rest.

My fingers find the knot in her hair and untie it with infinite care, as if she were already drifting off to sleep and I were unwrapping a treasure for her.

She does not move, but I can feel her smile all the way to the sensitive ends of her hair, which spread apart as if that same smile opened them up the way the breath of spring suddenly opens a large flower at nightfall.

A mysterious moment, as when the believer communicates with his god in a tangible form.

A human face is flesh and bone, pierced by the vigilant senses. A head of hair is a living mass that fills the hand and has weight.

But this face is nothing if not an airy fruit of my soul, these tresses like those extraordinary sentiments in which the soul remains suspended, freeing itself from the accident of time.

These locks smell of childhood, the way bouquets of lily flowers smell of annunciation. By age five she already had so much hair.

At the time, in a white house by the sea, she used to appear in the doorway to my room, to interrupt my work when it dragged on too long, when my spirit was a tireless tongue of perpetual fire and my art the very essence of requited love.

She would appear without a sound, like one of those birds that light upon a delicate branch and wait for it to stop swaying to begin their song.

Her grace used to catch the corner of my eye as I leaned over my papers.

Sometimes, so as not to let any fleeting images escape me, I would not turn around at once, but hold her in the crease of my eyelids the way one holds back a tear of emotion to prolong the pleasure of the moment when the soul overflows.

In her long dress like those of the Infantas, she would smile, and ever since, her smile has passed through the waves of her hair and divided the ends in two, the way a smile cleaves the mouth.

When the Sultan was in the arms of the fairest of his beauties, were a fire to break out in his city of wood, a silent female messenger dressed in vermilion would appear at the threshold of his secret room.

Dearer to me than the fairest of beauties was my art. I embraced her with a love oblivious to all other good things. But that wordless little messenger announced a wondrous, faraway event to me, which I was about to enter like some unexplored region of myself. *Memento vivere.*

My fingers released the pen and caressed the childish mane of hair, which seemed to swell with song like a nightingale's feathers.

Now I am no longer anxious about time.

My hands are nothing if not forms of my spirituality, as they were then.

I have a musical touch that corresponds to something deeper than my consciousness.

The smile of my tired, happy child seems immortal.

As then, I know where, here and there, her hair lightens; I feel the two-pointed tips, the split ends, on her shoulders.

Renata has closed her eyes. Her long lashes touch my heart.

"Are you asleep, child?" I ask her.

She rouses herself and rises. In her deep head of hair, her face is like an *Ave.*

At my feet stands the fullest-maned of Melozzo's angels, bringing me the evening's blessing.

She shares a brief meal with me. At the end, we both eat our oranges voraciously; they have already been prepared, freed of their skin and pips, all juicy pulp. We quench our thirst.

Now she bows her head, with the same gesture as a bird about to hide it under the wing.

"Are you sleepy, child?

"So sleepy."

My heart flutters. Until today, she has taken care of me. And now it is I who will take care of her.

"Lie down on my bed and sleep a little."

"If I fall asleep, I'll never wake up."

"I shall wake you myself."

She stands up with effort, her entire body sagging, and weakly approaches the bed.

She lies down in the spot hollowed out by my suffering, lays her head on the pillow of my sleepless nights.

It is a slender pillow, thinner than the arm a man uses for support when he falls asleep on the naked ground.

"How can you sleep with your head so low?" she asks in a subdued voice.

It is the pillow of pain, upon which I kept my eye immobile for weeks and weeks as upon a small pile of ash, a live ember under the incessant breath of a demon bent upon raising sparks and flames.

I am on my feet, and she is lying down. I am near the headboard, as she was before, and she is supine, as I was before.

She says: "I could never sleep this way."

I cannot lean over her, because I must always keep my head tilted slightly back when I am standing.

"Would you like another pillow?"

I tread with cautious step to where I had so recently reclined near the window. I take a pillow and return to the bed.

My heart swells with a sweetness so pure that it feels as if my daughter's childhood and my own were flowing together in it.

"There."

She raises her head, and I put the second pillow on top of the first. I feel as if I am imitating her same gesture of compassion.

"Is that all right?"

"Perfect. Thank you."

The kindness has been reversed. Her kindness and compassion fill my heart. She repeated my exact words, in the tone of my own gratitude!

At once she falls asleep, lets herself go. She no longer hears. She barely breathes.

She lies on her back, but her face is turned to the right, resting on her hair, while her feet are one on top of the other, as if pierced by a single nail. And I see a buckle shine.

Her arms are turned upwards, like those of virgins awaiting the stigmata; but her hands are closed.

She sleeps with fists clenched, the way she did as an infant; she sleeps on my bed of pain as in the cradle of her innocence.

I watch over her, walking gently from one side of the room to the other.

My footstep is silent. I am wearing woolen slippers.

I have regained a little of my flexibility below the waist.

I keep my torso stiff, my neck erect, my head tilted backwards.

I wear my infirm eye on my hollow face the way the martyred Saint Lucy carried hers on a dish.

If the dish were full of blood or tears, not a drop would fall, so adroit am I in my caution.

Each time I pass before the mirror, I see a stranger in the shadow with his head in bandages.

When I approach the bed, my foot becomes lighter on the rug, like the paw of a nocturnal animal crossing a meadow.

The doctors have allowed me to pace between these four walls, to help induce sleep, my enemy.

I stop. The sleeper seems not to be breathing.

She lies motionless in her brown dress. On either side of her face are her clenched fists.

A bouquet of red roses smells of a hothouse with golden windows: tomorrow's roses. The silence is perfect, the same in light as in shadow.

Where I have suffered, where I have hoped, where I have despaired, where I have wrestled with monsters, talked to the angels, bled, and wept, there sleeps my child.

How small she is this evening! She weighs no more than the dying little girl I once held in my arms for an entire night.[29]

It is a memory returned from afar, like a wave whose brunt the chest cannot withstand.

Pity, despair, terror, the desire to give blood and breath, the waiting for a miracle, the fateful splendor of the Great Bear, the Milky Way, near as a path that forks in the earth's road and climbs towards another sorrow; the alternating movement of unknown forces between mountain and sea, the swift passage of a god who neither hears the prayer nor sees the offering, the invincible quiver of the flesh, the will armed against death.

I was walking as now, in a much vaster room, with the same cautious, nimble step.

I was going from a door open onto shadow, where a bed and cradle shone white, towards a window gaping wide onto the stars.

In my arms was the baby, but a few months old, weak from illness, paler than her own linens, with something dark around her nostrils that terrified me.

I encountered death in the doorway, I encountered death on the windowsill. I stared straight at it, with the hard, wild eyes of a fighter.

The house was in a secluded spot in the country near Resìna.

It was a night in June.

The volcano had been active for several days; from the window we could see the fires in the crater, the wide, flaming fissures, the long, red-hot lava flows, the overhanging cloud reflecting red.

The doctor had left, placing his last hope in sleep as in a divine remedy. The child had stopped crying and dozed off when I took her in my arms and started walking slowly about.

I felt my body only as a form of cadence.

I did not whisper, did not sing, almost did not breathe, but my step was like a lullaby, my bending elbows like a rocking cradle, and all my limbs obeyed a music of persuasion.

The refrains my wet-nurse had once sung to me rose up from my depths and guided me.

My mouth recalled having sucked a poppy capsule, wrapped in a wet handkerchief.

My thoughts incessantly wavered between shadow and sleep, between life and death, between the light of heaven and the fire of earth.

Walking towards the window, I heard the crickets chirping, heard their quiet nighttime melody. Walking towards the door I heard a deep throbbing that seemed as mysterious to me as the voices of my endless wake.

And, for a short while, every time I turned around, that throbbing set the tempo for the melody of the earth, and thus my waves of fright began to dissipate.

Finally, however, when I reached the doorway where death stood, the throbbing increased and became terrifying.

The horror set my heart racing. I froze, lost.

I felt as if that frightful palpitation was being communicated to me by my dying child's fragile body.

I imagined a terrible fever, a ghastly, sudden agony tightening her tiny throat and allowing no more cries or moans to come out.

I bent my head to look at her haggard face, and then breathed into her half-open mouth.

The face was at peace, the mouth calm, and the sweetness of sleep filled the closed fists.

Nature's wonder was revealed to my anxious heart. All at once I recognized the throbbing of the veins that swelled my tired arms.

The slightest impatience might disturb her miraculous sleep. I accepted my torture. I continued pacing with my quiet step, carrying the life of my life.

I nursed her with my will, fed her with my suffering.

All the power of my soul was concentrated on sustaining my feeble arms, and yet I felt the beauty of the night as in a rapture of Apollonian inspiration.

The patient lullaby turned into an ecstasy of song throughout my body. The flaming crater became for me the myth of the Eternal Mother who tempers mortal flesh in roaring fire.

My labored pulse cadenced the poetry of the universe.

Never since have I felt such yearning for happiness upon seeing the stars tremble and fade at the first breath of dawn, nor have I ever again possessed in me the measure of that unexpressed song— until this moment, brought back to me by the mystery of goodness.

It is Good Friday. Rome's Christmas.

All those who have died in battle have given their lives as the price of this world.

All those who toil and huff to feed the battle give their exertions as the price of this world.

All those who shall suffer, fight, and die in the most just of wars shall suffer, fight, and die for the price of this world.

On what Calvary is the Son of Man sacrificed today?

The Son of Man is martyred for us today on the wild mountain named after Saint-Michael the Swordbearer, the mountain of four peaks and four wraths, in the shadowless, waterless Carso. And our bile-burnt mouths again breathe spirit and hope.

There the infantry find eternal life. I see them storming the summits again, alone with the flash of steel and the eyes of the Nation. I see them again rise up against the thundering sky. They look at first like storm-tossed bushes and brambles. Then they become bristling men. They become the teeth of the furious rock. They bite into eternity.

I have my four brotherly crosses.

Giuseppe Miraglia is crucified on his wings.

Luigi Bailo is crucified on his wings.

Alfredo Barbieri is crucified on his wings.

Luigi Bresciani is crucified on his wings.

I do not possess the linens of the disciple from Arimathea, nor the balms of Nicodemus.[30] But I have given them a new monument "wherein was never man yet laid."[31]

My mother's holy face of love and sorrow is veiled today by an angel with a violet cloth, who takes pity on me.

It is Holy Saturday.

The sudden pealing of the bells disturbs the funereal silence in great waves, as I lie in bed, wrapped tightly in linen, swaddled like Lazarus, a shroud over my head.

After so stirring my sadness, the bells now stir my hope.

Today ends the ninth week since my return, since my sentence, since my body was nailed to the darkness. I was fooled by an omen of Sirenetta's. But in this air of Resurrection, this air of Ascension, do we not feel the breath of miracle?

No voice calls for me to come outside, for me to rise again. I remain immobile, overcoming the urge to get up.

My body wastes away, drop by drop, ravaged by the piercings of salutary needles.

Here and there in my muscles, the intermittent pulsation of the fibrils makes me shudder indescribably, as if I were inhabited by a small beast moving frantically through my limbs, trying to open a pathway with its paws and muzzle.

My unruly heart throbs in my throat, thunders in the nape of my neck.

Peace, peace, peace. But the holy announcement does not allay my ills.

I cannot resist the temptation to put myself to the test. Little by little, I free my arm from its bandages, lift the edge of the bandage covering the injured eye, and raise the lid.

The shadow is still there, unchanged. The good omen has failed.

For the first time, I am allowed to go down to the garden.

A false sense of vigor uplifts me. With childish joy I cast off the senile trappings of the disabled veteran. I become a white Lancer again.

My riding breeches, which once fit so snug at the knee, now have a few folds in them. With a flutter of hope I see the flyer's insignias on the sleeves of the jacket, the golden wings reddened by the Adriatic brine. I can almost smell the altitude. These gray garments have known the blue beyond the clouds, were suspended at four thousand meters in a desert of air; they clothed an ecstasy of devotion that seemed to stop the wing in a sky over Trent rattled by thunder and rent by lightning streaking with twofold wrath. The talismans were in the breast pocket over the heart: my mother's old ring, with a little worn-out death's head between two tibiae for its gem, and a bullet that had lodged in the wood of the cockpit on August 7, near my elbow.

I smile to hear my spurs jingle as they are rubbed one against the other by the person crouching at my feet to fasten them. But I do not let him put them on. No horse is pawing the ground outside the door; nor, alas, is there a hydroplane rumbling at the dock, ready to take wing. I am a convalescent still in danger.

My knees are unsteady. My heart beats wildly. I am about to cross the threshold so long forbidden me.

I descend the staircase with infinite caution, carrying my eye in the reliquary of my raised head.

Sirenetta is right there, ready to support me.

Now the last stair.

Now the ground floor room.

Now the blaze of green behind bay windows covered with lace.

Now the sharp air which, like an unfamiliar drink, fills my eager mouth with its new flavor.

Now the garden, now the leaves, now the flowers.

My hand goes to my blindfold. It is more severe than usual. Not white, but dark. Not linen, but silk. My eye is dressed in mourning, wearing the weeds.

With her childish grace, Sirenetta takes my wild hand, leads me towards a rose-bush trained to flower on a tall stem, and says:

"Look at this little rose."

O mysterious voice that can make a single creature of a maiden and a rosebush!

As she holds the stem between her ring and middle fingers, the little rose seems to grow out of the hollow of her hand, as if to begin the metamorphosis of spring.

She is wearing a striped dress, white and green, that looks made in the image of one of those silvery poplars that tremble in all their fresh young branches at each gust of wind on the riverbank.

The little rose is grafted onto her; it is the flower of her tenderness.

It is so pure, so fragile, so delicately constructed that it cannot be compared to anything corporeal but only, perhaps, to a chaste, ineffable idea.

There is no form of childhood equal to it.

One can but bend the knee and worship it.

Its perfection is most fleeting.

I feel as if I can see its petals unfolding moment by moment.

By nightfall it will be already open and empty.

The inertia of so many days had imprisoned me in a sense of only my own transience amongst inanimate things. But now I am regaining the ear of a poet seated on the banks of time's river. I hear again the melody of the perpetual stream.

Sirenetta knows the garden's secret fable in minute detail. She knows where to find the caterpillar, where the bee, where the spider, where the beetle; and she knows what they do.

She knows which branches are sick; she knows how many buds there are, which are late to bloom, and which about to open.

She complains about the lazy gardener. She picks up a small bellows and blows a salutary powder onto a rosebush teeming with greenish insects.

She leads me with hesitant pity to a large white rose whose inner heart is being devoured by a beetle.

"Why don't you shake it and chase the bug away?" I ask.

"The rose is lost by now," she replies. "And if the beetle doesn't eat its fill on this one, it'll go find another."

I sense that her pity is divided between the insect and the flower, just as the Seraph of Assisi understood at once the ravenous bird and the worm in its beak, the burning fire and the burnt garment, the ailing flesh and the herbs pressed to heal it.

I pause before this spectacle of devastating passion.

The insect is lodged inside the flower's sweetness with a hunger resembling perdition or rapture.

It is as splendid as gold leaf shining through polished emerald.

It is a gorgeous gem and a savage force.

It is oblivious to everything, all risk, all surprise, all danger, immersed in its bliss as in a crime that fears no punishment.

Again I feel, as in early youth, what divinity there is in hunger and thirst.

The whole heart of the rose is ruined. Inside a crown of petals still intact, the color is yellowy, as from a residue of honey.

The wound is nectary, the killing sweet.

Insatiable love knows no guilt.

Whosoever feeds on beauty grows in beauty.

I wish I could linger awhile, to glimpse the beetle at the moment it spreads the wings of its golden armor and flies away on a sunbeam.

The afternoon wanes. There is no longer any trace of wind. The new leaves breathe and hope, the old ones ponder and remember.

A great flowering of wisteria covering the whole wall up to the roof, growing out from a vine-stock that looks like a tangle of rope, reminds me of a fishing net I once saw hauled onto the Atlantic shore, full of useless, pale violet medusas.

The swallows furiously squabble and screech, and my old wounds smart as if I were run through with arrows.

In a corner I see two upended watering cans. I'm not sure why, but they evoke a sense of silence for me, a pause in the piercing cries of the birds.

"There's your talking laurel," says Sirenetta.[32]

It is a rounded laurel on a slender, naked stalk, tall as a man.

It has an allegorical presence I cannot explain; it looks as though transplanted from a garden in Poliphilus's dream.[33]

All that it lacks is the flourish of a scroll, halfway up the trunk.

The foliage is so dark, hard, and dense that the Muse could never insert her hand in it without being injured by the leaves' sharp edges.

And from its evergreen boughs, smaller, young leaves emerge at rhythmic intervals, so lively they look like little impatient tongues that "wish to speak."

Sirenetta's fresh soul hears the soundless rhythm at once.

The laurel speaks. Is it saying: "So as not to sleep?" Or: "So as not to die?"[34]

Never was sleep so alien to me; never, amidst so much death, have I so yearned for immortality.

There is still a song deep in my tempered heart.

The sun sets beyond the bend in the canal, which is now green as the speaking laurel.

The bells are silent, but the air seems to tremble, awaiting their angelic sound.

My covered eye is full of luminous wisteria; the other, unaccustomed, daydreams.

Outside of time, a slow harmony unfolds.

Corè's house is nothing but a vast garland borne by the lions' heads leaning over the water.

From Palazzo Dario to the Church of the Salute, the brick and stone in the rosy light become almost fleshly.

The façades lean one against the other, like women supporting each other to keep from falling, invaded by April's sudden languor.

A large black boat, laden with radiant sulfur and propelled by long oars, passes like an apparition beyond the millennia and memory.

It has an ancient broad-blade rudder with a long helm shaft maneuvered by a man who looks like a Phoenician steersman.

The sulfur assumes an ineffable hue as it enters the shade.

The yellow has the force of an unexpected motif that suddenly lifts a waning symphony to sublime heights.

A strange silence forms inside me.

I no longer hear the swallows.

And my heart beats with dread, lest a tolling bell should interrupt this soundless music.

It is Easter. The Resurrection of Christ.

A battle companion has sent me the gift of a print of the sublime drawing Michelangelo sketched of the Resurrection with a plume plucked from the eagle of John the Favorite.[35] *Resurgit et insurgit.*[36]

The titanic Christ, having forced open the heavy lid of the sepulcher, still has one foot in the hollow stone. But with head high and arms raised, and the force and violence of his passion, he casts himself up towards the heavens.

Was my heart thus not mad enough? Did it not beat fast enough?

Did I need this impassioned image of power to feel how wretchedly small I truly am?

No disciple has erected a new monument to me. I lie here in the same bedsheets, the same bandages, the same sweat and tremors. I do not rise.

I am paying for yesterday's indulgence. I feel even more exhausted, as if from the coup de grâce. This listless flesh is held together not by my carcass but by anger.

I see green. My hands in the shadow look green to me. The whole room is green, as under a dense arbor. It is as if my head were wrapped in the round laurel bush, which has now turned entirely into fissured glass.

Has Oreste Salomone emerged from the grave to come to my bedside today?

He has come unexpectedly, without forewarning. From the threshold on the calle and up the stairs, step by step, he tramples on my empty heart. He enters the way I entered the little room at La Comina.

What has he brought me?

Will he throw the riddled head of Alfredo Barbieri into my lap?

He is even more emaciated than he was then, in the little camp-bed. His dark eyes, even bigger than before, consume his gaunt face. My sight turns him green, as if he has been dead for four days.

Why has he come to frighten me?

What is this burden weighing upon my cold feet?

Fur jacket and helmet and knee breeches and gloves.

Have they been brought to me by that footsoldier who still cannot swallow his bite of dark bread?

Be calm, heart. Let me tell the living from the dead.

Let me recognize the voice which on that February noon spoke to me not from deep in my bed but from the depths of sacrifice.

He spoke softly. Today, too, he speaks softly.

Have nine weeks passed? Or nine centuries?

This hero knows nothing of his transfiguration in me upon my burning. Were I to give him my first sibylline scroll to read, he would not understand.

"O sister, why have you twice let me down?"

He is returning from leave. He is returning from convalescence. He has known the leisures and honors of Capua.[37] He has not yet recovered. The anguish of Gonàrs still eats away at his stomach. His eyes in their cavernous, black-ringed sockets are as though oiled and sparkle insistently, as if still reflecting the swift route to the heavens lit up by the glistening blood. And they are lonely, unmoving between unbatting lashes. They are as lonely as those that span, from temple to temple, the faces of martyrs aligned in the mosaic gold of Ravenna's basilica. All the rest is opaque and returned to the earth.

There are heroic acts in which the astonished hero remains forever imprisoned.

Here comes an eagle to lay a lead ball and chain at his feet.

I know not why, but I feel that he shall remain oppressed by the need to surpass himself.

And I want to weep with him.

And I see him down there, an exile in his own land, feet stuck in the unseeded mud, focusing the despair of his aviator's eyes on the crest of Mount Vulture.

"I shall return to La Comina in two or three days. I'm only passing through Venice to embrace you."

"And will you already be able to return to battle?"

"Not yet. But I'll be the camp commander while I wait. What about you?"

In my fantasy he looks up at his mountain. And I am at the mouth of my river, with half of my body in the silt. And my mother is there, crouching, looking as if she is taking root in that spot, to take upon herself all the misfortunes of her people and her land.

O mother, from what darkness must I be reborn?

Her motionless eyes have no reply. Her inclined head is far away, like the last snows of the Maiella, looming in the distance like a breast.

I am spent, as if I had two holes in my head again and were dangling again in the void from the edge of the vibrating cockpit.

I know I am delirious, and overcome my delirium.

I am thirsty. I am all thirst and agitation. The image of the river overwhelms me, submerges me, washes over me.

To the languishing hero who on his chest wears the glorious stretch of sky between Ljubljana and Gonàrs reduced to a slender band of azure silk, I say: "At times I despair of regaining my strength, so exhausted do I feel, as now. My eye is lost. No matter. One will suffice. The cyclops is valiant in any foundry. But what if I remain disabled? What if the devastation wrought by my long torment is irreparable? What if I am broken in two, as I felt I was yesterday evening when my dear jailors laid me back down on this grill?

"Tell me yourself if we can go on living without a heroic reason for living. Tell me yourself if we can continue to be men without knowing for certain that the hour of transhumanizing will return, Oreste."[38]

Words fail me; they break against my metal palate. I am chewing steel again. Thirst screams inside me without a sound. The streaming river flows again, turns me over, splashes around me.

"Aged, bent, broken, blind, with wobbly knees and creaking elbows, here I am, calmly waiting on the banks of my river. Which is my river?

"I mean the river of eternity, Oreste.

"Heroic inspiration breathes upon the injured, too, breathes upon the human stumps, breathes upon impotent carcasses.

"I want to tell you a story of greatness, Oreste, you who were supposed to bring my sacrificed body back to the Fatherland.

"We have no wings. There is a glory of the heights, and there is a glory of the depths. One can die a good death, and one can die an even better death.

"It is a true story, but I want to situate it outside of time, beyond all limits.

"Can we no longer fight? I am a peasant from Pescara, you a peasant of the Vulture.

"A nameless peasant painfully tills his field on the banks of the river. His country is at war. His country is invaded. He will sow his seeds to feed the combatants.

"Since morning he has been watching his countrymen ford the stream, seeking safety on the other bank, where they can regroup, reorganize, and rearm themselves for resistance.

"Their pursuers arrive. Menacing horsemen arrive and ask the peasant to show them were the ford is.

"He leans over his spade and does not answer.

"They renew their demand.

"He cuts the clods of earth. And says not a word.

"And so they seize him, they tie his arms behind his back, they push him to the riverbank, and say: 'You shall cross the water first, ahead of us.'

"The ford is right there.

"He steps into the water. And he begins to bend his knees to make it look as if the water is getting deeper. Then he walks with his knees on the bottom. Then he crouches and disappears. He remains submerged. He lets the river of the Fatherland flow over his dark, silent sacrifice."

From where does this silence come to us?

It flows like the river in which that man laid himself down.

Little by little, my heart finds peace.

My comrade's hand is in mine, which rests on the bedside.

"What are all these strips of paper?" he asks, seeing the sibylline sheets scattered across the bed.

"I use them to write down my dreams in the dark, one line at a time."

He marvels at this. And in his wonderment, his smile takes on unexpected freshness.

"And how do you write?"

"Like this."

I take the board, set it at a slant on my slightly raised knees. I take a blank strip, spread it out, and write on it, shaking as I did the first time I tried it.

My hand is followed by the eyes that saw a dying Luigi Bàilo lie down on the footbridge between the two copper fuel tanks, saw the miraculous spray burst forth from Alfredo Barbieri's leather helmet and into the raging wind.

"Here. See if you're able to read what I've written."

The hero takes the strip, stands up, goes over to the half-open window, and tries to decipher my writing. He hesitates.

From what pits, what graves, does this silence come to us?
His hands tremble a little, under his aquiline profile.
He reads, in the same muffled voice he had on that field cot.
"But what if there were an even better way to die?"

O liberation, liberation,

I call to you in my evening without Hesperus, I call to you in my night without Ursa, I call to you in my morning without Lucifer, yet you will not release me!

O liberation, liberation,

to you I dedicate these bandages soaked with weakened blood and cold tears, to you I dedicate this pupil of mine which no longer sees nor wishes to see other than the dark dawn I raise within myself.

O liberation, liberation,

keep far from me the pity of those who love me and the love of those who pity me, and this music, and this raving, and all this softness unworthy of my straw bed.

O liberation, liberation,

come and release me; come and make my kneecaps and elbows and wrists whole again; come and mix salt and iron into my blood again; come and remake me with only my arid liver; and hurl me back into the battle.

This commentary on the shadows was written, one line at a time, on more than ten thousand strips of paper.[1] The writing is misshapen to greater or lesser degrees depending on the severity of my suffering and the urgency of my visions.

In the months of May and June 1916, my daughter Renata worked on deciphering the majority of the bands of paper, while in subdued light I wrote the *Envoi*, later added to my *Leda Without Swan*, using the same procedure, although able, this time, to straighten the lines with an occasional glance.

Her interpretation was read to me, and then—not without reluctance on my part—sent to my publisher, who printed it in autumn of the same year. It included the text of this book up to the episode of the blind soldiers in the field hospital, a few other fragments of the second part, and all the passion of Holy Week, up to the end.

The difficulties of deciphering and organizing, however, proved so daunting that they soon discouraged my very patient transcriber. The paper strips, having slipped out of their clasps, had got mixed up. Many of them, written at moments of tremendous distress, contained two or even three intersecting and overlapping lines. Others—such as, for example, those that describe the apparitions of my mother's face—had been turned over to my faithful nurse with the order to set them aside and not show them to anyone.

I myself have trouble recalling the vicissitudes of my effort: the sudden inspirations, the brusque interruptions, the frantic resumptions. The slightest pause would break up the flow. If my hand stopped for even an instant, the incandescent mental masses would collapse, and immediately new material and new aspects would arise and command my attention.

For several weeks, as I lay on my back, awake, suffering from relentless insomnia, there was a forge of dreams inside my damaged eye which my will could neither control nor halt. The optic nerve drew from every layer of my culture and prior life, projecting countless images into my field of vision with a swiftness of transition unknown even in my boldest flights of lyricism. The past became present, its forms in such full relief and such sharp detail that their emotional intensity was immeasurably increased thereby. One can imagine how the danger of madness hung perpetually over my bandaged head. And one can understand how my desire to externalize such tumult was an attempt at salvation.

When those close to me tried with increasing insistence to persuade me to transcribe the paper strips that I alone could decipher or divine, my aversion to placing so obscure a part of myself at the mercy of strangers only grew. Nor would my remaining eye, still disturbed and distressed by the infirmity of the other, have tolerated so intricate an effort.

My sadness, moreover, grew increasingly fierce as the frequent news of the war was brought to me by breathless comrades still smelling of battle, the way the butcher smells of blood and the reaper smells of hay.

The days of Santa Gorizia turned all anguish and impatience into resolute desperation.[2] I learned then the meaning of Michelangelo's words: "Not a thought is born in me that does not have death sculpted within it."

The only way I managed to regain control of myself was by resolving that I would overcome all obstacles to win back the wings that belonged to my will.

Against me stood the prognoses of science and the apprehensions of affection. To the daughters, sisters, and mothers of servicemen, I declare with pride and gratitude that in my struggle I had an intrepid ally in the offspring of my flesh and blood. She knew how vitally necessary I was; and she knew that the danger I carried in me was more certain than that which I was going out to meet. She rebelled against the prohibitions and was able to smile at the others' astonishment.

O day of Parenzo, turbid, bright September afternoon, by what sign shall I mark you in my votive tablet?[3]

I led the second group of hydroplane bombers. Luigi Bologna, who again was my pilot, was aware of my experience and supported it manfully, with unfailing heart. The rim of the cockpit, on my right, was open by design. Between my legs I had taken an extra load of four bombs, to be launched by hand; and before the altimeter loomed the prospect of sudden blindness.

Starting at two thousand meters, I alternated visual observation with smoke signals to keep the assembled group behind my blue flame.

At three thousand meters, the cyclops could see. A three thousand two hundred, he could see. At three thousand four hundred, he could see, "even with his one eye."

From time to time the pilot turned to me and gestured. With another gesture, I communicated the result of my observation. An unforgettable dialogue of martial friendship at high altitude, where nothing petty or timid can survive.

The leading group in the fog had yawed towards Rovigno. I was the first to arrive over the anti-aircraft battery's position. I reduced altitude for the attack. Executing a maneuver of the boldest elegance, Luigi Bologna descended to sixteen hundred meters, from one firing zone to another. Despite the abrupt change of pressure, I could still see. I pulled the pins from the bombs between my legs and tried to silence the enemy and my fate. At that time I had not yet rediscovered the primitive cry of my race,[4] which now wears woolen jambeaux instead of bronze greaves; but my raised arm could have plucked a star from the empyrean, so far did elation vault it beyond humanity.

After we had descended into the Sant'Andrea canal and ascended the slipway, my expectant young comrades lifted me onto their shoulders, as if to hoist me up to the summit of their youth, the peak of their wings.

I was reborn.

The date of my rebirth was the 13th of September, 1916. And I was rebaptized in a sea of bile.

Intumuit mascula bilis.[5] And then came the days of Vallone, of Doberdò, of flight-level 265, of the Veliki and the Faiti.[6] Having to wear a bandage over one eye was cumbersome and a terrible bother during aerial duty. Thus I grounded myself for a few months. I had difficulty gauging the unevenness of the rough Carso terrain. Continually struggling, in my crude hobnail boots, to reestablish "lateral equilibrium" through the jagged rocks, the red mud of the trenches, and the tunnels, I thought of an old Italian motto that seemed to fit my efforts: *Senz'ali non può*— Without wings, it's not possible.[7] I would fall and get back up. One evening I arrived at Vallone from Faiti with my hip and knees bloodied. I started out again in the company of an unknown foot-soldier who held me by the hand. And the same man who in times of cowardice had sung of heroes was, in times of valor, celebrated by a hero in a song of vindication.

The yellowish stain covering the chin, mouth, and nose of any face I gazed upon was a lugubrious thing. When, just before a mission, I would take leave of a comrade heading into danger by a different route, the yellowness I saw seemed to presage dissolution; and I did not know how to defend myself from the sinister omen. But as night began to fall, the stain would change into rings of light, floating haloes. Thus one evening I happened to be leaning over a wounded man whom I had seen off in the morning, having suffered that grim sign. When I took off his helmet, I saw the halo around his glorious head.

That halo has forever remained around my mother's head, around her sanctified beauty.

She never ceased appearing to me at the start and the climax of every mission. She no longer had that look of terrible forlornness that had so grieved me as I lay on my back in torment. She wore instead the resolute, courageous face of her adult years of misfortune and struggle.

One November evening, on the evening of Saint Charles's day, after the two victories on the two Calvaries, in the doline of La Bandiera, we were at table in a cave, belatedly celebrating All Saints' Day, when Colonel Perris, flower of valor and courtesy, gave me the gift of a bouquet of red roses that an unknown footsoldier had brought to him from I know not where, across the carnage and wilderness, for his name day.[8] It was like the "miracle of the blood."[9] We were stunned and speechless, as if we had never seen a fresh rose before. Then, in the darkness at the back of the cave, my mother appeared to me, beautiful again in her spirit, as if from beyond the grave.

Later, one evening in January—January 27, 1917—a messenger of Luigi Cadorna brought the terrible news to my bedside, to which I had retired with a high fever. I got up, wrapped myself in my aviator's furs, and departed. Through snow and ice and fever I retraced the same steps I had taken that March before my exile. I crossed the Tronto again. I saw the mouths of the small rivers again. Along the coastal road I saw the oxen again, and the carts and the donkey man driving his beast of burden. I passed under the brick arch again. And I pushed open my half-closed door. I smelled the terrible scent of flowers. The staircase was full of them. The first room was full of them.

And there was the coffin.

During my nights of atonement, had I not contemplated "death dressed in I know not what heavenly modesty"? Had I not thought of the art of that god who, on the newborn day, "shall refashion the faces of his elect in the image of his own recondite beauty"?

She was even more beautiful than her apparition in the cave, more beautiful than any human being I have known in all my years. Her face was refashioned according to the traits of her soul. Therefore her soul could not have departed. It was still there, burning at the summit of her consumed body, like the small flame at the top of a candle. And her consumption was not decomposition. After more than three days, she showed no sign or odor of impurity. She was preserved by the fragrance of her heart.

The people kneeling thought it was sainthood. They thought it was a miracle.

By the end of the fifth day, her body in the church appeared immune to the fate of the flesh, on full display to the eyes of the people who never tired of gazing upon her. The Mystic's "love without shape" and "goodness without shape" had assumed this form at the threshold of eternity. Death thus was no longer a dark passage between two lights, but the bright conjunction of two lights.

And so it was for me, from that point forward.

The sealing of the coffin, the lowering into the grave, the rite of burial seemed to me but impositions of custom. Atop the mound of earth we planted a crude cross made of the main rib and beam of an old *trabàccolo* sailboat of ours: a crude, black cross covered with tar.

But from the stone of our mountains we shall cut gigantic

statues of the nine mantled Muses, who under broad, columnar folds shall suffer the passion of future beauty; and we shall erect them to support the round sacrarium into which the humble heroine will be translated. And she shall welcome me into the same tomb. She shall take with her the part of me that will perish, and the part of me that shall never die.

To her I owe, in this harshest of wars, my loftiest hours of perfect peace. With the dark transit between two lights effaced, every departure for the most desperate of missions was the start of an ecstasy comparable to none but that of the rarest of spirits who hurl themselves toward the mystical apex of life and attain it.

O night raid on Pola! O Franciscan night of Cattaro![10] Overseas crossings fulfilling a vow forever renewed!

It is written, in one of my flight logs: "I am so full of life that, when I lean out from the prow, I feel I am overflowing."

Then came the great winged exploit, the following May, over the assault of the infantry; and the dominion achieved in the skies over Mount Hermada, and the mournful Pentecost on the Timavo. And then came the other names etched in the votive tablet: the Sky of the North Adriatic, the Sky of the Carso, the Mouths of the Cattaro, the Bay of Buccari, the Daytime Bombings of Pola, the Sky of Vienna, the Sky of the Piave,[11] the March from Ronchi, the Capture of Fiume,[12] the Zara Expedition, the Defense of Fiume, the Return to silence and solitude.

We had taken up arms again, after the injustice of the armistice. Alone with the flower of the soldiery, I had chased the thieving Serbs and insolent allies from the city on the Carnaro. In the place of a city of traffic, I had founded a city of life, there to rekindle the fires that had died on the altar of the Fatherland and to resuscitate the images of Victory and Grandeur that had been struck down in the thick mud of Rome.

To prevent the city from being undone in the spiritual space in which I had raised its towers and beacons, fraternal blood had to spill. The inexpiable crime, the insuperable trench, had to cleave the new Italy from the old. We had to bear witness, with wounds and deaths and ruins, that the new Italy forever rejected all reconciliation, all contamination.

So I wished, and so have I done. The tragic will to sacrifice shall avail me in the eyes of generations to come. The drama of the Carnaro is but the drama of the whole nation.

In the open tumult I never thought more loftily than when deep within my closed spirit. A Bonaparte well knew that "courage comes from thought."

Thus was I able to overcome my aversions and consent to finish interpreting these sibylline pages, though I have not fully dispelled the doubt in me that it were better to cast them to the scattering winds.

"She laid these pages upon the altar; if the wind dispersed them, their words were without virtue or efficacy; but if they remained immobile, they were possessed of virtue, and efficacy."[13]

I do not lay them on the much-frequented altar. I go back into my deserted home where my mother, ever since she first removed her white bridal footwear, never once let the fire in the hearth go out, but renewed each night the art of burying under ash an ember, that it might last until the new day. And all the people knew this art, and all the people remember it.

I go back into my home; I pass from room to room; I climb the three steps and enter the fifth room. The vast bed fills the space, the bed in which I was conceived and begotten, in which *I was well born.* Upon the pillow that held my mother's holy face transfigured as perpetual beauty, I lay the pages of my passion and devotion, *that they may remain immobile there.*

My effort as interpreter and transcriber was very painful. Too often I felt as if I were reopening my innermost wounds and working inside them with a surgeon's precision tools. Too often I felt as if powerful ghosts were leaping at my throat and strangling me. Unable to overcome an almost bodily fear, more than once I interrupted and abandoned a sheaf of paper strips.

Yet how prescience enlightens my aspiration! The unarmed spirit seems already to venture where it will later venture when armed. Words spring from the silence that will later rise to my living lips to rally my comrades and followers. And do not the "three planks of the bridge," where the Thirty of Buccari shall huddle together, already vibrate in one of my musical imaginings?[14] And does not the rhythm that will become the ideal law of the fighter back in the "forge in which the new substance is being smelted" return in the nocturnal refrain?

And only one constellation
for the soul alone:
the Good Cause.

And in that fiction of the river and the ford, recounted to console myself and the hero riveted to the ground, is there not a sort of premonition of the riverbank in which we later planted victory, "mutilated and bloody, against the invader"?

The Easter dialogue between glory's chosen and death's malcontent was not in vain. I saw Oreste Salomone again, there on the field in Puglia, on the eve of the bombing of Cattaro. He had come back, anxious to give himself again, persecuted and thwarted by sedentary souls. He asked me to take him into my crew, even in the place of the aft-turret machine gunner. I was unable to overcome the obstacles put up, and he remained grounded, wrathful and humbled.

Then, one night, on a test flight by starlight with one of my Cattaro faithful, the white lancer Mariano d'Ayala, Oreste lost his life due to manual error while landing on the airfield at Padua. And along with his life the top of a beautiful tree was felled.

Light a fire for him each year on Mount Vulture!

The battle's last eagles fall one by one. On the same lagoon bottom in which Giuseppe Miraglia had fallen, Luigi Bologna also broke his wings and bones one clear morning last September. In the same death chamber in Sant'Anna hospital where together we kept vigil over our comrade from the first war, I raised a corner of the flag and recognized the same strong face that, on the day of Parenzo, had turned toward me with a gesture not unlike that of farewell.

And the day before yesterday, my extremely daring pilot, the pilot of the first naval squadron of torpedo bombers, the pilot of the San Marco squadron, which included my beautiful Sparrowhawk SIA 9B, Luigi Garrone, fell when within sight of the Isonzo, which no longer drags the bodies of the dead, but dashed hopes, out to sea.

Never again shall I see his sickly face under the straight hair, his pale, contemplative eyes, and all that quasi-feminine frailty which his bladelike energy enclosed as in a sheath of glass. But I do see him clearly again in that sudden, soaring pull-up into the sun and sky over Mount Grappa, between the four explosive shells in the front and back of the wings of our Sparrowhawk. And I see him again returning from the bombing and reconnaissance along the Piave, that evening when the searchlights had not yet come on over the field of San Nicolò and we crashed to our ruin against the cement runway and walked away from the wreckage unscathed. I see him again in the October offensive, on one of our two daily sorties, when the bomb-laden aircraft veered wildly on the runway, not responding to the controls, and smashed with all its load into the embankment of an artillery battery and miraculously burst apart without exploding. Despite the collision I heard the terrified cries of my drill squad, gathered together for the *alalà*,[15] and as I turned around I caught a glimpse of them with hands over their eyes in a gesture of horror, and found myself in the machine gun circle beside my companion, smiling as he removed a crumb of earth and a blade of grass from his gaunt cheek.

On the same day three years later, perhaps at the same hour, luck abandoned him. And in a place where the memory of heroism has since vanished, in a place without spirit, his scornful heroism was cut down.

One goal at a time, one death at a time. And beyond.

As I was sadly transcribing the example of that unnamed peasant entering the ford and kneeling in the middle of the stream, etching his sacrifice into the water itself, inside the basilica of Aquilea a grieving mother was choosing, from eleven nameless coffins, the one that would be lowered into the monument.

In my mind I imagined her looking like the Mary in the Crypt, who with her slender, divine hands holds the sorrow of all creatures aloft, aflame in her head as in an eternal lamp. How many centuries of our misfortune, how many Italian centuries of suffering and patience, how many centuries of iniquity and servitude wept within her?

And why was the bier of the Great Martyr not draped in the flag of the Timavo, the one in my care, called the "shroud of sacrifice" and the "footsoldier's banner," the one that was spread over the coffins of my dead from Fiume, lined up one beside the other on the ground?[16]

What first remained was the effigy of only one dead hero; but it is now the image of all the dead, for those who have died for the Fatherland all resemble one another in the Fatherland just as Giovanni Randaccio in his stone sarcophagus resembles the unknown foot soldier laid between four planks of wood.

Indeed, today he removes the halo of glory from his head and offers it up to the nameless. Just as he decided one day, when alive on this earth, out of humility toward the thousands and thousands of unknown heroes, to remove the sky-blue insignia from his chest. And I did the same.

Last night I gave mine to the flames.

O Aquileia, did not your antistes, the pure man the Lord sent to guard you, see my mother descend over your cypresses in the form of a snow-white dove?

So he told me. It was May 15, 1917.

The basilica, too, was wounded. And it saw God's sky through the gash. The splinters of the rafters, the rubble and shards of glass cluttered the Roman flagstones. And another suffering was added to the suffering of the Christ sculpted by a soldier who was left buried under the debris and rose again after four days like Lazarus.

I headed towards the cemetery. Giovanni's bier lay beside the baptistry, still empty, neglected. Behind the ancient cypresses young laurels were coming to leaf; and in the enclosure wall, which looks out onto the countryside, the tenacious ivy rejuvenated.

The day was waning. The cannon thundered at Monfalcone and throughout the valley. Soot and smoke covered the mountains of wrath. A few spans from the wall, between grassy banks bristling with willows, flowed the bright Natissa in which the four martyrs of Christ were drowned: Euphemia, Dorothea, Thecla, and Erasma.

The banks were painted with flowers both yellow and white. Along the grassy edge was a strip of tilled land. Side by side the furrows followed the course of the stream. Low flying swallows seemed to imitate the work of the ploughshare. Emitting their cries, they turned about and swiftly ploughed without plough.

Behind me the graves lay silent, like somebody holding his breath. And an evening nightingale intoned its ode to the lengthening shadows.

Then I saw a gray soldier approach along the bank, poorer than God's Pauper, feet bare in his clogs, trousers torn at the knees, tunic worn at the elbows.[17] He looked as if he were of a single color, so much did his clothing blend with his skin. His head was bandaged white.

He was carrying a square fishing net suspended from a rod by four stays.

He chose a spot and settled in. Then he lowered his net into the Natissa and waited with his impoverished face bent towards the water, not breathing, unaware that the water was sanctified by an ancient martyrdom.

Perhaps his heart knew.

Thecla, Erasma, Euphemia, and Dorothea prayed for him.

The water was clear by the right bank, and bronze by the left, green like the bronze of sacred doors. The pruned poplars had new leaves on their blunted branches, similar to misshapen candelabra awaiting votive candles to illuminate martyrdom's river. And the swallows continued to plough; and as the land darkened, they brightened it with the white of their breasts.

The fisherman stood there, immobile, rod in hand, gazing at the water, patient. He caught nothing.

Thecla, Erasma, Euphemia and Dorothea prayed for him.

He bestirred himself and pulled the empty net out of the water, walking backwards. He chose another spot, lowered the box again, resumed his patient pose, and waited.

No divine voice had said to him: "Cast your net again. Do not despair."

Little by little the noises faded. The boom of the faraway

cannon was like the dull rumble of a storm. From each grave a column of glorious silence rose to meet the stars' first tears.

The nightingale's ode accompanied the ascension with a rapturous force greater than the skylark's solar delirium.

Death was singing, life was singing. *O mors, ero mors tua.*[18]

Behind me were the graves of two boys of my acquaintance, two first fruits of the offering: the grave of Lapo Niccolini Alamanni and that of Corradino Lanza d'Aieta. I picked an old laurel leaf and a new one; and I broke them as though following a ritual. The old one was more fragrant; but the new one, damp with sap, promised the water that slakes keen yearnings.

I could no longer leave. Night was falling. The swallows had ceased their ploughing. Between the black cypresses the Latin basilica had turned an ironlike color, as if entirely dressed in armor, and saying of its wound: *Non dolet.* It does not hurt.

The unknown foot soldier said nothing of his own wound. But his arms were beginning to tremble.

He raised the net from the water. Set the rod on the grass. He knelt and bent forward to rinse his hands.

And the bell tolled the Angelus.

For a while the prayer dominated the hymn. Then it seemed as if the nightingale caught the last tremor of solemn bronze to storm the heavens with a more fervent melody.

The poor fisher had made the sign of the cross; he had removed his clogs and sat down at the edge of the stream, his poor feet dangling, skimming martyrdom's water.

Dorothea, Thecla, Erasma, and Euphemia prayed for him.

He sat there with head bowed; on his left were his pair of clogs, on his right, the empty square net. And the rents in his trousers revealed bony knees.

He raised his face towards God's singing creature.

He took his bandaged head in his hands, and towards the song raised a gaunt face that surely resembled that of God's Pauper in the grace of rapture.

What anguish rose up from his human depths to darken that radiant goodness?

Again he took his bandaged head in his hands, as though the wound had reopened. And he cast his face down again, towards martyrdom's waters. He seemed to be crying.

Then from the water came the four martyrs, and they kissed his poor feet.

Last night that nameless, graveless foot soldier was with us at the crossing of three roads, and there we lit the fire for him.

The Little Pauper of Italy was of a single color, as if his God had remodeled him in the clay of the Piave. And the flame was of a single splendor.

We had made a bed for the embers with five stones arranged in a circle. A peasant from the hills and his young son helped to pile bundle upon bundle of wood. We burned olive and hornbeam and cypress. But in the hollow space between the stones I had placed a good firebrand of oak, in memory of my hearth.

We crouched round the fire, in silence.

Only the soldier and the flame were standing.

The flame was beautiful, and the soldier in his divine poverty was beyond all beauty.

The flame roared, and the soldier pressed his lips together.

All the fires of my sere and sterile blindness never roused me to such passion as did that fire on the ground.

When the bundles had burnt up and we had gathered the vine shoots and sticks around us to burn them all, I took my armful of laurels and threw them onto the embers.

We remained in suspense, watching, listening.

The laurel threatened, then burst into flame with magnanimous rage.

We all shone with its light, were dazzled by it, ravished by it.

Now the unknown soldier had no body but this.

And the voice that had called Lazarus, this same voice said to the pauper who had cast his net into martyrdom's stream in vain: "Fear not. Hereafter thou shalt be a fisher of living men, or spirit."

Then, when even the laurel was consumed by flame, and my people had left, and the crossing of the three roads was deserted, I rediscovered my mother's art of placing the end of the firebrand under the embers.

"Suso in Italia bella"[19]

G. d'A.
November 4, 1921[20]

What follows is the transcription of one complete string of "scrolls," the narrow strips of paper on which the blindfolded poet composed the short sentences later recast in Notturno (Archivio Personale del Vittoriale, LXXIX, 4; no. 1639, cc. 22503–30; fasc. IV).

yearning for immortality. I have never
theless a song deep in the
tempered heart
The sun sets beyond the
bend in the canal that is now gre
en like the speaking laurel. The bells
fall silent, but the air seems to trem
ble awaiting their angel-
ic sound. My covered eye is full
of luminous wisteria; but the other
one, now out of the habit, daydreams.
Outside of time, a harmony slowly takes
wing. Coré's house is
but a vast garland sup-
ported by the heads of the lions lean-

ing over the water. From Palazzo Dario
to the Church of the Salute, brick and
stone in the roseate light turn al
most fleshly. The façades lean
one against the other, like wo-
men supporting one another to
keep from falling, invaded
by the sudden languor of April.
A large black boat, loaded
with brilliant sulfur, propelled
by long oars, passes like
a portentous apparition.

It has an antique, broad-
blade rudder with a long helm

shaft held by a man who looks like
a Phoenician steersman.

The sulfur assumes an indescrib-
able hue as it enters the shade. That

yellow has the power of an
unexpected motif that suddenly lifts

a waning symphony
to sublime heights. An odd silence

arises in me. I no longer
hear the swallows. And my heart
beats with the dread that a peal-

ing might interrupt this
soundless music.

The text of *Notturno* is a veritable thicket of literary allusions and echoes, historical references both ancient and contemporary, and invocations of myth, art, and scripture. What follows is a basic guide to the most important of these many references, so that reader may more fully appreciate the richness of D'Annunzio's culture and grasp some of the meanings hidden in the poetic shorthand he often uses to express this culture. For many of these of notes I am greatly indebted to the Italian D'Annunzio scholar Elena Ledda, whose massive apparatus of notes to the 1995 Garzanti edition of *Notturno* constitutes the most exhaustive annotation of this text to date.

The translations of the quoted passages of Dante and other authors in these notes are my own.

Stephen Sartarelli

First Offering

1. *Et in tenebris/Aegri somnia:* Lat., "And in darkness"/"Dreams of the sick one."

2. *burns like Dante's paper, as the brown slowly effaces the words on it:* Cf. Dante, *Inf.* XXV, 63–65: "come procede innanzi da l'ardore/per lo papiro suso un color bruno/che non è nero ancora e 'l bianco more" ("the way before the flame/a brown color moves over the paper/that is not yet black, as the whiteness dies").

3. *Per non dormire:* It., "So as not to sleep."

4. *Vincenzo Gemito:* Gemito (1852–1929) was a prominent Neapolitan sculptor about whom D'Annunzio had written on several occasions.

5. *killing my comrade:* Namely, Giuseppe Miraglia, D'Annunzio's young copilot on a variety of missions before the one alluded to here. His

death, and the poet's response to it, are among the principal subjects of *Notturno*.

6. *the way the milk of the goddess gleams eternally white in the night*: In Greek myth, the Milky Way was created from the milk spilt by Hera, Queen of the Gods, when suckling Heracles.

7. *the dead man who stares at me with embers for eyes*: An echo of Dante's "Caron dimonio con occhi di bragia" ("the demon Charon with eyes of ember"), especially as D'Annunzio uses the archaic *bragia*, instead of *brace*, for "ember." *Inf.* III, 109.

8. *My comrade lies on the island of the dead*: Giuseppe Miraglia is buried on the island of San Michele, the "cemetery island" of the Venetian lagoon, known in Venice as the "island of the dead."

9. *Cinerina*: La Cinerina was a nickname of American painter Romaine Brooks (1874–1970), recalling the dominant ash-gray tones of her pictures. (For more on Brooks's relationship with D'Annunzio, see the references provided by Elena Ledda on p. 21, note 2, of the *Notturno* edition cited above. Subsequent citations of Ledda's annotations will henceforth be abbreviated to EL, with relevant page and note numbers.)

10. *two men "inside a fire," but the fire is not divided. [. . .] And they needed no brief exhortation to make them eager*: Dante, *Inf.* XXVI, ll. 52–54: "chi è in quel foco che vien sì diviso/di sopra, che par surger de la pira/dov'Eteocle col fratel fu miso?" ("Who is in that fire, which is so divided/on top that it seems to rise from the pyre/where Eteocles was laid with his brother?") And Dante, *Inf.* XXVI, ll. 119–23: "Li miei compagni fec'io sì aguti/con questa orazion piccola, al cammino,/che a pena poscia li avrei ritenuti" (With this brief exhortation I made/my companions so eager for the journey/that after I could hardly restrain them.")

11. *sack of messages*: On several of these flying missions over majority-Italian cities under Austrian rule, such as Trieste, D'Annunzio would scatter leaflets, written by himself, with messages to the population to stand fast, for they would soon be liberated.

12. *Beppino*: That is, Miraglia. Beppino is a diminutive for Giuseppe.

13. *The young Veronese's physical type*: That is, the physical type of Bresciani, who was from the Verona region.

14. *the Lions sent as a gift to the Republic by Francesco Morosini*:

Morosini (1618–1694), who was doge of Venice from 1688–94, famously defeated the Turks when Captain-General of the Venetian fleet, seizing the islands of the Pelopponese and several cities in the Morea. In 1687, he sent the famous "Arsenal Lions" to Venice, where they remain to this day, outside the main gate of the Arsenale shipyards. (EL, p. 53, n. 1)

15. *the bas-relief of Zara:* The baroque façade of the Church of Santa Maria del Giglio features, at the base of the pilasters, bas-reliefs of a number of Italian cities, including Bologna and Padova, as well as Dalmatian towns which were formerly part of the Venetian empire, such as Zara and Spalato (now called Zadar and Split), and are now part of Croatia. The missions of the aerial squadrons of which D'Annunzio was part around the time of the events recounted in this book included the reconnaissance and bombing of these towns in the attempt, ultimately unsuccessful, to recapture these Austro-Hungarian cities for Italy.

16. *Pola:* Pola (Pula in Croatian) was a majority-Italian city in Istria on the eastern Adriatic shore which, after Napoleon, had fallen into Austrian hands, and which the military effort of which D'Annunzio was part intended to recapture. Pola did indeed rejoin the Kingdom of Italy after World War I and until 1943 but was finally ceded to Yugoslavia in the settlements the followed the end of World War II, leading to a mass exodus of ethnic Italians.

17. *peate:* A kind of Venetian barge.

18. *the wooden bridge:* The Ponte dell'Accademia, the only wooden bridge over the Grand Canal.

19. *sandalo:* A flat-bottomed rowboat.

20. *Rosalinda:* Miraglia's woman.

21. *palazzo of the Lions:* Called the "truncated house" (*casa mozza*) later in this text (see p. 238), this building was the residence of the Marchesa Luisa Amman Casati Stampa. Nicknamed "Corè" by D'Annunzio (see the Third Offering of the present book), the marchesa was a flamboyant socialite who became friends with D'Annunzio in 1902 and remained close to him until the end. See also Third Offering, note 2. (EL, p. 66, n. 1)

Second Offering

1. *Carso . . . Tarnova . . . Isonzo:* The author is recalling his flight over the region of Friuli in northeastern Italy. In WWI the "Carso," the great

limestone plateau between the eastern Friuli and western Slovenia, was the site of pitched battles between Italian and Austrian forces, and it was in the Isonzo region that the famous battle of Caporetto took place in October 1917, when Italian forces were severely routed by the Austrians.

2. *the brown relic that quickly turns back into fiery liquid in its vial:* A reference to the "miracle" of San Gennaro, a thrice-annual ritual in the Neapolitan cathedral of the same name, in which the saint's supposed blood, inside its two vials, usually liquefies before the waiting congregation. Liquefaction bodes good fortune, while failure to liquefy presages hard times ahead.

3. *the evening of the Campidoglio:* On the evening of May 17, 1915, D'Annunzio delivered an historic speech "from the balustrade of the Campidoglio," as it is called ("Dalla ringhiera del Campidoglio"), exhorting the Italians to make war, after Italy had secretly agreed to the London Pact a month earlier. (EL, p. 77, n. 1)

4. *my exile:* D'Annunzio is alluding to the years he spent in France, from spring 1910 to spring 1915, when he fled to escape his creditors in Italy. He will make repeated reference to this period throughout the text of *Notturno.* (For more about this period, cf. EL, p. 77, n. 2 and *passim.*)

5. *Marcus Aurelius' green horse:* The famous ancient Roman equestrian bronze that used to stand at the center of Michelangelo's Piazza del Campidoglio. It was replaced by a copy after the original was attacked, without significant damage, by political extremists in 1979.

6. *Nino Bixio:* A fervent *garibaldino* whose feats in the wars for Italian unification became legend, Bixio (1821–1873) was one of the organizers of Garibaldi's "Expedition of the Thousand," which wrested control of southern Italy from the Bourbon crown.

7. *the mother of the two Tribunes:* Daughter of Publius Cornelius Scipio Africanus, Cornelia (Africana) became famous for having raised her two sons Tiberius Gracchus and Gaius Gracchus, who became Tribunes of the plebs, to love their country to the point of sacrifice. The Romans erected a statue to her, and it is in reference to this that D'Annunzio speaks of the women of the people as "sculpted." (EL, p. 80, n. 1)

8. *the red flag of Trieste:* Trieste at this time remained one of the *città irredente,* one of the cities "unredeemed" by the Italian republic, and was

thus a motive for making war against the Austro-Hungarian empire, which still ruled it.

9. *decuman surge:* In Pliny, a *decumani fluctus,* or decuman wave or surge, is the tenth in a series of waves and arrives with a force "greater than the nine preceding waves and greater than the nine subsequent." (EL, p. 81, n. 1)

10. *Freedom's hill:* The Aventine hill in Rome has been associated with liberty since ancient times. The Icilian law of 456 BC gave theAventine to the ancient plebs. (EL, p. 82, n. 1)

11. *the pierced door through which so many eyes fix their gaze upon the airy Dome through the palm trees:* The "airy Dome" is the cupola of St. Peter's, and, thanks to a remarkable bit of geometrical and architectural engineering, through the keyhole of this door one can glimpse Michelangelo's dome in the distance, in perfect perspective.

12. *five ambiguous summers in the extreme West:* Another reference to D'Annunzio's "exile" in southwestern France from 1910 to 1915. Since that region is on the far western shores of Europe, D'Annunzio refers to it as the *estremo Occidente,* as a Western counterpart to the *estremo Oriente,* as the Italians call the Far East. I could not, however, translate *estremo Occidente* as "Far West," as this might create a false association with the Far West of the United States. I have therefore chosen to call it the "extreme West."

13. *the myth of Aetolia. When will my own mother put me back in her hearth to be consumed?:* D'Annunzio here sees himself as Meleager, son of Althaea and Oeneus, king of Caledonia. When Meleager was seven years old, the Moirae (Fates) predicted that he would die the moment a brand was consumed in the hearth. Althaea removed the brand and preserved it. During the expedition of the Argonauts, Meleager took part in the hunt for the boar of Caledonia. During the chase, he killed his two maternal uncles. In revenge, Althaea placed the brand back in the fire, and Meleager died.

14. *the Lande of my exile:* After fleeing first to Paris (see note 4 to the present Offering, above), D'Annunzio went to live in Arcachon, a town on an Atlantic inlet on France's western coast. The bay of Arcachon lies at the northwestern corner of a vast triangular area the French traditionally call

la Grande-Lande, the "great moorland" or "wasteland," which is situated between the Atlantic coast and the Garonne and Adour rivers. (Administratively the area known as the Grande-Lande is somewhat smaller.) Originally a broad, flat expanse of heaths, with low, scrubby vegetation, it was reforested in the early modern era. With the present and subsequent references, D'Annunzio is referring to this general area when he uses the term "la Landa," which I have translated as "the Lande," though the reader should bear in mind the Italian and French terms' symbolic implications of "wasteland" as well.

15. *campiello:* Venetian dialect for "small square."

16. *Imbres effugio . . . Fons signatus, Hortus conclusus . . . Onustior humilior, Tantummodo fulcimentum:* The first phrase means "I flee the rain." The second, "sealed fountain" and "enclosed garden"; originally drawn from the Song of Solomon, IV, 12, both the *Fons signatus* and *Hortus conclusus* symbolized the Blessed Virgin's purity in medieval Christian iconology. The *Hortus conclusus* was also the concept behind the monastic cloister and was supposed to be a microcosm of Paradise. The third phrase above means "The more burdened I am, the more am I humbled," and "Only a support," respectively.

17. *Archbishop Ubaldo's Camposanto was closed, huddled in silence round its fifty-three ship-holds of soil from Calvary:* The Camposanto, or "holy field," is the monumental cemetery in the cathedral complex of Pisa, where many of the local civil, military, and religious notables were buried over several centuries. According to legend, the Camposanto was founded in the twelfth century when Archbishop Ubaldo de' Lanfranchi returned from the Second Crusade with many ships laden with "sacred soil" from Mount Calvary, which was then transposed into Pisan ground. The actual construction of the Camposanto was begun in 1277. Architecturally it consists of a cloistered quadrangle of marble, with delicate Gothic tracery articulating the arcade; the outside walls on the Piazza present blind marble arcades. The tombs lie along and inside the cloister's inner walls, which were decorated with major fresco cycles in the fourteenth and fifteenth centuries. (See note 18.)

18. *And our music had the face of the woman in a dress leaning forward:* A reference to the Camposanto's famous fresco of *The Triumph of Death*

(1336–1341), by Buonamico Buffalmacco. The woman with the psaltery is part of a group of young ladies in a garden who appear placid and un-harmed amidst the apocalyptic destruction, though Death with its scythe looms over them. D'Annunzio's specification that she is "in a dress" is perhaps due to the fact that many of the dead and damned in the painting are naked. And her "face," to which he likens "our music," wears a playful, slightly mocking and intense expression, as she looks out at the viewer

19. *Ghìsola:* The nickname of Eleonora Duse (1859–1924), the great Italian actress of the stage and silent screen, with whom D'Annunzio had an intense and very public relationship.

20. *Vide cor meum:* Lat., "Look at my heart." Dante, *Vita nuova,* III, XXII.

21. *"What my son? . . . that which destroys kings":* Proverbs, XXXI, 2–3: "What, my son? And what, the son of my womb? And what, the son of my vows? Give not thy strength unto women, nor thy ways to that which destroyeth kings." (King James Version)

22. *let me regain what I have given:* A self-conscious echo of the motto written over the entrance to D'Annunzio's estate, the Vittoriale: "I have what I have given."

23. *Ausa:* The river that marked the boundary between Italy and Aus-tria from 1866 to 1915.

24. *under a rain of fire, liked the damned in the third circle. [. . .] And I cannot beat back the burning with a "dance of wretched hands":* The damned in the third circle of Dante's *Inferno* (XIV, 40) are the violent. The "dance of wretched hands" is from *Inf.* XIV, 40–42: "Sanza riposo mai era la tresca/de le misere mani, or quindi or quinci/escotendo da sé l'arsura fresca." ("The dance of the wretched hands/was ever without pause, now here, now there/beating back the fresh burning.")

25. *"mad flight":* D'Annunzio quotes the exact words used by Dante, *"folle volo,"* to characterize Ulysses' final voyage. *Inf.* XXVI, 125: "de' remi facemmo ali al folle volo" ("we made our oars wings for the mad flight"). The phrase is repeated elsewhere in *Notturno* to evoke literal flying.

26. *Né dolcezza di figlio . . . Nor a son's fondness:* Dante, *Inf.* XXVI, 94. The quote is from Ulysses' speech in the *Inferno,* in which the hero lists the family ties that failed to keep him from setting out to sea: "Né dolcezza

di figlio, né la pieta/del vecchio padre, né 'l debito amore/lo qual dovea
Penelopè far lieta,/vincer poter dentro a me l'ardore/ch'i' ebbi a divenir
del mondo esperto . . ." It is curious to note that D'Annunzio's reading of
né dolcezza di figlio is at odds with the standard reading of this line in the
English translations of Dante. Just before the quote, D'Annunzio writes,
"Why did my love of destiny prevail over my filial love?" He thus inter-
prets *dolcezza di figlio* as the love *of* the son for the parent, not that of the
parent *for* the son, as is the case in the Longfellow, Mandelbaum, Sin-
gleton, and Ciardi translations, among others. I have therefore preserved
D'Annunzio's reading, or misreading, as the case may be, in my transla-
tion of the line: "Nor a son's fondness . . ."

27. *this Great Mother:* That is, Italy.

28. *And being, to my bitter regret, "like those who cannot move"* . . . :
"You are dead.": Variations on a passage of Dante, *Vita nuova*, XXIII, 1: "A
few days thereafter it happened that a painful infirmity struck a certain
part of my body, whereby I suffered terrible aches continually for nine
days; and this made me so weak, that I was forced to remain *like those who
cannot move.*" (My emphasis.) And XXIII, 4: " . . . and as my imagination
began to wander, faces of disheveled women appeared to me, saying: '*You
too shall die.*'" (My emphasis.) (Cf. EL, p. 122, n. 2.)

29. *the Swabian sultan:* That is, Frederick II of Hohenstaufen (1194–
1250), "Stupor Mundi," Holy Roman Emperor and King of Sicily.

30. *the "flower of Syria":* A quotation from the canzone "Oi lasso, nom
pensai," attributed to Frederick II by E. Monaci, in *Crestomazia italiana
dei primi secoli* (Città di Castello: Lapi, 1912), 74. (EL, p. 124, n. 1)

31. *the Bovolo staircase:* An external spiral staircase in the courtyard of
the Palazzo Contarini del Bovolo in Venice. Built in the late fifteenth
century, it takes the form of a cylindrical tower reminiscent of the Tower of
Pisa. ("Bovolo" is Venetian dialect for "snail.")

32. *the sleep of Ilaria in her tomb at Lucca:* A reference to the early-
Renaissance *gisant* tomb sculpture of Ilaria del Carretto, by Jacopo della
Quercia (1374–1438), in Lucca Cathedral.

33. *as the Mystic would say:* The "Mystic" is Jacopone da Todi (ca.
1236–1306), a Franciscan friar and one of Italy's first vernacular poets.

34. *"The façade of the house is already all dressed up in green like Ornella"*: An allusion to the lines of Ornella in D'Annunzio's play, *La Figlia di Iorio:* "Tutta di verde mi voglio vestire/Tutta di verde per Santo Giovanni/ch'in mezzo al verde mi venne a ferire" ("I want to dress up all in green,/All in green for Saint John,/who came through the green to wound me"). (*Tragedie sogni e misteri*, I, Atto I, scena I, ll. 6–7.) (EL, p. 128, n. 2)

35. *Florentine chancel [. . .] Luca's living marble:* D'Annunzio is referring to the chancel (*cantorìa*) sculpted by Luca della Robbia (1400–1482), in the Museo di Santa Maria del Fiore in Florence, in which cherubs beat drums.

36. *"Io vedo pur con l'uno"*: Dante, *Inf.* XXVIII, 85: "Quel traditor che vede pur con l'uno" ("That traitor who still can see with only one.")

37. *traghetto:* In Venice, a gondola that affords passage at various points across the Grand Canal.

38. *"Ah, alas, my child! Irish girl, you wild, adorable girl!"*: The last lines sung by the unknown sailor to open scene I of Wagner's *Tristan und Isolde:* "Weh, ach wehe, mein Kind!/Irische Maid,/du wilde, minnige Maid!"

39. *the foam from which the Voluptas of mortals and immortals was born:* In other words, Venus. D'Annunzio's phrasing and imagery echo the opening of Lucretius's *De rerum natura:* "Aeneadum genitrix/hominumque divumque voluptas." (EL, p. 164, n. 2)

40. *Impavido; and the destroyer and the entire crew and I all have the same true name: Impavido* means "fearless."

41. *And wherever the sì is heard, the whole sea belongs to Dante: Inferno,* XXXIII, 80: "del bel paese là dove 'l sì suona." The "beautiful land where the *sì* is heard" is, of course, Italy, and D'Annunzio here invokes Dante to assert the "Italianness" of those cities on the eastern shore of the Adriatic in most of which the majority of the population was, at the time, ethnically Italian and Italian-speaking. In the Middle Ages, the dialects of Italy were called the language of *sì*, French the language of *oïl* (which later evolved into the modern *oui*), and the dialects of what is now southern France the language of *oc*.

42. *the Libyan hero:* Umberto Cagni led the occupation of Tripoli when Italy conquered Libya in 1912. D'Annunzio dedicated a "Canzone" to him in *Merope*. (EL, p. 175, n. 1)

43. *"the cold orb of all daring"*: A self-quote by D'Annunzio from "La Canzone dei Dardanelli," l. 307, in the *Merope* cycle (1912), the fourth book of his *Laudi* tetralogy. All of the phrases set off in quotes (apart from dialogue) or in italics on this page and the following, up to "vie for victory," are from the same cycle, in which D'Annunzio fully embraced the martial style that was later to be seen as a decline from the lyric heights attained in *Alcyone* (1903), the third book of *Laudi*. (For more on Cagni and the *Merope* cycle, cf. EL, p. 175, n. 1 and *passim*.)

44. *Mario Bianco:* An Abbruzzese sailor about whom D'Annunzio wrote a poem, "La canzone di Mario Bianco," in *Merope*. While overseeing the unloading of two cannons near Benghazi during the Italian attack, Bianco was surprised from behind by a host of Turks and Arabs and shot in the groin. Though losing a great deal of blood, he continued to rally his sailors before falling into a trench. (EL, p. 177, n. 10)

45. A *skylark soars in space, singing, never sated:* Cf. Dante, *Paradiso*, ll. 73–75, where the skylark is in fact sated: "questa lodoletta che in aere si spazia/prima cantando, e poi tace/dell'ultima dolcezza si sazia." ("That skylark that soars in space/first singing, then falling silent/sated with ultimate sweetness.")

46. *"Take them, God, for I hurl them at you!"*: A direct quote of Dante, *Inf.* XXV, 3: "Togli, Dio, che a te le squadro."

47. *beaver, "which is both beast and fish"*: D'Annunzio draws his definition of the animal from a fourteenth-century poem by Fazio degli Uberti (ca. 1306–ca. 1370), the *Dittamondo*. (EL, p. 183, n. 2)

48. *Titian's painting:* The painting of Titian cited and described here by D'Annunzio is *Venus and the Organ Player*, at the Prado Museum in Madrid.

49. *as if towards an expiatory chasm:* D'Annunzio is alluding to the story of Marcus Curtius, the young Roman cavalier who, according to legend, sacrificed himself for his country in 362 BC, throwing himself, arms and all, into a chasm that had opened up in the Roman Forum. According to the oracle, the chasm would close back up only after "what

was most precious to Rome" was thrown into it. As Livy tells the story, Rome at that time was at war with the Sabines, and Curtius decided that what was most precious to Rome were valor and arms. And so, armed from head to toe, he got on his horse and, at a full gallop, rode straight into the chasm. (EL, p. 196, n. 2)

50. *Aeschylus' brother:* That is, Cynegeirus, son of Euphorion. After he helped defeat the Persians at Marathon, the latter tried to board their ships and flee over the sea. Herodotus tells that Cynegeirus, after seizing an enemy vessel, had his hands cut off by an axe wielded by a Mede. (EL, p. 198, n. 2)

51. *Are the Salamanders singing?:* In medieval bestiaries and various esoteric traditions it was believed that salamanders could survive fire.

52. *Cybele without towers or lions:* Cybele was the "Great Mother" goddess of Phrygia, and her cult eventually spread throughout the ancient world, including Rome. Primarily a goddess of fertility, she also symbolized wild nature and was believed to protect her worshipers in times of war; thus two of the principal attributes with which she was often represented were lions and a crown of turreted walls on her head. The image here presented by D'Annunzio is that of the goddess celebrated on the March 22, the day of the Dendrophoria, when a long procession would carry the sacred tree, a pine, to the Temple of the Great Mother on the Capitoline Hill. The cult of Cybele had spread into mountainous areas, as a cult of the tree-goddess who oversaw the activities of the Roman "dendrophores" (carpenters, tree-cutters, firemen, etc. as well as those who carried the trees during sacred processions). (Cf. EL, p. 202, n. 1)

Third Offering

1. *the Canticle:* That is, the "Canticle of the Creatures," by St. Francis of Assisi, from which the phrase is quoted ("humele, pretiosa, et casta").

2. *Corè's garden:* Corè (Italian for Kore, another name for Persephone) was D'Annunzio's nickname for the Marchesa Luisa Amman Casati Stampa, who used to live in the "truncated house" visible from D'Annunzio's window. For more on the marchesa, see note 21, First Offering.

3. *Venier:* Venier D'Annunzio, Gabriele's third-born child by his wife Maria Hardouin di Gallese, born in Pescara in 1887. He took part in World

War I under the rank of lieutenant, later becoming a pilot and ultimately an aircraft designer for the Isotta Fraschini firm at their American office. He eventually became a U.S. citizen and died in New York in 1947. (EL, p. 223, n. 3)

4. *Arion's ship:* Arion was a Dionysiac poet of ancient Greece, credited with inventing the dithyramb, but he is chiefly known for the legend recounted by Herodotus in *Histories*, I, 23–24. Returning home by sea after winning a musical competition in Sicily, he was kidnapped by pirates eager to steal his winnings. When given the choice between suicide and burial on land, and being thrown overboard into the sea, Arion asked if he could sing one last song on his lyre. He sang a song of praise to Apollo, god of poetry, and the ship was soon encircled by dolphins. Throwing himself into the sea, he was saved by one of the dolphins, which carried him to safety at the sanctuary of Poseidon in Cape Taneiron, Greece.

5. *Bayram:* The Turkish word for "celebration" or "festival." Egypt was under Ottoman Turkish rule at the time of D'Annunzio's sojourn there.

6. *Khamsin:* A hot, dry wind that blows across the desert, bringing with it the reddish sand of the dunes.

7. *Aziyeh:* A village near Cairo.

8. *Rakush:* The horse of Rastem, in the *Shah Nameh* of Firdausi (940–1020 AD), the national epic poet of Greater Khorasan (and thus Iran), comprising parts of modern day Iran, Afghanistan, Turkmenistan, Uzbekistan, and Tajikistan. Also called Reksh.

9. *a Styx not allowed to bend:* In Greek mythology, the Styx, the river separating Hades, the Underworld, from the world of the living, winds round the Underworld nine times.

10. *on the night after All Saints' Day, when we would wait for it to bring us presents:* In parts of Italy, especially the South, on the night after All Saints' Day, that is, the eve of All Souls's Day—or, as they call it, The Day of the Dead (il Giorno dei Morti)—the souls of the dead are supposed to leave presents and sweets (called Dolci dei Morti) for children.

11. *O cessate di piagarmi . . . O lasciatemi morir:* The opening lines of an aria from *Il Pompeo* (1683), an opera by Alessandro Scarlatti. The lines mean "O stop wounding me/O let me die."

12. *Non so più cosa son cosa faccio . . . :* The opening line of the aria by

Cherubino in Mozart's *The Marriage of Figaro*. It means "I no longer know what I am or what I am doing." Cherubino is Count Almaviva's page.

13. *"The plastic of the first man . . . the first protoplast.":* Quoted from second page of the first volume of *Notizie de' Professori del Disegno da Cimabue in qua, opera divisa in secoli distinti per Decennali,* by the Florentine art historian Filippo Baldinucci (1624–1697). (EL, p. 260, n. 1)

14. *Et remotissima prope:* Literally, "faraway things are near."

15. *Prometheus the Fire-Bearer:* Aeschylus (525–456 BC), the early Greek dramaturge, is reputed to have written anywhere from seventy to ninety tragedies, of which only seven have survived. One of these, with some caveats from modern literary historians, is *Prometheus Bound,* about the Titan who was chained to a rock by Zeus for having brought fire to man. It is believed to have been the first part of a trilogy, of which the other two lost tragedies would be *Prometheus Unbound* and *Prometheus the Fire-Bearer.* D'Annunzio here imagines the latter of these two being brought to him.

16. *Here is Glaucus Marinus . . . the Niobean trilogy . . . the Theban trilogy . . . Shepherd of souls . . . Ixion . . . Sisyphus:* In this string of Aeschylean references, D'Annunzio appears to be thinking of the lost tragedy of *Glaucus Potniaeus* ("Glaucus of Potniae"), but his addition of "Marinus" points unmistakably to myth of the fisherman Glaucus (Ovid, *Metamorphoses,* XIII, *inter alia*), in an apparent conflation of the two Glauci by the poet, since Glaucus of Potniae could hardly be called "marinus." The "marine" Glaucus was in fact a fisherman who noticed one day that the fish he had caught in his nets were coming back to life when tossed onto the grass. Thinking this marvel due to the grass, he ate some and immediately felt the need to jump into the sea, whereupon he became immortal, turning into an oracular god of the sea. The prior mention of Aeschylus, who wrote a (now lost) tragedy of *Glaucus Potniaeus* ("Glaucus of Potnia") may have led D'Annunzio to think of Glaucus Marinus, though he is not the same Glaucus.

In the "Niobean trilogy," D'Annunzio appears to be imagining the existence of an Aeschylean "trilogy" on the myth of Niobe, probably on the basis of the surviving fragments of a tragedy of Niobe by the same

Greek playwright. Similarly, the "Theban trilogy" mentioned here apparently refers to another "lost trilogy" by Aeschylus, of which only the third part, *Seven Against Thebes*, is extant, the first two plays, *Laius* and *Oedipus*, having been lost.

The "Shepherd of souls" refers perhaps to Hermes Psychagogue (the aspect of Hermes that guides the souls of the dead to the Underworld), or, more simply, to Jesus Christ.

Ixion was king of the Lapiths. Invited to the table of the gods, he wanted to seduce Hera, but Zeus, divining his intentions, sent a cloud, Nephele, in the guise of Hera, to deceive him. From Ixion's union with Nephele the Centaurs were born, but for his transgression, he was cast into Hades and bound hand and foot to a fiery wheel, eternally in motion.

Sisyphus was condemned in death to roll a great boulder up a high slope, only to have it roll back down just as it was about to reach the summit. Another of Aeschylus' lost tragedies appears to have been about Sisyphus.

17. *the singer of Capaneus . . . the tragedian of the "fierce Erinyes"*: Dante and Aeschylus, respectively. Dante puts Capaneus, who was one of the Seven against Thebes, in the seventh *girone* of the third circle of Hell, where the damned try to dodge a rain of fire with "the dance of their wretched hands" (*Inf.* XIV, 46). The "fierce Erinyes," *Inf.* IX, 45, are of course the Eumenides, about whom Aeschylus wrote a play of the same name.

18. *intonaco:* The plaster upon which the fresco painter applies his pigments while the plaster is still wet, thus binding the color with the support.

19. *crude sonnet . . . belly was hanging just under his chin?:* This is the famous caudated sonnet by Michelangelo, written in 1509, which begins "I'ho già fatto un gozzo in questo stento" ("This strain's already given me a paunch") and talks about the artist's efforts painting the Sistine Chapel ceiling and the physical contortions required of him. The D'Annunzio passage cited above contains two indirect quotes from the famous sonnet: "e 'l pennel sopra 'l viso tuttavia/mel fa, gocciando, un ricco pavimento" ("and dripping over my face, my brush/turns it into a colorful floor"); "a forza 'l ventre appicca sotto 'l mento" ("my belly hangs under my chin").

20. *he was not "in the right place" . . . he was not a painter:* Another indirect quote from the famous sonnet—the final line, to be precise: "non sendo in loco bon, né io pittore" ("not being in the right place, nor a painter").

21. *"harpylike breast":* Another quote from Michelangelo's sonnet, where he says he has "the breast of a Harpy" ("e'l petto fo d'arpia").

22. *compiuta donzella:* Literally, the "complete maiden," the Compiuta Donzella was the pseudonym of a mysterious thirteenth-century Italian poetess, three of whose poems remain extant. Here, however, the name serves as a *senhal* (in the Troubadour tradition, a fictitious name for a real person in a poem) for Giselda Zucconi, an early love of the adolescent D'Annunzio. (EL, p. 267, n. 2)

23. *Canto novo:* An early collection of verse (1882) by D'Annunzio.

24. *Thibaut de Champagne:* Being count of Champagne and writing in the *langue d'oïl*, the medieval precursor to modern French, Thibaut is actually not, as D'Annunzio calls him, a troubadour, but a *trouvère*, that is, one of the northern French imitators of the troubadours, who for their part wrote in the *langue d'oc*, or, as it is now called, Occitan. In fairness to D'Annunzio, Thibaut is sometimes called the "troubadour king," though in French he is just "le roi chansonnier," having also been king of Navarre.

25. *Accessus morbi:* With a nod to Seneca, a fit of passion (*accessus*) is seen here as a bout of illness (*morbi*). (EL, p. 277, n. 1)

26. *Giorgio Aurispa:* The protagonist of D'Annunzio's novel *Il trionfo della morte* (1894) who, like his uncle Demetrio, ends up a suicide, clutching his mistress-companion and leaping into the void.

27. *the crypt at Aquileia:* The crypt in the Patriarchal Basilica of Aquileia, in northeastern Italy, contains a remarkable cycle of twelfth-century frescoes, including the scene from the Passion of Christ evoked here.

28. *Colleoni . . . covered with sacks:* Verrocchio's bronze equestrian statue of Bartolomeo Colleoni in front of the church of San Giovanni e Paolo (which D'Annunzio did everything in his power to safeguard during the war years) was protected with sacks from possible attacks.

29. *the dying little girl:* Renata herself, who fell gravely ill when only a few months old. (EL, p. 290, n. 1)

30. *the disciple from Arimathea:* Joseph of Arimathea, a New Testa-

ment figure remembered as the man who persuaded Pilate to let Jesus be buried and offered his own private sepulcher for this purpose.

31. *wherein was never man yet laid:* John, XIX, 41.

32. *talking laurel:* Here and in the passage that follows, D'Annunzio takes his cue from Ovid, *Metamorphoses*, I, 450–567.

33. *Poliphilus's dream:* A reference to the *Hypnerotomachia Poliphili* ("Poliphilo's Strife of Love," in English), a fifteenth-century "romance" believed to have been written by Francesco Colonna.

34. *The laurel . . . "So as not to die":* Probably a reference to the crown of laurel, accompanied by the motto "Per non dormire" etched into D'Annunzio's embossing stamp. In the frontispiece of the 1917 proof of *Notturno*, D'Annunzio changed "Per non dormire" into "Per non morire." (EL, p. 301, n. 4)

35. *the eagle of John the Favorite:* St. John the Evangelist, considered Jesus Christ's favorite, is often depicted in Christian iconography with an eagle, or as an eagle.

36. *Resurgit et insurgit:* "He rises again, and rises up in arms."

37. *the leisures and honors of Capua:* In Italian, the phrase *ozi di Capua* means a long period of idleness amidst luxuries and comforts, with specific reference to the period of inactivity spent by Hannibal's army at Capua in 216–215 BC, while awaiting reinforcements from Carthage, thus losing their opportunity to march on Rome.

38. *transhumanizing:* That is, transcending the limits of human nature to attain the divine. From the Dantean verb *trasumanar* in *Paradiso* I, 70 ("Trasumanar significar per verba/non si poria"; "Transcending humanity cannot be/signified in words").

Post Scriptum

1. *more than ten thousand strips of paper:* In reality, they numbered no more than three thousand. (EL, p. 319, n. 1)

2. *days of Santa Gorizia:* An allusion to the sixth battle of the Isonzo, at the foot of Monte Santo, which led to the Italian capture of Gorizia on August 16–17, 1916.

3. *day of Parenzo:* September 13, 1916, when the bombing raids against the hangars of Parenzo were carried out. This was the first military action

taken by the poet after the injury sustained at Grado and the convalescence recounted in the present volume. As can be gleaned from the program of instructions published by the commander of the naval district, Admiral Revel, D'Annunzio did not figure among the men planned for the mission. It was the poet himself who requested inclusion in the action, as a spotter-officer on the hydroplane of the Grado squad piloted by Bologna. (EL, p. 321, n. 2)

4. *I had not yet discovered the primitive cry of my race:* A reference to the cry of *eia eia eia alalà!*—which D'Annunzio chose for his comrades in aviation for the raid on Pola, claiming it was once the battle cry of the ancient Greeks. It replaced the foreign "Hip Hip Hooray." The *alalà*, as it came to be called, was later taken up by Mussolini's Fascists as a vocal equivalent to the Fascist salute.

5. *Intumuit mascula bilis:* [My] manly disdain grew.

6. *And then came . . . the Faiti:* After the Parenzo mission, D'Annunzio had himself assigned as liaison officer to the command of the 45th infantry division, which he joined on September 21, shortly before the eighth battle of the Isonzo (October 14–16). He was with the Brigata Toscana when he took part in the capture of Veliki and the Faiti, and the attainment of flight level 265. (EL, p. 323, n. 2)

7. *Senz'ali non può:* From Pietro Bembo, *Prose della volgar lingua* (1525).

8. *the two Calvaries:* That is, Mounts Faiti and Veliki.

9. *the "miracle of the blood":* See note 2 to Second Offering.

10. *O night raid on Pola! O Franciscan night of Cattaro!:* On the night of August 2–3, 1917, thirty-six Italian airplanes bombed an enemy base in Pola (Pula in Croatian), fully succeeding in their intent and all returning unharmed to their bases. D'Annunzio flew with the 8th Squadron, as a spotter. And on the night of October 4–5 (the 4th is St. Francis's feast day), fourteen Italian planes bombed the enemy naval base at Cattaro (Kotor in Montenegrin and Croatian). Twelve of them reached their destination and effectively struck submarines and torpedo boats at anchor. D'Annunzio once again took part only as a spotter. (EL, p. 326, n. 4, and p. 327, n. 1)

11. *Sky of the North Adriatic . . . Sky of the Piave:* The operations here

mentioned took place between November 1917 and August 1918. In addition to the first three aerial missions, D'Annunzio also participated in an important incursion into the Bay of Buccari (Bakar in Croatian), on the night of February 10–11, 1918, aboard an MAS 96 (a torpedo-armed motorboat), an operation that came to be known as *La beffa di Buccari* ("the Jest of Bakar"), when the Italian navy penetrated fifty miles past the Austro-Hungarian coastal defenses and into the Croatian bay of Bakar, managing to fire six torpedoes. He also took part in the flight over Vienna on August 8, 1918. (For more references, cf. EL, p. 327, n. 6.)

12. *the March from Ronchi, the Capture of Fiume:* The capture and "rule" of the Istrian city of Fiume (Rijeka in Croatian), during which time the poet even drew up, together with the syndicalist Alceste De Ambris, the Charter of the Carnaro, a highly eccentric "constitution" for his ideal mini-state, make up one of the more colorful episodes of D'Annunzio's life. During the fourteen-odd months in which the poet held the city with a militia of rebellious Italian soldiers, he instituted many of the superficial features that would soon come to characterize Mussolinian Fascism, including declaring himself *duce* and having his militia wear black shirts.

The question of Fiume, the "city of the Carnaro" mentioned below, arose from the Italian request, sent on February 7, 1919, to the members of the Paris Peace Conference, to have the city annexed to Italian territory (in opposition to the Treaty of London, which assigned it to Croatia), and from the request of Yugoslavia claiming for herself the territories assigned to Italy by the same Treaty (Dalmatia and Istria, including Trieste). Incidents between the city's population and the Inter-Allied forces (French, British, and American) in July 1919 led to the establishment of a Commission of Inquest. Meanwhile, the order came from Paris to disband the National Council of Fiume and the Legion of Fiuman Volunteers, and for Italian troops and ships to leave the city. At this juncture, D'Annunzio, who had been ready for some time to make his move, left Ronchi (near Trieste) with a force of some 2,600 rebellious Italian soldiers and militarily occupied the city of Fiume on September 12, 1919, eventually assuming full civil and military powers with the establishment of the Italian Regency of the Carnaro. Meanwhile, negotiations between Italy and Yugoslavia led to the Treaty of Rapallo (November 12, 1920), whereby Fiume was recognized as a free and independent state. Approved by the Italian parliament, the Treaty was not recognized by D'Annunzio, who on November 28 launched a resistance against the troops of General Enrico Caviglia, not relinquishing power to a new, provisional government until December 31, after the so-called Christmas of blood.

Good sources for this episode and the poet's life in general include J. R. Woodhouse's biography *D'Annunzio: Defiant Archangel* (Oxford: Oxford University Press, 1998); and Anthony Rhodes's *D'Annunzio: The Poet as Superman* (New York: McDowell, Oblensky, 1959). (Cf. also EL, p. 328, n. 1.)

13. *"She laid these pages . . . efficacy"*: The quotation is from Napoleon Bonaparte's *Memorial de Sainte-Hélène* (Paris: Lecointe Libraire, 1828, tome premier), 228.

14. *"three planks"* . . . *imaginings*: The author is alluding to his verses inspired by Scriabin's music. See pp. 138ff of the present text.

15. *alalà*: See note 4 of the present section.

16. *Great Martyr*: That is, the unknown soldier.

17. *God's Pauper*: Saint Francis.

18. *O mors, ero mors tua*: "O death, I shall be your death." A quotation-variation of Hosea XIII, 14: "O grave, I will be thy destruction." (King James Version)

19. *"Suso in Italia bella"*: "Up there in beautiful Italy." Dante, *Inf.* LXI, 20.

20. *November 4, 1921*: D'Annunzio finishes, or claims to finish, his text on the third anniversary of the end of WWI, when the body of the "unknown soldier" was transferred from Aquileia to Rome and buried in the Altare della Patria, the massive Monument to Vittorio Emanuele II in Piazza Venezia in Rome. (EL, p. 338, n. 3)